THE ACE
and THE ASSISTANT

A New Orleans Revelers NOVEL

JIFFY KATE

Books by Jiffy Kate

Finding Focus Series
Finding Focus
Chasing Castles
Fighting Fire
Taming Trouble

French Quarter Collection
Turn of Fate
Blue Bayou
Come Again
Neutral Grounds
Good Times

Table 10 Novella Series
Table 10 part 1
Table 10 part 2
Table 10 part 3

New Orleans Revelers
The Rookie and The Rockstar
The Ace and The Assistant

Smartypants Romance
Stud Muffin (Fighting For Love, book 1)
Beef Cake (Fighting For Love, book 2)
Eye Candy (Fighting For Love, book 3)

Standalones
Watch and See
No Strings Attached

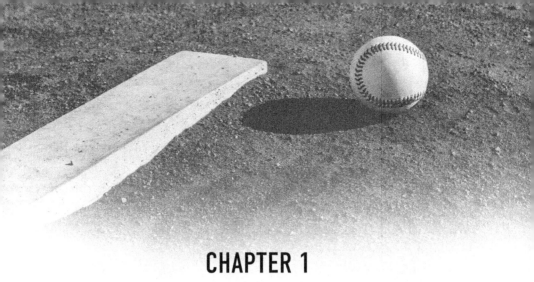

CHAPTER 1

Ross

ROCK, PIVOT, LIFT, THROW.

Thwap.

Rock, pivot, lift, throw.

Thwap.

"Shit!"

Come on, Davies. Get your head outta your ass and hit the fucking target.

Yogi Berra once said, "Baseball is ninety percent mental and the other half is physical" and fuck if he wasn't spot on.

The physical side of my game, I still have. I can throw the damn ball and make it land where it needs to be, *when* I'm focused. Which means, it's the mental part that's kicking my ass. Clearing my mind and thinking of nothing but doing my job is the struggle and has been for the last six months.

Well, longer, if I'm being completely honest.

Not only did my marriage implode before my eyes but so did the New Orleans' Revelers' chances for going to the playoffs last season. I take full responsibility for letting my team down but the demise of my seven-year marriage, that's not all on me. Marriage is both people giving one hundred percent, a fifty-fifty partnership at the very least.

But Felicia gave up on us.

Felicia Davies, my college sweetheart who promised me she'd always stick it out, through good times and bad, decided she was tired of being my wife… my *sidekick*. Her words, not mine.

Felicia Davies, the woman I thought I'd spend the rest of my life with—have a family with, experience the highs and lows of life with, grow old with—decided she was done *living in my shadow* and wanted the spotlight for herself.

Felicia Davies, *my ex-wife*—who now, from what I hear, is this city's biggest up-and-coming socialite, the Philanthropy Princess of New Orleans—checked out on me, our life, and our marriage.

Not that I give two shits.

Because I don't.

Rock, pivot, lift, throw.

Repeating the words in my head, I drill the ball at the strike box in my practice net like I've done more times than I can count. Instead of practicing at the field or in our team gym with the other Revelers during the off-season, I've stayed at home. Some may say I'm licking my wounds, and there's some truth to that, but I really just don't want to be around people yet.

I won't deny, after our divorce was finalized, I missed Felicia. We had been together so long and she brought a sense of belonging. Being my wife, she was part of my identity. So, of course, I missed her. But, now that some time has passed, I realize our relationship wasn't as solid as I thought it was. Or maybe that I pretended it was? That's what really has my head fucked up.

How am I supposed to be a leader to my teammates, my organization, and the league if I'm failing at my personal life and oblivious to my marriage falling apart?

During a particularly rough patch a while back, I thought about putting a picture of Felicia in my practice strike box. Let me be clear, I'd never hit a woman or joke about doing so, but I wondered if it'd help me concentrate on the target while getting some aggression out at the same time. Ultimately, I didn't do it, but now, I'm wondering if I should put my own face up there since I'm the one to blame in all this.

Rock, pivot, lift, throw.

Thwap.

Rock, pivot, lift, throw.

What the fuck?

"Lola?"

I must be losing my mind. After imagining Felicia's face in the strike box, followed by my own, I'm now seeing the face of Lola Carradine—world-famous rock star and girlfriend to my teammate, Bo Bennett—on top of my fence.

I blame the Louisiana humidity.

"Hey. We brought lasagna."

Okay, Lola can talk so that must mean she's real, right? Or Charlotte, rather, I'm still getting used to calling her by her real name, instead of her stage name—Lola—what the rest of the world calls her. In my head, I kind of still use both, interchangeably, but most of her family and close friends call her Charlotte. I think it helps her separate her public life from her private life and I get that.

But regardless of her name, she brought food and that's never a bad thing. Taking my chances that she's really here with my favorite dish, I motion to the house and tell her I'll let her inside.

Turns out, Charlotte and Bo really are here, along with an amazing lasagna. The three of us sitting around the table like this… eating, drinking, laughing…reminds me of better times, back when I wasn't embarrassed to show my face in public and could allow myself to have some fun. Of course, Felicia was never around but Charlotte's younger sister, Casey, would sometimes fill her void.

I miss those days.

"Is there someone you can call to catch up on stuff you don't want to tackle? Like open your mail and handle your finances… an assistant or something?"

Charlotte's questions pull me out of my memories and I look up to see her and Bo watching me, waiting for an answer. I glance around the room and see what they obviously see: dirty dishes piled up in the sink, the trash can overflowing, unopened mail, and who knows what else covering the opposite side of the table we're at. I've let this place—a fucking mansion—go to hell all because I can't get my shit together.

Embarrassment doesn't even cover it.

Shame comes close, though.

Wincing, I finally respond. "That used to be Felicia's job. She handled all of that… the mail, the bills, the house." I shake my head and stare into my mostly-empty wineglass. "I haven't taken the time to find someone. It's hard to know who to trust. I guess I could hire a firm or something, but that feels so impersonal and I have a remodel job that needs to be finished. Then, of course, there's Spring Training..." I add, drifting off. I realize there's no way I can leave my life in its current state and be in the right frame of mind while I'm preparing for the upcoming season.

"What about Casey?" Charlotte asks. "She's been the best assistant I could ever ask for and she might not have a college degree to back her up, but she has me as a reference and loads of hands-on experience. I'd trust her with my life… I *do* trust her with my life."

I try to school my reaction to her suggestion because, honestly, I'm shocked. Casey and I have always gotten along well, but I can't help but worry it might be uncomfortable having her here, with just the two of us. We've never been alone together because Bo and Charlotte are always around. Besides, wouldn't it be strange to hire someone I consider a friend?

"Plus, you know her, so it might make it an easier transition. With Spring Training coming up so soon, you wouldn't have to worry about leaving your affairs in the hands of a stranger."

Or I could look at it that way.

Maybe I'm overthinking this, like I have been with every other thing in my life lately. I haven't made any decisions and that's resulted in not going forward or backward, just staying stagnant.

"It's a good idea," Bo declares, and I can't help but wonder when our roles reversed—him helping me. It wasn't too long ago I was the one giving him advice.

Now, I'm wondering if I even knew what the hell I was talking about. Since Felicia ended things, I've started questioning everything.

Who am I?

How did I let my marriage fall apart?

What the fuck am I doing with my life?

I never pictured myself here—struggling to find my footing and my fucking identity.

"What do you say?" Bo asks, pulling me back out of my thoughts.

Sighing, I down the last of my wine and sit back in my seat. It's not a horrible idea and much better than anything I've come up with on my own, which is nothing. Casey's a smart girl and she's used to juggling busy schedules. The best part, with Lola Carradine as a sister, she's well-versed in discretion. I need some of that in my life right now, while I try to pick up the pieces and figure my shit out.

"Okay," I finally agree.

What do I have to lose?

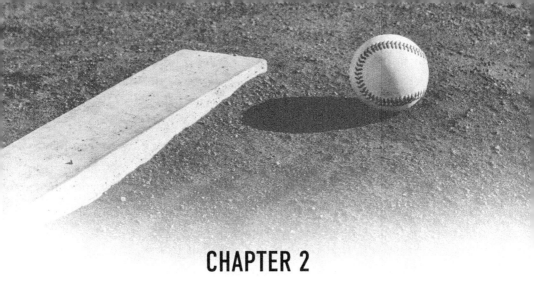

CHAPTER 2

Casey

SCANNING THE KITCHEN COUNTER, I MAKE SURE I HAVE ALL THE INGREDIENTS I NEED before popping my earbuds in and hitting play on my music app. Some people may like to belt out their favorite tunes while in front of their bathroom mirror, while others may prefer to perform while cleaning. Speaking for myself, I love putting on private concerts when I'm cooking. The kitchen is the perfect place to dance around and it's full of tools that can double as mics, guitars, and drumsticks.

Normally, my music is blaring but I don't think Charlotte and Bo are up yet and I'm nothing if not considerate, hence my earbuds. They were out pretty late last night, doing who knows what, so I thought I'd make a breakfast casserole we all can enjoy.

I quickly put together the dish, put it in the oven, and set the time. As I tidy up the kitchen, I take a few spins around the island while using a clean, wooden spoon for my mic. I'm so deep into one of my favorite albums, nothing in the world exists except me and the music. When I turn and see movement out of the corner of my eye, I forget about staying quiet and let out a scream rivaling the eighties hair bands I typically listen to.

"For the love of all that's holy!" Pulling out my earbuds, I toss them on the counter and brace myself.

"Sorry," Charlotte says, raising both of her hands in surrender. "I didn't mean to startle you, I swear!"

Glaring at my sister, I clutch my chest and try to get my heart rate to slow down to its normal rhythm. *Deep breaths in…. And out… in…*

Trying not to laugh, she continues. "I even called your name but you *obviously* didn't hear me. What were you listening to anyway?"

"Stevie Nicks, of course," I say with a wink, picking my earbuds back up and stuffing them in my pocket. Those little ninjas disappear faster than socks and hair ties combined, and cost a fortune to replace. "Disappointed it wasn't *The* Lola Carradine?"

Everyone knows I'm my sister's biggest fan, but real talk, she's no Stevie Nicks. Besides, I have to keep her grounded. That's what little sisters are put on this earth to do. Well, that, and if you're me, you also manage your big sister's life.

"Of course not. I'd be listening to Stevie, too, if I was cooking."

Still feeling like my heart is racing, I grab a glass from a cabinet and fill it with water, taking a large drink. "What are you doing awake anyway? I assumed you and Bo were sleeping in."

Charlotte picks a banana from the produce basket and peels it. "Nah, you know I can't sleep when the sun's up."

"What did y'all do last night?" I ask, digging for information without blatantly coming out with the nosey questions. "I must've fallen asleep before you got home."

She shrugs, leaning against the island. "We had dinner at Ross's house."

Without me?

That's my knee-jerk reaction, but I focus on schooling my features. She doesn't need to know it stings to hear I was left out of last night's dinner party. The four of us used to have dinner all the time, but since his divorce, we haven't seen much of him. Which is weird because you'd think it'd be the opposite. According to Bo, he's struggling.

Charlotte quickly takes a bite of her banana, as though she's trying to keep herself from saying more.

Why is she acting so weird?

I'm probably overreacting because Charlotte knows she can tell me anything. We have zero secrets between us.

Well, except one… you know, the one where I've had a crush on Ross Davies since the moment I met him. But, it's no big deal. It's a tiny, baby crush that will go away eventually, I'm sure.

When she continues to eat her banana in silence, it's on the tip of my tongue to ask how he's doing, but that seems too personal. Clearing my throat, I decide to play it safe and ask, "Anything interesting to report?"

"Oh, well, you know, he's still trying to cope with life after divorce," she hedges.

Must. Not. Roll. My. Eyes.

I hate that Ross is hurting, I really do, but why can't he see *whatsherface* was all wrong for him?

Thankfully, the oven timer goes off, saving me from saying anything that may sound suspicious.

I slip on my oven mitts and take the casserole out, placing it on a trivet so it can cool, before turning the oven and the timer off.

After a few more seconds of silence, Charlotte tosses her peel in the trash and walks over to where I'm standing. "He really needs an assistant. You know, someone to help him get his life straight…"

A non-committal hum is all I can muster while I reach into the cabinet and take out some plates and set them on the island.

"You know, someone to do for him what you did—and still do—for me," she continues.

No, I think as I open the drawer and take out three forks, *what he needs is a swift kick in his perfectly firm booty so he can focus on baseball.* But, of course, I don't say that. "Absolutely, he should totally get some help."

"I knew you'd agree!" Charlotte pulls me into a side hug and crushes me to her. "Don't worry about me. I can handle my own shit for a while. Getting Ross back on track is more important right now. So, focus on him. And, you're the best!"

Say what?

"Wait. I think I missed something," I tell her, pulling away with a scrutinizing gaze.

Did she drink too much wine last night?

Bump her head?

Do I need to call her doctor?

Letting out a confused chuckle, I place the forks methodically by the plates. "I'm confused. You make it sound like I'll be the one helping Ross."

Surely I'm misunderstanding her excitement.

"Because you will be."

"Umm. no." I grab a pizza cutter to slice the casserole into even squares.

"Case, please. You're the only one who can truly help him."

"Char, there are plenty of assistants out there who would kill to work for Ross Davies. Hire one of them!"

She growls in frustration. "You know he wouldn't agree to that. He may be kind of pitiful right now but he's still got his pride and doesn't want the whole world to know he's struggling. You can help him, I know you can. And it wouldn't be forever, just until he gets back on his feet and starts the season."

I close my eyes and take a deep breath. I get what she's saying. Really, I do. Being behind the scenes of her life, I know how much people who live in the spotlight value their privacy. But this is Ross Davies. The one I have the tiny, baby crush on. It's one thing to have pizza nights and dinners with him, but it's another to work for the man.

And he is a man, in every sense of the word. The manliest man I've ever laid eyes on.

Focus, Casey.

"Please," Charlotte begs, imploring me with her puppy dog eyes. Wouldn't the tabloids love to see this—Lola Carradine practically on her hands and knees, begging.

Could I do this? Could I work closely with the man of my dreams in his house *and remain professional? Could I whip his life into shape and not be tempted to whip him in the bedroom?*

Absolutely. I'm Casey freaking Carradine.

The better question is, will I?

"Fine," I finally say after an extremely long stare off that rivals the ones we used to have when we were kids. "I'll do it, but you owe me big time."

"That's what I'm talking about," Charlotte says, raising her hand for a high-five. I leave her hanging but that doesn't deter her excitement. "It's going to be great. You're exactly what he needs, I just know it."

Ha! I wish.

"Oh, and Ross wants you to meet with him at his place today for a little interview-type of thing, even though you're a sure thing. It's just a technicality, so don't be nervous."

My eyes go wide as I turn on her. "Why do I feel like I've been pimped out?"

Charlotte just smiles, knowing I'd do anything for her. And Ross.
"You are so going to owe me."

OKAY, CASEY, YOU NEED TO RELAX.

This is no big deal.

It's just Ross, your friend, and soon-to-be boss.

You can do this.

And, yes, it was totally normal to change your outfit six times before leaving the house.

Ha.

You know what else is totally normal? Talking to yourself in said friend's driveway. Totally normal.

Do not overthink this.

"Casey? Everything all right?"

I look out of my window and see *The* Ross Davies standing next to my car, watching me. At least, I think it's Ross Davies. He looks very different from the last time I saw him. His hair has grown out and the beard he's sporting is looking pretty wild but he still has those bright green eyes that always seem to look straight into my soul. It's not a bad look on him; it's just… different. I could work with it, no problem.

No, you can't, Casey. You are working for *him, not* with *him. Get your head on straight.*

I need to start making a list of all the ways I'll be making Charlotte pay for making me do this.

Number one: season tickets to watch the Saints play football since I'll never be able to watch another Revelers' game after working for Ross.

Grabbing my bag, I finally open the door of my car and step out to meet Ross. "Hey, Ross. I hear you need a kick in the nads to get ready for the new season and I'm supposed to be the girl to do it."

A strange noise seems to come from the back of his throat but he coughs to hide it. Maybe I should've softened my greeting but I have to admit I like being able to knock Ross down a peg or two. I think that's what made us fast friends, I didn't handle him with kid gloves, or *celebrity gloves*, and I never pull my punches.

"You heard right," he answers while peering down at me. "Thank you for helping me out. I really do appreciate it."

The sincerity in his voice catches me off guard and for the first time, I see the changes in him. Not just his looks, but beneath the surface too. Under the dark circles framing his green eyes, his usually chiseled face looks a bit thinner, there's somberness, and struggle seeping from his pores. Even his posture seems beaten down.

Not gonna lie, my heart breaks for him.

"Let's go inside and talk." Ross stuffs his hands into the pockets of his jeans and nods toward the house as he starts walking. I take a second to get my head on straight before jogging to catch up with him on the porch.

I can do this.

"Brace yourself," he warns. "It's not pretty in here."

I give him a small, reassuring smile before he lets out a deep breath and opens the door, holding it to allow me to enter first. The foyer appears normal enough but when I step into the living room, I have to stifle a gasp. I've been to Ross's house twice, and both times, it looked like something out of a magazine spread for *Better Homes and Gardens*.

That is not the case today.

Every surface has something on it—mail, newspapers, takeout containers, bottles, cans. Basically, it looks like he just gave up, which makes me even sadder for him but also angry he hasn't asked for help until now.

"Judas Priest, you weren't kidding, were you?" I blurt out.

Ross snickers and when I turn to face him, he's looking down at his feet while rubbing the back of his neck with his hand.

"I'm sorry," I tell him, pressing my lips together. "I have a bad habit of being brutally honest when it's not necessarily appropriate."

"You don't have to apologize," he says. "I know it's a mess. I was laughing at your word choice. I forgot how you don't say real cuss words."

My cheeks turn pink, but I shrug it off. "I think my version of expletives is more creative and fun."

When I glance over at him, our eyes meet and for a second, I'm held hostage by the moment.

Maybe it's his vulnerability or the way he's letting me see a side of him no one else is privy to? Or maybe it's the fact this is the first time we've ever truly been alone together? Regardless, there's something in the air between us. It might just be me and my tiny, baby crush, but I feel it.

"I agree. I'm glad you haven't changed, Casey."

Those words and the way he's staring at me when he says them almost have me cussing for real.

Almost.

Clearing my throat, I break our eye contact and walk into the kitchen, needing to put some distance between us and a chance to take a deep breath without my lungs being full of his intoxicating scent. Thankfully, it's not completely disgusting. The sink is empty, but the counters are just as cluttered and unorganized as the living room.

Who knew a professional baseball player would have so many papers and pieces of mail? And, if the kitchen and living room look the way they do, I can only imagine how bad his actual office looks.

When I turn back to face him, he's leaning against the wall, staring at a stack of papers. He looks so lost and overwhelmed, nothing like the powerful pitcher and team leader I know him to be... or what his team expects him to be.

That thought gives me the strength I need to power through my feelings and remember what I'm here to do.

"It's really not that bad," I say. "I've seen much worse at frat houses, so not all hope is lost." I give him a genuine smile, hoping it reassures him. When he still doesn't look convinced, I continue. "Ross, I can do this. Let me help you."

He sighs, leaning against the entry to the kitchen as I do the same on the counter beside the stove. Looking at him, I'm once again hit in the face with his current condition. He's tired, that's obvious. But there's more to it. When I first met Ross, or even before we were formally introduced and I just knew him as the ace pitcher for the New Orleans Revelers, he was the most confident person I'd ever seen. It wasn't cockiness, like a lot of professional athletes possess, it was just this air of assuredness. Mentally, I'd always placed Ross at the top of the list of people I'd call in a crisis.

Steady.

Strong.

Sexy.

All of those qualities are still there, but it's buried under defeat and sadness.

I hate she did that to him.

"How does five grand a week sound?" Ross asks, pulling me out of my thoughts.

My brows furrow in confusion, unsure of what he's referring to. "I'm sorry. What did you say?"

I must have missed something.

"I could probably do six..." he counters, squinting his face up as if he's uncomfortable.

"For what?" Maybe this has to do with the remodel Charlotte mentioned.

He cocks his head in confusion. "To pay you... for you to work for me..." He trails off and I realize then what he's referring to and nearly choke on air.

"Five grand?" I ask incredulously. "Are you flipping kidding me?" Scoffing, I push off the island and walk over to the large pile of mail that's haphazardly strewn about. Picking some up, I begin to sort the envelopes into piles. "If I had to guess, you don't have any idea what has and hasn't been paid. Charlotte mentioned an ongoing remodel that needs to be completed. And I'm sure you have new bills coming in due to your divorce."

Stopping, I slap an envelope from an attorney on top of the growing pile of people demanding Ross Davies' money. "Does that sound about right?"

His hand reaches back and squeezes his neck as he turns his eyes to the ceiling. I know this has to be uncomfortable for him, but if I'm going to work for him and be effective at my job, we're going to have to get past the awkwardness of it all pretty quick.

The team leaves for Spring Training in a week, so we don't have much time to figure all this out so I can put his life back in order while he's gone.

"Sounds about right," Ross finally says, bringing his eyes back to mine.

Tucking loose strands of hair behind my ears, I take a deep breath. "Let's say a thousand dollars a week," I tell him, even though that still feels like highway robbery. I'd do it for free.

The bottom line is—tiny, baby crush aside—I really like him.

Not the ace pitcher or magazine cover model.

Not the person other people idolize.

I like the guy who comes over and has pizza nights and crashes our family dinners.

I like the guy who donates his time to worthy causes and never uses it as a publicity stunt.

I like the guy who goes above and beyond for his friends.

I've seen it, been on the receiving end of it, and would like to return the favor.

"I would say I'd do it for free," I continue. "But I know you and I know you won't let me do that. And if I don't take this job you probably won't hire anyone else, which means your life will continue to crumble around you. And as a friend, I can't let that happen."

For good measure, I tack on, "Besides, we need a good season and that means having you at your best."

That gets a small smile from him which gives me hope.

"What do you say?"

Eventually, his eyes meet mine and we enter into one of those raw, real moments that make my stomach do weird things and my palms start to sweat.

"It's a deal."

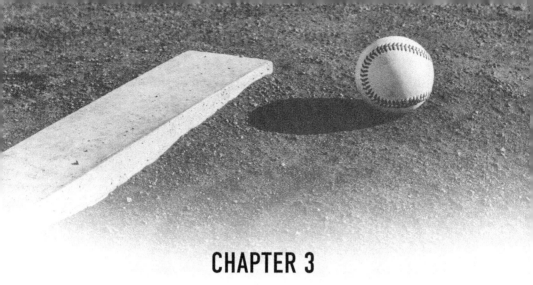

CHAPTER 3

Ross

WALKING DOWNSTAIRS, I SCRUB A HAND OVER MY FACE AND THROUGH MY BEARD. Typically, it's not this long. I always let my hair grow during the off-season, but it's definitely a bit out of control, even for me, which is basically my life right now.

But hopefully not for much longer. After mine and Casey's meeting, I could feel the black cloud that's been hanging over me for the past six months start to dissipate. Just her presence alone brought with it a sense of peace I haven't had in a really long time.

I hate to admit it, but if Bo and Charlotte hadn't staged their intervention, I'd probably still be throwing balls in my backyard while the rest of my life deteriorates.

Giving help is second nature. I'm used to being the one in the driver's seat, the one who's leading and guiding others, but this current state I'm in is foreign and unwelcome, which is probably why I'm having such a hard time digging myself out.

Most mornings, I head straight to my home gym and work out. It helps release all the pent-up energy and tension I've been carrying around and it's the only way to quiet the constant stream of thoughts that bombard me.

But this morning, Casey Carradine is coming here for her first day on the job.

I'm still trying to wrap my brain around her working for me and figure out how I feel about it.

Sure, she's more than capable and she's a close enough friend that I trust her with my personal information. She's used to handling the affairs of someone who lives in the spotlight. Being the younger sister of Lola Carradine, she's seen it all.

She's lived her entire life in the shadow of a celebrity. Some people might assume she's jaded or jealous, but I know she's neither of those things. Casey is the brightest ray of sunshine I've ever seen. She's quirky and fun and an all-around good person.

So, why am I so fucking nervous?

I've been asking myself that question since I agreed to her terms and we shook on an agreement, but I can't quite put my finger on what has me on edge.

My lawyer sent over some standard paperwork yesterday for her to sign, mainly an NDA. Not that I think we need one, but Jason, my lawyer, does, and since I know Casey won't think anything of it, I agreed.

NDA aside, I trust her.

Maybe I'm nervous because I'm finally doing something—taking action, moving forward? Maybe it's because this is the first step in regaining control of my life? I don't know. Regardless of the nerves, the thought of her being around and helping me work through my shit makes me the happiest I've felt in a long time. So, I'm going to embrace it.

As I start the coffee pot, I pop open my laptop and check my emails.

To the dismay of everyone around me, I hate text messages. Call me old school, but I prefer a good, old-fashioned phone call or an email. Being a pitcher, I have great hand-eye coordination, so I don't think it has anything to do with that. But I hate the way text messages replace human interaction, so if I can avoid them, I do.

After deleting all the junk, I'm left with an email from Heath, my agent, who also fills a PR/manager role when needed, reminding me about the upcoming Spring Training schedule, and another from Jason, reminding me to have Casey sign the documents before I hand over any personal information.

I would roll my eyes at their insistent reminding, but I realize I've given them reason to doubt my abilities to take care of business. The old Ross wouldn't need double reminders.

Fighting back the annoyance, I continue through my emails until I come to one from ccarradine0607.

It's short and to the point.

Ross,

I know you hate text messages and I'm not going to lie, that's a bit lame, but you're the boss, so if it's emails you want, it's emails you'll get.

Just letting you know I was able to call in a favor and I have our cleaning people coming to your house tomorrow morning. I should beat them there, but just in case, I wanted to give you a heads up. Don't worry, they've been thoroughly vetted. If Charlotte trusts them in her studio, you know they're on the up and up.

See you in the morning.

Casey

I smile to myself, for what might be the first time in six months. That girl doesn't mess around.

Girl? No, definitely a woman. She might be younger than me, but I'm not blind or an idiot. I can see her for what she is—gorgeous, confident, smart… Did I mention sexy as hell? Yeah, that.

Maybe I pushed that thought out of my mind for the majority of the time I've known Casey because I was a married man and even though Felicia tried to accuse me of cheating, I've never laid a finger on another woman or let my eyes wander.

I'm as loyal as they come. It's ingrained so deeply into my DNA I don't know how to be anything different, which is why this divorce has hit me so hard.

You know that saying about how it's hard to teach an old dog new tricks? I might not be old, although thirty-one isn't a spring chicken by baseball standards, but I did spend almost a decade loving Felicia and being committed to her.

Even when things weren't great between us, I made it my mission in life to do whatever I could to make our marriage better. There were times I knew it would be easier to give up, but I'd made a vow to her and I was going to see it through to the end.

Now that she's not a part of my life, I'm struggling to retrain my brain and my heart to do something new. It's not that I'm still in love with her. Actually, I might've fallen out of love a while ago. But the loyalty is harder to break.

However, the more she shows her true colors, the easier it is, but it still doesn't feel good.

Neither do the feelings of betrayal or abandonment.

The smell of coffee pulls me out of my thoughts and I grab a mug and fill it up. I need to get my head on straight before Casey shows up. I've spent long enough wallowing and feeling sorry for myself. Spring Training is almost here and I refuse to be the weak link in our lineup this season.

Speaking of loyalty, my team needs me.

"Knock, knock," a voice from the foyer calls out.

"In the kitchen," I call back, pulling out another mug and filling it with coffee.

Casey's smile brightens up the whole room when she walks in.

With her hair in a ponytail and her face free of makeup, she's definitely playing up the little sister vibe, but it does nothing to distract me from noticing her.

She's stunning.

And *holy fuck*, she's wearing yoga pants.

Clearing my throat, I turn my back on her and walk to the fridge. "How do you take your coffee?"

"Milk, no sugar," she says, cheerfully, unbeknownst to my inner turmoil or my dick that decided to wake up and make his presence known.

It's been a while.

Honestly, I can't remember the last time I had a visceral reaction to a woman who wasn't my wife.

Ex-wife.

And even then… it's been a while.

"Did you get my email about the cleaning service?"

I turn to see her pulling out a binder from her bag. After she takes out a pencil and highlighter, she perches her sweet little yoga pant-covered ass on one of the bar stools. Taking a cleansing breath, I reign in my reactions toward her and slide the mug and milk across the counter.

"I did." My reply is clipped but she has my head in a jumbled mess and I'm not quite sure what to make of it. It's a bit unsettling and that's counterproductive to what I was going for. What happened to that sense of peace and calm I felt after our meeting yesterday? Since when do I react this way to Casey?

Fuck.

Maybe this was a bad idea.

"Is that okay?" Casey asks hesitantly. "Because if you'd rather me call someone else, it's not too late to cancel. But they'll be here in the next hour, so—"

"It's fine," I say, cutting her off and feeling bad about it. When I turn to face her, I can see the questions piling up on her gorgeous face. Before she has a chance to ask, I try to cover up my mood and smooth the waters. "Sorry, I slept like shit and this is my first cup of coffee."

The crease between her eyebrows relaxes and she offers me a small smile. "It's okay. I know this is probably weird for you and you've been dealing with a lot. But that's why I'm here." Her shoulders rise and fall as she inhales and exhales. "I just want to help and I realize you're a private person, so if I overstep my boundaries, just tell me. I won't push."

"I know all of that," I assure her. "And I'm happy you're here. But you're right, I am a private person and I really hate asking for help, so this is difficult for me." *It's not the only thing that's* hard *right now*, I think to myself, but continue. "Thank you for calling in a favor with the cleaning service. I know I'll feel better once this place is back in order and that's the first step."

Casey smiles, reaching across the counter and placing her small hand on mine. "Good, I'm glad we got all of that out of the way." Sitting up straight, she pulls her hand back and I immediately miss the warmth. Brushing a stray piece of her blonde hair behind her ear, she opens the binder up and flips a few pages to an empty calendar. "Now, let's start with your schedule and any dates I need to know. Then, we'll work on the mounds of mail and any issues that entails."

She's back to being all-business and that should get my head out of the gutter, but it doesn't. Her take-charge attitude is sexy as hell. There are only eight days until I leave for Spring Training. Surely, I can keep myself under control until I leave.

Then, I'll be gone for a month and a half and by the time I get back, all of this pent-up sexual tension will be behind me, my affairs will be in order, and Casey and I can go back to just being friends.

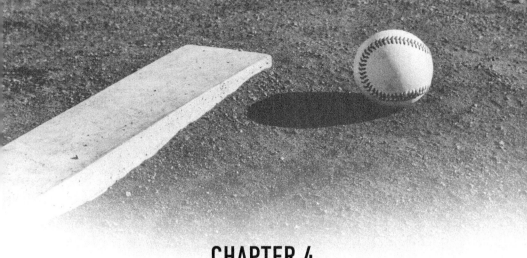

CHAPTER 4

Casey

AS I WALK UP THE STEPS TO ROSS'S FRONT DOOR, I PLACE A HAND ON MY STOMACH and will the butterflies to go back to sleep. You'd think after working with him in close proximity for the past five days I'd be past these feelings, but I can't help it.

I was attracted to Ross when he was married. I never would've acted on my attraction. I just appreciated him from a safe distance, whether that was across the dinner table or from the stands of a baseball game.

Now that he's divorced and I've been in his space, submerged in everything Ross Davies, my tiny, baby crush has grown. Even though I've told myself every day that it can't. It's like a defiant teenager and has a mind of its own.

And here I stand, with two bottles of wine in hand, getting ready to ring his doorbell.

He asked me to come over tonight so we can go over my progress and work out a game plan for when he's gone to Spring Training. If I can just make it through tonight without making a complete fool out of myself, I'll be in the clear.

In two days, he'll leave for six weeks and I won't have to see his gorgeous face every day.

Letting out a huff, I bring my hand up and hover over the doorbell. Not like it'll matter that he's gone, I'll still be here, in his house, surrounded by his things, handling his business. But that's what I signed up for and he needs me.

Before my finger can press the button, the door opens and Ross is there—disheveled hair, luscious beard, faded jeans, button-up shirt with the sleeves rolled to his elbows, and bare feet.

Holy Moses.

"Hey," he says, his eyes crinkling with a smile. Unlike five days ago when I showed up at his house, the dark circles aren't as prevalent, and the smiles are more forthcoming. It's as though me being here and helping him wade through his backlogged life has lifted a boulder from his shoulders.

He's not completely back to the pre-divorce Ross, but he's better.

"Hi," I say, stepping into the foyer and smiling as I see the fresh flowers on the table. "I brought wine."

The house looks better too.

After our first meeting, before I even made it to my car, I was on the phone with the lady who occasionally cleans for us, calling in a favor. Thankfully, she was able to move things around and clean Ross's house the next day. As she scrubbed, dusted, swept, and mopped, I made my way through the house collecting every loose piece of mail.

I spent the rest of the morning and afternoon organizing. Then, Ross and I sat down to go over everything. He gave me passwords and access to his accounts. Things weren't really as bad as they initially seemed. Most of his bills were set for auto-pay and he obviously has money in the bank, so that wasn't an issue. The main areas of concern were the things Felicia normally took care of—cleaning, organizing, grocery shopping, and general maintenance.

She'd been the one to manage their finances and run their household, so Ross felt detached from it all. After we went through everything and I was able to put all of his expenses into a spreadsheet, I could visibly see him begin to relax.

"Smells amazing," I call out, placing my bag on the hook by the door and following the sound of glasses clinking.

When I walk into the dining room, Ross is setting two wineglasses on the table. "I fired up the grill," he says, glancing up at me. "Hope you like steak."

"I love steak." My mouth is already watering at the mere mention, like a Pavlovian response.

I also love a man who can cook, I think to myself, but quickly push that out of my mind.

"What can I do to help?"

He pauses on his way back to the kitchen and gives me a smile that makes my insides the consistency of a warm chocolate chip cookie. "I've got it covered. Just sit down and pour some wine."

Between the way he looks tonight—relaxed and so sexy—the fact he cooked, and the way he's doling out smiles like they're candy at a parade, I *need* to sit because he's making my knees weak. So, I return his smile and nod my acquiescence as I set about opening one of the bottles of wine with the electric corkscrew he left on the table. It's fancy, like a lot of things in Ross's house, but not him.

Ross is laidback and the most unpretentious person I've ever met. After working closely with him these past five days, it's become even more apparent how down-to-earth he really is. While working through his finances, he made notes of superfluous accounts and expenses he wanted canceled, while instructing me on charitable organizations he'd like to send more money to.

All things that make me like Ross Davies, the man, even more than I already did.

Which is not good for my resolve.

This is just business, I repeat to myself as I pop the cork on the wine.

Eyeballing the three other bottles on the table, I pour myself a glass and take a sip. If he plans on us drinking all of this, I'm going to need some food in my stomach or I'll be in trouble. I'm no lightweight and can definitely hold my own, but for some reason, wine hits me harder than liquor or beer. But hopefully, this glass will calm me down and allow me to focus on the job I'm here to do and not the man making my insides a jumbled mess.

Pace yourself, Casey.

Ross comes back a few minutes later with a sizzling plate of steaks. I pour him a glass of wine while he serves me a steak. He scoops up a spoonful of roasted potatoes and places them on my plate while I toss the salad.

We continue to work in tandem until our plates are full and then we dig in.

It's funny, I never thought of what a working relationship with Ross would be like. Before this past week, I just knew him as Ross Davies, the ace pitcher for the Revelers, and then Ross Davies, Bo's best friend, and eventually, just Ross, my friend.

And then of course there's that tiny, baby crush that we don't speak of.

But this new dynamic is good too.

We work well together.

And that makes my mind go to places it shouldn't... like how well we'd work together with our clothes off... which leads to thoughts of Ross naked. Thanks to ESPN's Body Issue, I don't have to use too much of my imagination.

Long, lean muscles.

Toned torso.

Washboard abs.

"Are you sure you're okay with handling the remodel on the guest house while I'm gone?" Ross asks, thankfully pulling me out of my dirty, inappropriate thoughts.

Clearing my throat, I take a healthy drink of my wine before answering. "Yeah, absolutely," I assure him as I cut off a piece of steak, which is so tender I hardly need my knife. When I moan at the burst of flavor on my tongue, it's now Ross who's clearing his throat.

We eat in semi-silence for a few minutes. Occasionally, I compliment Ross on the amazing meal and he deflects my remarks. When I peek at him from the corner of my eye, I think I even see him blush.

Maybe it's the wine.

We're both nearly finished with our second glass and I know after I've had two I'm usually pink-cheeked and comfortably loose. I know Ross is considerably bigger than me, but I don't think he drinks much, so maybe it affects him in the same way.

And now I'm thinking about all the ways Ross is bigger.

Get it together, Casey.

"I'm sorry I'm leaving you with such a mess," Ross eventually says, picking up a new bottle of wine and using the corkscrew to open it. I watch as his forearms flex and swallow hard. *God, this was a bad idea.* Working with Ross is one thing, but eating what feels like an intimate meal with him, just the two of us, in his house, is another.

"No worries," I tell him, shoving another piece of food in my mouth to give myself a chance to cool off. The heat from my cheeks is moving down my body at an alarming rate. "That's what I'm here for and I'm good with messes."

He chuckles and shakes his head as he pours us both a third glass of wine.

"I guess that comes with the territory of having a rockstar for a sister."

Letting out a huff, I shrug my shoulders and take a sip of the new glass of wine. "Oh, this is good."

"One of my favorites," he says, bringing the glass to his nose and inhaling before taking a drink.

"I didn't peg you as a wine connoisseur," I tease. "You always come bearing a six-pack when you show up at the house for dinner."

Ross laughs again and I can't stop looking at the way his eyes crinkle and appreciating how beautiful his face is. I know, beautiful isn't a term often used to describe a man, especially one as masculine as Ross Davies, but it's true. I've always noticed it and tonight, I'm appreciating it more than usual.

Last week when I showed up at his house, he was not himself. So, seeing him peek out from under the debris that was his former life and watching his green eyes shine with amusement is more payment than necessary.

"I love wine," he admits. "But usually when I come over to hang with y'all, which I must admit I've really missed." He pauses and the sincerity on his face is disarming. For a second, I think he's going to reach across the table and touch my hand or something, but then he continues. "It was usually for pizza."

"Pizza and wine go great together," I tell him, laughing and hoping it doesn't sound as nervous as I suddenly feel.

The room seems to be squeezing in.

The air is thicker.

I pull at the collar of my t-shirt dress and fan it.

It's hot in here.

So hot.

Picking up the wineglass, I down it in one gulp, hoping it'll extinguish the heat blazing in my belly.

"Dessert?" Ross asks, standing from his chair and picking up his plate as he gestures toward mine. I've only eaten about half of what was on my plate, but I'm not hungry anymore. Well, I am, but not for anything that's on the menu.

Because Ross Davies is not on the menu.

He's *the* Ross Davies.

My friend.

Recently divorced.

My boss.

I continue to list off all the reasons why I should not be thinking about making him my dessert and while he's gone, I help myself to another glass of wine.

When he shows back up, he's holding a small King Cake from my favorite local bakery.

"'Tis the season," he says with a wry grin.

My mouth immediately begins to drool.

It's the perfect distraction from the buzz of the alcohol and my incessant mind thinking about getting Ross Davies naked. "The more King Cake, the better," I say, tipping up my wineglass and downing the last sip, along with my lust.

Ross sets it down in the middle of the table and instead of getting plates, he just hands me a fork and shrugs. "I figure it's small and what we don't eat you can take home with you or leave it here for tomorrow… or whenever."

"Why me?" I ask, my voice going up an octave.

"Because it's time for me to get on my Spring Training diet."

Already going in for a bite, I have the fork halfway to my mouth when I stop mid-air. "Wait, you have a Spring Training diet?"

Ross smirks. "You didn't think I got this six-pack from eating King Cakes and Twinkies, did you?" When he raises his shirt to drive home his point, I nearly drop my fork… and King Cake. Instead, I shove it into my mouth in the most unladylike maneuver ever.

Huffing a laugh around the bite, I inwardly cringe.

So attractive, Casey.

No, you know what. Actually, this is good. It's not like I'm trying to be attractive to Ross. I shouldn't be trying to get him to notice me. As long as

I can keep my thoughts and feelings to myself tonight, he'll be gone in two days and I won't have to worry about it anymore.

By the time he gets back from Spring Training, I'll have myself under control, along with his personal affairs, and we'll go back to business as usual.

Ross and Casey.

Casey and Ross.

Crap.

Why do I like the sound of our names together so much?

"What's wrong?" Ross asks, his brows furrowing as he takes another bite of cake.

"Nothing," I say, brushing a strand of my hair behind my ear and using my fork to stab at the delectable goodness. *Nothing, other than the fact, I want you.* Like more than I've ever wanted anyone in my entire life.

That has to be the wine talking.

"You sure?" he asks, his expression going serious. "No second thoughts about this gig or anything?"

"No," I tell him with a small smile. "No second thoughts. And don't worry about anything while you're gone, I can handle it. Just focus on kicking butt on the mound."

Ross rakes his teeth over his bottom lip and I don't think it's meant to have the effect it does on my body, but God, does it ever. My stomach flips and my core aches.

Needing a moment to get a grip, I excuse myself and go to the bathroom. Staring in the mirror, I take inventory of my flushed cheeks and glassy eyes. I'm not sloppy drunk, but I'm not merely tipsy. If this was any other night, if I was just at home having a wine and movie night with my sister, my current state wouldn't be a problem. I'd say I'm perfect… in that blissful state between not remembering and not caring.

But I'm not.

So, I splash my face with water, give myself a brief pep talk in the mirror about minding my manners and keeping my hands to myself, and walk out.

When I get back to the dining room, Ross has already cleared the plates and is in the kitchen. There's water running and music playing in the background. It's soft and low, but just loud enough I can make out the words and soulful melody of a Chris Stapleton song. It's not my normal choice of music, but I can appreciate it and somehow, it's so Ross.

Gritty.

A little rough around the edges.

But so well defined and precise.

Calm.

Mellow.

And so sexy.

Leaning against the entryway to the kitchen, I just watch for a minute, taking him in and admiring the view.

I should leave.

I should tell him I have to get home and walk out that door, but I don't and it feels reckless but I can't find it in me to care. He's leaving in two days and I'll miss him. Call me crazy, but over the past week, I've gotten even more attached.

Like a magnet to steel.

Pushing off the wall, I walk over and give him a nudge. "You cooked; I'll clean. That's the rule at our house. If Charlotte cooks, I clean. If I cook, she cleans. She might be a bigtime rockstar, but when she's inside the walls of our house, she's just Charlotte Carradine, my big sister."

Ross smiles down at me and I realize that's something I love about him too. Inside these walls, he's just Ross Davies, a regular guy who's trying to respond to the curveball he was thrown and figure out what this new season of his life is going to look like.

We lock eyes for a long moment and I'm forced to swallow down the lump in my throat. Just when I'm getting ready to avert my gaze, Ross raises his hand... and flicks me with soapy water.

"Oh," I say on a screech. "You did not just do that."

"Yeah," he says, his voice dropping low and gravely. "I did."

I laugh and so does he and the next thing I know, we're having a full-fledged water fight in his kitchen. My hair is a mess as strands begin to stick to my face. When I go for the big guns and pull out the sprayer from the sink, Ross holds his hands up in surrender.

"Okay, okay," he says, still laughing and the rumbling sound stokes the ember that has settled in my stomach. "Truce?"

"I don't think so, Big Shot," I say, mocking him with his nickname from college. Yeah, I've looked up everything there is to know about Ross Davies. I know his stats from high school to the big leagues and everything in between.

"Big Shot, huh?"

In one ridiculously athletic move, he braces his arms on the island that's between us and launches himself over. The next thing I know he's standing in front of me, chest heaving and brushing against mine, sending a bolt of need straight to my core.

"Ross," I murmur, bringing my hand up and placing it on his chest, right between his pecs. He's so hard, everywhere, except right under where my palm resides. His heart is anything but hard and that's probably the sexiest thing about him. He could be cold and jaded, but he's not. He's still himself, even though he's still a little broken, but he's still there… and he's standing right here in front of me, exposed and vulnerable and so real that I can't help myself.

Pressing up on my tiptoes, I brush my lips against his.

"Casey," he whispers. My name sounds like a plea and I want to give him whatever he wants, unless he's getting ready to ask me to leave… I don't want that. But I will, if he asks me to. If this is too soon or if we're not on the same page…

"I can go," I tell him, leaning forward and kissing his cheek.

"Don't you dare."

We stand there for a moment, breathing the same air, giving ourselves a chance to catch up and bail, but neither of us does. When I feel his hands grip my hips tightly, I respond by wrapping my arms around his neck and crashing my mouth to his, taking what I've wanted all night.

The way Ross kisses me back is straight out of a romance novel.

He doesn't just kiss me, he claims me.

It's possessive and wanting.

When I wrap my legs around his waist, he brings his hands up to my hair, gently pulling it as he tilts my head back and claims my neck like he did my lips.

At some point, he walks us out of the kitchen and to the stairs that lead to his bedroom, but we don't make it more than two steps before he stops and takes my dress off.

Then my bra.

Halfway up the stairs, he lays me down and begins to kiss his way from my neck to my panties, paying special attention to my boobs. I can't think straight for the way his skin feels against mine and the delicious way his scruff leaves its mark down my body.

This is stuff fantasies are made of.

My fantasies.

For a brief second, I think about pinching myself to make sure it's real, but then decide against it as Ross's teeth nip at the waist of my panties.

If this is a fantasy or a dream, I don't want to wake up.

When I hear the rip of fabric and then the bite against my skin as Ross discards my panties, my eyes fly open and I glance down to see a look on Ross Davies' face that I've never seen before.

Need.

Want.

Like an animal on the prey.

He's the lion and I'm the gazelle, except I'm not unsuspecting or a silent bystander, I want this more than he'll ever know.

Holding my gaze, he lowers his mouth to my center and my eyes roll.

Oh, God.

I know this is not an appropriate time to bring God in to this, but *Sweet Jesus…*

Okay, or Jesus.

But this man is a gift from heaven and his tongue has been blessed by the angels. There's no other logical explanation for how he's making me feel right now.

When his mouth sucks my clit as he plunges two fingers inside me, the room spins and my body burns with an impending orgasm. Usually, it takes me a good five minutes to come, but in less than two, Ross has me teetering on the edge.

The heat travels up my torso and before I know it, my entire world explodes.

When I finally open my eyes, a smirking Ross is hovering above me and my hands are still in his hair. "Did you like that?" he asks smugly and I groan as his jean-clad erection thrusts against me, making me want more.

Since when am I so greedy?

"You know I did," I retort, leaning forward to kiss him. Tasting myself on him does something to me. I've had men go down on me before, but never with that much fervor. I want to return the favor, but Ross doesn't give me the chance.

When our kiss gets heated, he uses the rail to stand up on the step below me, and then he lifts me into his arms. Before we make it to the top, I have his jeans halfway down his muscular hips and I can feel the head of his erection at my entrance. Using my feet to push the denim further down his legs, I let out a loud, satisfied groan of approval when I feel him enter me.

It's only an inch or so, but it's enough to let me know Ross is big everywhere, especially *there.*

"Oh, God," I say, panting as my arms wrap tighter around his shoulders and he angles me against the wall. "Yes."

Ross grunts his approval and kisses down my bare shoulder, giving me a minute to adjust to his girth before thrusting his hips and filling me completely.

Kissing down his neck, I sink my teeth into that sexy-as-sin muscle between his neck and shoulder. "Ross," I moan, holding onto him as he begins to pound into me.

Never.

Never in my twenty-three years have I ever felt like this, had sex like this… been completely and utterly owned like this. He's taking what he wants and giving me everything all at once.

"So good." My words come out in a choppy pant. I'm usually not a talker during sex but I can't help it, not with him. It's so good, I have to tell him or I'll combust. "Never," I say, throwing my head back and meeting the wall behind me but not caring. Nothing could take away from the euphoria that's racing through my body as another orgasm builds. "I've never felt like this."

"You like my cock," Ross says and I'm a little caught off guard, not expecting the dirty talk.

When I laugh, Ross groans as his hands tighten on my thighs.

"You're gonna kill me," he says, moving his hips even faster and deeper, hitting a spot I didn't even know was possible.

"The feeling is mutual," I tell him, meeting his eyes. With one hand on his scruff-covered cheek, I use my other hand to brush the hair out of his face.

It's an intimate, sweet moment in the middle of the hottest sex of my life and I can't stop the soft smile. I want to say so many things, but I know I can't. It would freak him out and as far as I know, this is just a one-night deal—good sex to blow off steam.

"Come for me," Ross demands. "I need you to come for me."

Slipping a hand between us, he finds my clit and I detonate.

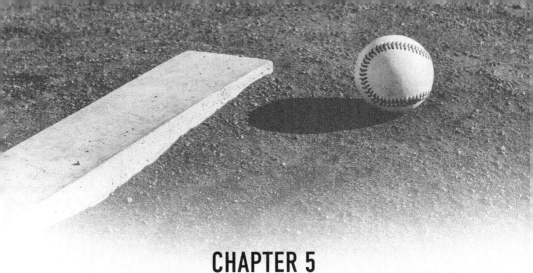

CHAPTER 5

Ross

FUCK.

I don't want to wake up but there's a sudden chill in the air and I can't seem to find any of my blankets. I keep my eyes closed as I feel around the bed, trying to grab anything to cover up with but come up empty handed.

I must've had some wild dreams or something because I don't normally kick the bedding off. I'm typically a very sound sleeper and barely change positions.

Maybe it was all that wine I drank last night.

At that thought, images begin to flash through my mind.

Long, blonde hair.

Rich, brown eyes.

And silky, soft skin.

So much skin.

Touching me.

Under me.

Casey.

When there's a soft rustle in my otherwise quiet bedroom, my eyes pop open... just in time to see Casey and her bare ass tiptoe out of my room.

Part of me wants to pretend I'm still asleep and let her go, because she's obviously trying to escape undetected and probably trying to avoid an awkward conversation. And although we do need to have a conversation, it's fucking early. And if she's feeling anything like me, she's still trying to wrap her head around what happened between us last night.

But a bigger part of me wants to grab her and pull her back in bed and have my way with her.

Again.

The more I remember about last night, the more I want a repeat and now that I'm fully awake, I know I need to act fast before she leaves my house.

Even if last night was a one and done kind of deal, I don't want it to ruin the friendship we've developed over the past year. I'll kick my own ass if that happens, because Casey's been a lifeline I didn't even know I needed. In just a week she's helped me get my life back in order and feel good about leaving for Spring Training.

And don't even get me started on what last night did for me. Not only did I need a release, but I also needed to be reminded that I'm a man and I can still feel. The last year of my life has been such a fucking roller coaster and it's been a long damn time since I've just lost myself in a woman, even my ex-wife.

We stopped having sex a long time before we divorced.

Rolling out of bed, I quickly rifle through the blankets on the floor until I find my boxer briefs and attempt to pull them on, not-so-gracefully, as I rush out of the room.

I'm halfway down the stairs when I hear her car come to life and by the time I make it to the front door, she's driving away.

Shit.

Slumping down, I sit on the bench in the foyer, staring at the front door. When I lean my head back and inhale deeply, I can smell her sweet scent lingering and a vision of last night's activities flood my mind.

Everything happened in such a frenzy.

One minute we were playing around in my kitchen and the next Casey was kissing me.

I can't remember the last time I let loose like that and just did what felt right—from the water fight to taking Casey against the wall…

What the fuck have you done, Davies?

After I mentally berate myself for a few minutes, I eventually get up and go into the kitchen for coffee. I leave bright and early in the morning for Spring Training and I still need to pack. I also need to call my parents. They usually come and spend a few days at the beginning of each season and I need to make sure they're still coming this year.

Everyone has responded to my and Felicia's divorce in their own way.

My dad was very matter-of-fact about it.

Well, Son, sometimes things just don't work out. As long as you gave it your all, that's all you can do, and now you just have to move on and figure out your Plan B.

That's my dad, always with the words of wisdom.

My mom was sad about it.

But not for the obvious reasons. She was just disappointed because she's not any closer to getting grandchildren. She and Felicia butted heads quite a bit over the years, usually over trivial things, but they never bonded like I always hoped they would.

Maybe that was my first sign and I just refused to pay attention.

Things changed so fast after we got married. We went from young love and having our whole lives ahead of us to being married and then thrust into the world of professional baseball.

I remember a talk we had before I proposed, where I specifically asked Felicia if the career I hoped to have was something she was willing to take on. I knew being the wife of a Major League baseball player wasn't going to be an easy task and I needed to know she was onboard and in it for the long haul.

Of course, she said yes—*Anywhere you are is where I want to be.*

And now I wonder if all of that was a lie.

Or did we just grow apart?

Fall out of love?

And that brings me back to the vicious cycle of thinking I've been in for the past six months. How does that happen? What did I do to cause it? Could I have prevented it? Did I not fight hard enough?

The therapist I saw the first few months after the divorce told me no one plans a divorce and if we all saw it coming, we'd either never get married or fix our problems before they become too big to handle. She helped me take responsibility for my part, because it is a partnership and we're both responsible, and also try to let go of the things out of my control.

As much as it goes against what I believed for so long, I wasn't responsible for Felicia's happiness, she was. Sure, it was my job to do everything I could to make her feel loved and cherished and protected, but ultimately, her happiness was her responsibility.

When my phone rings, it makes me jump, and I realize I've been standing at the kitchen sink with the water running for who knows how long. I never even put the coffee grounds in the filter.

Swiping my thumb across the screen, I answer before it goes to voicemail. "You'll never be able to convince me you don't have a sixth sense," I say, securing my phone between my ear and shoulder as I finish prepping the coffee pot.

"You sound chipper this morning," my mom says.

I smirk, shaking my head as thoughts of Casey and the things we did still roll through my mind. "I leave for Spring Training in the morning," I tell her, going the safe route. Not that she would judge me for what happened last night. She started encouraging me to *get back out there* a couple of months ago.

One night on a FaceTime with her and my dad, who are way more tech-savvy than I am, they basically insinuated I needed to get laid to get my pitching game back on track.

"How are you feeling about that?" she asks. "Do you need anything?"

The worry begins to creep in and I feel bad. I know I've given them plenty to be concerned about lately and I hate it. "I'm good, Mom," I assure her, glancing around and taking in the organized, clean house. Even after the dinner I made for Casey last night, it's still tidy. Although there are a few dishes that need washing.

We kind of got sidetracked.

"Better than I've been in a while," I tell her. "Are you and Dad still planning on coming before the home opener?"

"We wouldn't miss it."

At that, I smile. My parents have always been a constant source of support and I appreciate it now more than ever. I could tell my mom really wanted to hover after Felicia left, but she gave me my space and let me grieve and wallow and find my own way out. But I know she would've been here in a heartbeat if I had needed her.

That's both the upside and downside of being an only child, having your parents' complete attention at all times.

"Unless you need us to sit this one out," she adds.

"No, I want you here."

The coffee finishes brewing and I pull a mug from the cabinet and fill it all the way to the top, inhaling before taking a tentative sip.

"The guest house should be back in working order by that time," I tell her, walking over to pop my laptop open and check emails. The first thing I see is my flight itinerary and another email telling me a car will be by to pick me up in the morning at six thirty.

Back to the grind.

"Oh," she says, surprise in her tone. "You decided to go ahead and get that finished?"

This is her tiptoeing around a sore subject without coming right out and asking about it.

"Yeah, I figured I should do that," I say, scrolling through the rest of my emails and deleting the majority of them. After Casey helped me organize my physical inboxes, she helped me tackle my virtual ones too. "Who knows, maybe I'll sell this place and buy something smaller?"

There's something about logging in and not seeing thousands of unopened emails that frees up space in my brain. It's as if those thousands of emails were keeping me from being able to focus and now that they're gone, I can use that space for other things, like Spring Training and the upcoming season.

"It's such a great house," she says. "I'm sure you wouldn't have any trouble selling."

"Especially once the guest house isn't a construction zone. It's kind of hard to put it on the market with it torn all to pieces."

The guest house remodel was one of Felicia's projects she abandoned.

And, I'm not proud of it, but I also took some anger and frustrations out on the walls at the end of the season when I felt like my life was spiraling out of control.

"How are you going to take care of that when you're gone?"

Opening up a new email, I type in the beginning of Casey's email address. I should call her, but maybe an email would be easier?

"I hired someone to help out for a while," I tell her, my fingers resting on the keyboard as I try to think about how to start. "She's going to oversee the remodel and handle everything around here while I'm gone."

"She?" I hear the smile in her voice and can't help the one that creeps up on my face.

"Yes, *she*," I tell her. "Casey Carradine, Charlotte's sister." I almost say *little sister*, but after last night, the last thing I want to use as a qualifier for Casey is little sister. She's so much more than that.

"Oh," Mom says. "I thought she stayed pretty busy with helping Charlotte."

My parents have met Casey and Charlotte at a few games, so they've gotten to know them pretty well.

"Charlotte was the one who volunteered her services." As soon as the sentence is out of my mouth I want to shove it back in and choose new words, but I press on and hope my mom doesn't catch on to the double entendre as visions of Casey in compromising positions flood my mind. "She's great," I continue, clearing my throat. "It took her less than a week to have this place in tip-top shape and she's already been in touch with the contractors for the remodel."

I hear my dad in the background, asking who she's talking to, and then wait as she catches him up to speed, finishing with the newest information of me hiring Casey.

"I like her," my dad says. "She's a go-getter."

Yes, she is.

After a few more minutes on the phone with them making tentative plans for the home opener, I say my good-byes. Then, it's just me, my half-full cup of coffee, and an open email to Casey.

Subject: About last night...

Subject: Sorry.

Subject: Can I see you again tonight?

Subject: Hello

Casey,

I was going to call but I wasn't sure if you'd want me to do that, so I'm sending this lame-ass email.

About last night... I should probably apologize, but I'm not sorry. I should probably also regret it, but I don't. I was on my way downstairs to bring you back to bed when I heard your car start up. I hope you took time to put some clothes on because I don't want the rest of the world to see that sweet ass.

If this is too weird for you, we don't have to talk about it again.

If it's not too weird, feel free to call me... or come back over tonight.

I'm leaving the ball in your court...or field.

Sorry, my jokes are as lame as these emails.

If I don't see you again before I leave in the morning, I want to say thank you for everything. Not just for the best sex I've had in a long time, possibly ever. But for stepping in and helping me work through my shit and taking care of everything while I'm gone. I appreciate it more than you'll ever know.

Feel free to email me or call me anytime for anything.

Ross

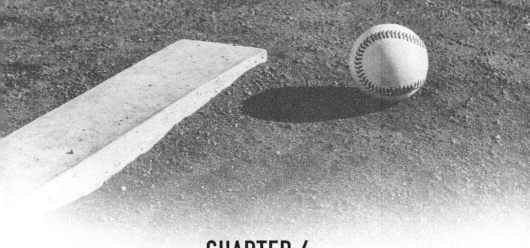

CHAPTER 6

Casey

BANGING MY HEAD AGAINST THE KEYBOARD OF MY LAPTOP, I TAKE DEEP BREATHS.

What did I do?

Ross, that's what. You literally did *your friend AND BOSS, Ross Davies.*

It's been a week and I still can't stop thinking about it.

Today, I'm going to try a new tactic where I only focus on the negative aspects of our night together, rather than acknowledging the fact it was the best sex of my life. I've learned, if I think about how Ross's lips felt all over me—tender one moment, full of passion the next—I can't stop craving him. When I remember how safe and warm I felt as he wrapped his huge arms around me, I shiver in response, like there's an actual chill in the air. But worst of all, when I allow myself to go back to that night and think about how amazing Ross felt inside me, my body starts to physically ache for him.

Which is why a list is needed.

Number one: Ross is your boss.

This job may only be temporary but it's important for me to remind myself that it is a job and Ross is my boss. I've always prided myself on being a hard worker and keeping things professional. Well, at least until last week.

Number two: Ross is your friend.

It was blatantly obvious our night together was something we both wanted—needed, even—but I also know neither of us wants to hurt our friendship.

Which brings me to number three: If we are such good friends, why haven't I been able to respond to the email he sent before he left for Spring Training?

Because, even though he said he was leaving the ball in my court, I know I can't admit to having any kind of feelings for him. That's too risky. I can't take the chance of him brushing it off as a one-night stand, which I've *never* had before, or a rebound fling. All of the logical explanations for what happened would crush me and I can't have my heart broken by Ross.

That would ruin everything—our professional relationship, our friendship, my long-lived crush, my love affair with the New Orleans Revelers... everything.

Some grownup, you are, Casey Marie Carradine.

I know I should write him back but what do I say? *"Hey, Ross, things are going smoothly at your house. I'm able to get work done even though I can't stop thinking about that time you put your man business inside my lady bits. Have a great day at Spring Training"* just doesn't seem right.

And now, I'm afraid I've wasted too much time and made things weird and he's probably given up on a response from me.

But, maybe that's what needs to happen. He obviously enjoyed sleeping with me but it doesn't mean he wants a repeat or anything more than that. The guy has been single for less than a year; I'm sure he's ready to play the field once the season starts, both literally and figuratively. So I need to pull up my big-girl panties—without thinking about Ross ripping them off—and move on.

Coffee. Coffee first then, email.

I close my laptop and walk downstairs to Charlotte's kitchen. It's been raining off and on all day, so the construction at Ross's house was postponed until tomorrow. I decided to stay here for the day so I wouldn't be tempted to put on one of Ross's t-shirts and sleep in his bed, engulfing myself in his manly scent. I let myself do it once, the day after he left, but vowed to never let that happen again.

Okay, maybe once a week, tops.

As my coffee starts to brew, I take out my favorite mug and glance out the kitchen window. I love overcast weather like we have today but it makes me want to shuck all my responsibilities and everything on my to-do list and snuggle up on the couch with a thick book.

Or a thick man.

Like, Ross.

Stop it, Casey!

I swear, I've never had thoughts like this after sleeping with someone. Typically, once I'm done, I'm done. Maybe I'm reacting this way because it had been quite a while since I was with a man and I'd forgotten how good it could be. That can't be true, though, because I didn't know sex could even be that good until I was with Ross. How sad that I didn't even know how unsatisfying my previous partners had been.

The sound of Charlotte's laughter coming from the living room pulls me out of my pity party so I quickly fix my coffee and head her way. Spending time with my big sister is exactly what I need to get me out of my funk.

"Oh, my god, Bo. You better be wearing sunscreen every day. A sunburned head is no laughing matter," Charlotte says in between giggles.

"Excuse me, your sister is in the room. Please stop all dirty talk immediately," I warn.

Charlotte only laughs harder and waves me over. "Come say hi to Bo."

I hesitantly walk over to the couch and stand behind my sister so I can look at her laptop screen over her shoulder. It takes a moment for my brain to catch up with what my wide eyes are seeing. "Bo Bennet, what the fudge happened to your hair? You're completely bald!"

"Hey, Casey," Bo greets me. "It's a Reveler's Spring Training tradition for every team member to shave their head. Don't worry, it's usually grown back in by the time the first game rolls around."

"That's... crazy," I say, still in shock over his nonexistent hair. "But it actually doesn't look bad. I just wasn't expecting it. Be glad you have a nice, smooth head," I add, before realizing how that sounds and wanting to take the words back.

Then I hear a ruckus of laughter coming from the other end.

"Wait," I say, my cheeks flushing pink. "Where are you?"

Bo tries to hide his amusement but fails. "Clubhouse."

At this, Charlotte falls over on the couch, dying. "This is FaceTime gold."

"Shut up," I tell her, picking up a pillow and whacking her upside the head. "You know what I meant. You all knew what I meant... get your heads out of the gutter." My voice gets louder when I get flustered, and I'm totally flustered, especially when I see the person I've been avoiding for the past week walk into view.

"You should really stop talking about heads," Charlotte mutters, still laughing.

Dear, Lord, take me now.

Ross seems to be frozen behind Bo and I wish I could zoom in on his face, because I can't tell if the look he's giving me is angry or hot or both. To be honest, I'd be okay with either. Anything other than indifference. That would hurt too much.

What I do know is, with or without hair, he's still the best looking man I've ever seen.

Trying not to be too obvious, I wait until Bo and Charlotte start talking about some television show they've been binging before I lift my hand and give Ross a quick wave. His eyes seem to soften minutely but it's enough of a change for me to notice.

And it's enough that it makes me wish I hadn't put off writing that email for so long.

Is it weird to miss someone who's supposed to be just a friend... and your boss?

Leaning over, I give Charlotte a big, sloppy kiss on her cheek. "I have some work to do but I'll be back down later," I say, smiling at the camera. Deciding to lean into my embarrassment, I wave at the camera. "Bye, Bo! Take care of your head. Don't want to get a nasty burn."

Taking one last glance at Ross, who's still hovering in the background of Bo's FaceTime call, I give him a small smile before jogging back upstairs.

CHAPTER 7

Ross

WHEN CASEY WALKS AWAY, SO DO I, HEADING IMMEDIATELY FOR MY LOCKER. SINCE we're finished for today, I grab my bag and go straight to my rental car. Once I'm inside and the A/C is blowing, I turn my phone on and open my email.

There's still no response from Casey.

I've given her an entire week to reply, but nothing.

Complete radio silence.

Now that I've seen her, the pull I've been feeling is even stronger. Unable to stop myself, I open up a new email.

Subject: Talk to me

Just making sure you're okay... we're okay... everything's okay.

Ross

It's short and sweet, but I need to know I didn't fuck everything up.

When my notifications immediately go off, my heart speeds up like I'm still doing drills. Her ears must've been burning, or whatever is supposed to happen when someone is thinking about you, because sure enough, there's a response to my original email waiting to be read.

Subject: re: Hello

Ross,

First, I'm sorry for taking so long to reply to your email. That's really unlike me. I'm typically a take-care-of-business kind of person. But our night together kind of threw me for a loop and it took me a few days to wrap my mind around it. Actually, I'm still working on that.

I also feel like I should apologize even though I don't regret it either. The reason for my early morning walk of shame was just that... a walk of shame. I felt like that kiss I initiated started everything and that maybe I took advantage of you and your situation. I know you said in your email that you enjoyed it... or at least that's what I'm taking from your "best sex" line... but my head still says we shouldn't have done what we did.

I'd never want to do anything to jeopardize our friendship.

You're also technically my boss...

Speaking of that, everything is going smoothly. The remodel has been delayed a little due to the rain, but the contractors have promised me we're still on schedule and the remodel should be complete by the time you're back from Spring Training.

How's ST going? Dominating the mound?

Wait, did that sound dirty? Seems as though I'm good at that today.

To answer your second email... I'm okay, we're okay, everything is okay.

Casey

The relief I feel due to a simple email is ridiculous, but damn it, I can't help it. The not knowing has been killing me. I realize she could totally be bullshitting me right now and lying about everything being okay, but Casey isn't typically a bullshitter. She's honest as the day is long.

It's one of the many things I like about her. Admire about her. For someone so young, she has integrity and a great work ethic, aside from banging her boss.

That makes me smirk and think about all the things I'd love to do to her right now.

Shit.

I should've known one night with Casey wouldn't get her out of my head. If anything, it only made me think of her and want her more.

Quickly, I type out a reply.

Subject: re: re: Talk to me

Just to clear things up...

You didn't take advantage of me. If anything, I'm the employer and you're my employee, so I was the one taking advantage of you. But I have to warn you, the HR department is shit.

I enjoyed it. Immensely.

Now that we've deduced that we were two consenting adults, let's forget about the regrets. My only regret is that we won't get a chance to do it again for the next five weeks.

I'm glad to hear everything is going well on the homefront. The contractor emailed me to tell me they'll be working a Saturday or two to make up for the rain delays. Don't feel like you have to be there on the weekends. They have the code to the gate and keys to the guest house.

How's everything else going? Other than taking care of my shit, what's a day in the life of Casey Carradine like?

Ross

P.S. I've heard I'm pretty good on the mound. ;)

Just as I hit send there's a loud bang on the hood of my rental car. Glancing up, I see Bo and Mack standing there with their arms crossed over their chests. Once they have my attention, they walk around to the driver's side and motion for me to roll the window down.

"Where the fuck do you think you're going?" Mack asks, bracing his arm on the door as he leans in and checks the backseat like he's going to find something or someone. "You hauled ass like your pants were on fire. Gotta hot date we don't know about?"

Squinting into the hot Florida sun, I look up at them. "Just ready for some A/C and a steak."

"Oh, no," Bo says, reaching for the door handle. "You're not going back to the hotel room before dark again tonight."

"Yes, I am."

Locking the doors, I reach for the button to roll up the windows, but Bo beats me to the punch and reaches his arm through to pop the locks, and then the door is open. "Out."

With a loud huff, I reluctantly step out of the car. "Didn't your mama teach you to respect your elders?"

"That's what we're doing," Mack says, slapping my back. "Showing our respect by not letting you forget how to have a little fun."

"You've been there for us and now we're here for you," Bo says, his face going a little more serious than I've seen it in a while. Well, since the day he and Charlotte showed up at my house for their intervention.

He's a good friend, so is Mack, which is why I let them win. I abandon my original plan of dinner to-go and another night alone in my hotel room, and I follow them to Mack's SUV.

Ten minutes later, we're all sitting around a table, with a few of our other teammates, in the back of Shortie's, a pub we frequent often when we're at Spring Training. I'm usually the one enforcing these evenings on rookies and now, it's me being forced into having a little fun.

Crazy how things change.

That blindsided feeling creeps back up on me as I sip my beer.

"I'm going to give you back a little of your own advice," Bo says, tossing a peanut in the air and catching it in his mouth. "You need to get laid."

Smirking, I shake my head and take another drink of beer to keep from saying something I'd regret. Not that I'm ashamed of what Casey and I did. I was being honest with her when I said we don't have anything to be ashamed of. But Bo is basically her brother-in-law and I don't know how he'd respond to knowing I had sex with his girlfriend's little sister. Besides, I've never been one to talk about what happens behind closed doors… or on staircases… or in hallways.

God, just thinking about it, Casey's name conjures up images that make my body respond.

Thank goodness for this table hiding my dick.

I'd hate to have to explain why I'm now sporting a stiffy.

"Maybe he already has," Mack says with a cocked eyebrow. "I mean, have you seen the heat he's been throwing?" He pops a peanut into his mouth, shaking his head. "Not gonna lie, after the end of last season, I was worried, but man… you're back."

I'm back.

He's right, I have been throwing some good shit, better than I expected, if I'm being honest. I'm not sure what to attribute it to. Maybe it's the solitude I allowed myself in the off-season? Maybe it was working relentlessly on my pitches?

Therapy, Bo and Charlotte's intervention, getting my affairs in order, letting shit go… all of those things definitely attributed to my mental clarity and my ability to be the ace pitcher I've worked so hard to be.

But somewhere in the back of my mind, one word echoes: *Casey.*

Casey.

Casey.

Casey.

She wasn't planned or prescribed and maybe that's what makes her so perfect. I've always been a sucker for spontaneity and serendipity. Some of the best things in my life have simply dropped in my lap. Take baseball for instance, I'm not a kid of a coach or ex-pro ballplayer.

My parents let me play every sport under the sun. They never pushed me to excel at something, but merely let me explore until I found something that stuck. Crazy enough, baseball was the last sport I tried and I didn't even pick up a bat and ball until I was in junior high. Most of the boys on my first team had played together since little league. But not me, I stepped on the field and gravitated toward the mound. The rest was history.

I graduated from a small high school who'd never had a player go to a D-1 school until me. A scout was in my area on his way to another high school when he stopped into a convenience store in my town and overheard people talking about my last home game and how they can't believe I hadn't been picked up by a college yet.

Again, the rest was history.

Casey feels like another one of those moments, like she just dropped into my lap, literally and figuratively.

Even if she's just here for a season—someone to remind me of what it feels like to want someone and be wanted in return—I'm glad she's here… or there, rather. And I'm hoping we'll be able to pick things up where we left off when I get back.

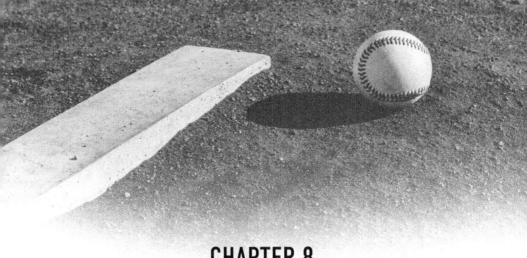

CHAPTER 8

Casey

STANDING ON ROSS'S FRONT PORCH, I WAVE TO PHIL AS HE DRIVES OUT OF THE GATE. He's the guy who's doing most of the remodel on the guest house and he's super nice. He's also probably the same age as my dad and as round as he is tall. We've become fast friends over the past two weeks.

I bring him coffee every morning.

He shares his homemade cookies his wife sends with him for lunch.

It's a pretty sweet deal.

When my phone rings from my back pocket, I pull it out to see Ross's name flash on the screen.

"Hello?" I answer, trying not to sound as breathy as he makes me feel.

"Hello," he replies in his deep, smooth voice that shoots straight to my core.

Clearing my throat, I turn to walk back inside and pretend like I'm unaffected. "Hey, Ross. So, uh, how's Spring Training going?"

Stupid question, Casey.

Slapping my forehead, I lean against the counter. I already know the answer to this. Thanks to the dozens of emails we've exchanged over the past two weeks, I know a lot about Ross Davies, including how Spring Training is going. He just gave me a full rundown last night.

"Good," he says, drawing out his response with a chuckle. He's onto me, I know it, but thankfully, he lets my awkwardness slide. "Just wanted to call and see if you'd do me a favor."

His tone shifts when he mentions me doing him a favor, like he hates asking. I want to tell him I'd do anything for him, but that might sound desperate.

And if he's thinking sexual favors, I'm more than happy to oblige.

"Sure." The pitch of my voice rises and I clear my throat and try again. "I mean, of course, I am your employee, so whatever you need…"

He sighs and I can almost see him running a hand over his now-bald head.

I'd love to do that for him.

"I hate even asking, but I kind of haven't hired a publicist. My agent handles most of those duties out of the kindness of his heart, but he's tied up and I need someone to coordinate a few interviews for when I'm back in town, mostly local stuff…"

He's rambling and it's adorable. "No problem," I tell him, unable to hide my smile when he sighs again, this time in relief. "I'm well versed in being a stand-in publicist. Forward any emails my way and I'll field them and get everything scheduled."

"I owe you," he says. "More than what I pay you."

"No, you don't," I reply flatly.

There's a moment of silence and I'm getting ready to ask him if there's anything else when he begins to speak again. "I'm sorry for the phone call… I just wanted to hear your voice and the favor was a good excuse to call you. I could've put it in an email, but sometimes those start to feel even more impersonal than fucking text messages."

"What's your deal with text messages anyway?" I ask, partly because I want to know and partly because I want to keep him talking for as long as possible. *Especially* now that I know he called because he wanted to hear my voice.

"Hate them." He doesn't even hesitate with the reply and I feel like there's a story there but I won't pry. I know Ross, and if he wants to share, he'll share. And if he doesn't, he won't. "I think they leave too much room for misunderstanding. And don't even get me started on all the acronyms and one-letter replies."

"And an email is so much better?" I retort, knowing I'm playing devil's advocate and loving every moment of it. When Ross Davies is passionate about something, it's a total turn-on. Not that I need to be any more turned on by him than I already am, but whatever.

He laughs and it's literal music to my ears. "Oh, an email is so much better."

"I'm going to need something to back up that claim," I tell him, perching on one of his barstools and wishing he was next to me… in front of me, behind me… inside me.

Stop, Casey.

"First, when you have something substantial to say, it's ridiculous to send a text message. No one wants to read a fucking book through text message. I'm not huge on small talk, so typically, if I have something to say, it's better suited for email."

Nodding, I reply, "Good point. I'll accept that. But what about when you just need to send a simple, short reply?"

"Well, then it falls back to principle." There's a rustle of sheets in the background and my mind is officially picturing Ross naked, in bed. "I can see where text messages have their place, but since I've taken such a strong stance against them, I feel it is my worldly duty to uphold my position and therefore only send emails. It's like when you pick a baseball team. No matter how much they suck, you have to support them. If you don't, you're a fucking fair-weather fan and nobody likes those bastards."

Now I'm laughing and wishing we were having this conversation face to face… in bed, naked.

"Team Email," I say, punching a fist in the air. "Solidarity."

"Make fun all you want, but it's my loyalty that's so attractive, admit it."

For whatever reason, speaking about his attractiveness makes my cheeks flame.

"That's not the only thing attractive about you," I say, my voice dipping an octave.

Who the heck is that seductress and where did she come from?

Ross Davies' bed, I hear the voice in my head reply. And she's not wrong. Ever since our night together, my hormones have felt like they're firing on all cylinders. All I think about is Ross and sex. And even when I'm not thinking about one or the other, a mere mention of something related to him or sex has my mind jumping right back in the gutter. I feel wound up tighter than an eight-day clock, which is crazy. After having the best orgasms of my life, you'd think I'd be good for a while, but no. Ross has turned me into a sex fiend and without him here to get my fix, I'm a mess.

I obviously need a little me time… tonight… in Ross's bed.

"Casey?"

"What?"

He laughs and I bite down on my lip to keep from moaning at the way my name sounds coming out of his mouth.

"You were saying…"

"Oh." My cheeks flush again. Actually, my entire body flushes. "Huh," I laugh nervously. "Well, it's not like you need me to tell you that you're attractive."

"Oh, but I do."

Standing from the barstool, I begin to pace his kitchen, fanning my shirt. "It's hot in here. I think your air conditioner is on the fritz. Maybe I should call the repairman…"

"You're at my house?" he asks.

Glancing around his kitchen, I nod and then remember he can't see me. "Yes, I'm at your house. Phil just left and I was finishing up with paperwork in your office… and probably staying the night. If that's okay with you."

He told me when we made the arrangement that his house is my house while he's away. Even though I have a perfectly good house I share with my sister, it's nice having a place to myself, even if it is only for a short time. Besides, Charlotte is on her way to see Bo. Since her schedule is so flexible, she can do that.

Don't think I didn't consider hopping on that plane with her, but since no one knows about me and Ross, I didn't think it'd be a good idea.

"Charlotte's on her way to Florida," I add, because if he's not going to talk, I feel the need to keep explaining myself. "And Phil has been coming so early. It's just easier if I'm already here…"

Ross grunts and then speaks, his voice sounding gruff. "I love that you're at my house."

"Are you sure?" If he's uncomfortable with me being here, all he has to do is say the word and I'll go back home. "I just thought… well, you said—"

"And I meant what I said." There's a finality to his words that does things to my insides. I love gruff Ross... and sweet Ross... demanding Ross. Actually, there's not a version I've seen so far that I don't love.

"Okay."

The phone goes silent again and once again I'm left wishing he was here.

"I would just rather be there with you." His confession comes out just barely above a whisper and I close my eyes as I fight back another smile. Ross Davies knows how to turn me inside out with just a few words and I'm not even sure if he realizes what he does to me.

"I would rather that too..." I confess. "Not going to lie. When Charlotte told me she was flying out today, it took all I had in me not to insist on going with her. I mean, I normally do... she wouldn't have thought anything of it and I could've just gotten my own room. And maybe we could've..." I let my words drift off before I get too far ahead of myself. "But I'm here, taking care of your affairs. That's what you hired me for and if nothing else, I'm responsible."

I hear a loud sigh and I wish I would've kept all of that to myself. Ross needs to be focusing on baseball. He's had enough on his plate and he definitely doesn't need me complicating things.

"Not going to lie," he starts, throwing my words back at me. "I wouldn't hate it if you showed up. But..."

Of course, there's a but. He knows as well as I do that if we were seen together it would spike a media frenzy. Not only is he recently divorced, but I'm already connected to the team through Charlotte and Bo. No telling what the tabloids would make out of the two of us being together.

I've seen the damage paparazzi can cause. They made my sister's life a nightmare and put her life in danger. I wouldn't wish that on my mortal enemy, so there's no way I'd want that for Ross.

It's better if we keep whatever happened between us behind closed doors, a secret between the two of us.

"But it's better if I don't," I finish for him.

"Probably." He sounds regretful and I feel that regret deep into my soul, wishing things were different. If he was just Ross Davies and I was just Casey Carradine and we didn't have any of our other defining characteristics, I can see us being something special.

There's definitely a connection here.

I can feel it and I hope it's not one-sided.

I hope he feels it too, if for nothing more than to know that there will be someone else out there for him. He might be a little banged up, but he's not broken. Life might have thrown him a curveball, but he'll recover.

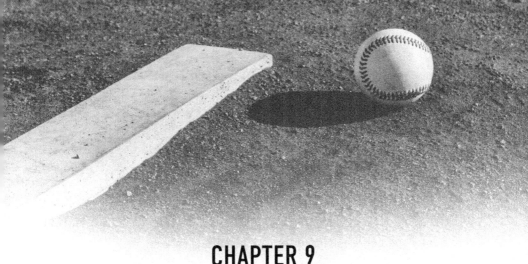

CHAPTER 9

Ross

STANDING ON THE MOUND, I WIPE THE SWEAT FROM MY BROW AS I WAIT FOR THE sign from Mack.

When he drops two fingers, signaling for a curveball, I shake my head in disagreement. I know Mack is banking on Hager chasing it, but after his last swing, I'm leaning toward a two-seam fastball.

Mack, on the same page as usual, signals for the exact pitch I was thinking.

Nodding, I take my stance, drifting past the balance point as I lean toward the plate and release the ball, which meets Mack's glove in less than half a second.

Don't blink, motherfucker.

When the ump calls the strike, Hager mutters something I can't hear, but I see the smirk on Mack's face as we leave the field, which tells me everything I need to know.

"That was some easy cheese," Mack says, hitting my arm with his catcher's mitt.

We're at the bottom of the fourth, which means that was probably my last pitch of the game. Since we're still in the fourth week of Spring Training, I'm slowly working my way up to a full game, but not quite there yet. Give me another week or two and I'll be ready to go all nine innings.

Glancing up into the stands before I step into the dugout, I lock eyes with Charlotte Carradine.

Most people don't realize the famous rockstar is here but that's because they don't recognize her. She's currently rocking a ginger wig full of curls tucked under a Revelers baseball cap. The big sunglasses hide her insanely identifiable face, so I can't see her eyes, but she gives me a small wave as I pass by.

Smirking, I give her a nod in return.

She's been at Spring Training more days than not. I don't think she and Bo made it three days apart before she was booking a flight to Florida. Every time I see her, I can't help but think of Casey.

But then again, the fucking red dirt makes me think about Casey.

The bright blue sky makes me think about Casey.

My right hand makes me think about Casey.

"Nice heat," Buddy says.

"Thanks, Skip."

Taking a seat on the bench next to Bo, I grab a cup for some Gatorade. "I see Charlotte's here again."

Bo can't fight the smile that breaks across his face at the mention of her. "Yeah, I tried to get her to stay for the last two weeks, but she said she needs to be in the studio. She's working on some new music and producing for someone..."

"It's about time we get a new Lola Carradine album."

"Yeah," Bo says, running a hand over his barely there hair. "I just hate that with every new song or album comes a new onslaught of media attention."

"I thought that was getting better."

The paparazzi put Charlotte through the wringer for years, but after it all came to a head a year or so ago, they've laid off and given her a little space.

"It is," Bo says, nodding as his eyes drift up, like he can see her behind the dugout. "But until the day they leave her alone for good, I'll always worry. I want to protect her from every evil, you know?"

I do know what he's talking about. I've felt that way before. I felt that way about Felicia. When she was mine, I would've done anything to protect her. Even after the divorce was final, I still struggled with letting go and reminding myself she was no longer my concern.

It wasn't until I ran into her around Christmas and saw her with someone else that the tether broke. She isn't mine and probably hasn't been for a lot longer than I realize.

Our conversation comes to an abrupt halt as Sanchez blasts one out of the park, giving us two more runs. Even though these games don't technically count, it doesn't mean we still don't want to win, but it does make the atmosphere more relaxed.

When Sanchez enters the dugout, we all stand and salute, then everyone breaks out into a ruckus—stomping feet, high fiving, back-slapping… it's a spectacle, but nobody cares. This might be a job, but deep down, we're all still a bunch of kids playing our favorite sport.

"Come out with us tonight," Bo says as we make our way into the clubhouse, after we beat LA by four runs. "Charlotte has to fly back home in the morning and I know she'd like to see you."

I've been making an effort to go out with my team every night. Part of Spring Training is strengthening bonds and I've always valued that aspect of the sport. Besides, my philosophy is balance—on and off the field. The past six months haven't been my best months, but I'm trying to make up for that going forward.

"You can bring someone if you want," Bo adds with a wink. "I've seen all the girls outside the hotel waiting to catch your attention."

"Oh, Ross," Mack says in a high pitched voice. "Let me make you feel better."

"I'll be the new Mrs. Davies," Sanchez says, jumping in on the ribbing.

Salito walks by, chuckling under his breath.

"You're the new most-eligible bachelor on the team and you haven't even cashed in on it," Jason Freeman says with a scowl. "What the fuck are you waiting for? Your dick to shrivel up and die?"

He's only pissed because he'd like that title to belong to him, but he's an asshole and everyone can smell him from a mile away, even the women.

"According to the gossip blogs," Sanchez says, pulling a clean t-shirt over his head, "he's already on the rebound. There's a new pic circulating with you and some smoking hot chick."

My heart stops and feels like it drops out of my chest. There's no way the gossip blogs know about Casey. That's fucking crazy. We've only been together in the privacy of my home… and she's really good about flying under the radar.... And there's no way she'd—

"Oh, yeah, I saw that," Mack says with a knowing smile and a quirk of his eyebrows. "Susan, the redhead."

I close my eyes in what I hope appears to be annoyance, but in reality, it's sheer relief that this has nothing to do with Casey. My guilty conscience was obviously getting the best of me and sending my paranoia into overdrive.

A few months ago, Mack was on a mission to get me out of my house and on the town. He set me up on a couple of blind dates. Both were awful. Susan, the red head, was the worst of all. She had arms like an octopus and I ended the night feeling violated.

That night, I went home, showered twice, and drank three glasses of Jack Daniels.

I also vowed that when I was ready to be with a woman again, it'd be on my own terms.

"Susan is the exact reason I won't be taking anyone out tonight," I deadpan, making eye contact with Bo. "But I will go to dinner with you and Charlotte." What I don't mention is that if I were to take anyone to dinner it would be Casey...his girlfriend's little sister.

Yeah, I definitely don't mention that.

Subject: Blind dates

Have you ever been on a blind date?

If not. Don't do it. Worst idea ever.

Also, if you happen to read gossip blogs and see a picture of me with a red-head, that's old fucking news. It's also not news at all. Her name is Susan and she was a blind date Mack set me up on months ago. It was horrible and I spent the entire night playing defense. I swear, the woman had invisible sets of hands.

In other news, how are you? How's the remodel going?

Did I mention my parents will be at my house for the first game? If not, I'm sorry I didn't mention it before now. If you don't mind asking Alice to make sure the spare bedrooms and bathrooms are ready for company, I'd really appreciate it.

Ross

"SO, BO TELLS ME BIG SHOT IS BACK IN BUSINESS," CHARLOTTE SAYS WITH A WINK.

Groaning, I shake my head and laugh into my beer. "Did he now?"

She gives me a knowing grin. "He did, but you can thank Casey for the nickname. Seems as though she's got all the insider information. Why don't they use that during games? It's so good… Ross *Big Shot* Davies." Her eyes grow wide. "The ladies would go nuts."

Bo just about busts a gut as he tries to hold back his laughter.

"They don't because it's in my contract," I tell her with a leveled stare. "And I'd appreciate it if you'd keep that little nugget to yourself."

Her hands go up in surrender. "Fine," she says. "It'll just be our little inside joke." She glances at Bo and then back at me, her lips twitching with a smile. "But I can't promise my sister won't use it in one of her mid-game tirades. You know how passionate she gets and when she's in the moment, she can't hold her tongue."

Suddenly, my neck feels hot and I pull at the collar of my t-shirt, then chug the remainder of my beer and hold the empty mug in the air for a refill.

"You know," Bo says, saving me from having to respond. "I've never seen someone get so heated without ever letting a cuss word fly. Have you ever heard her use anything stronger than freaking or flipping or *shut the front door?*"

His mimic of Casey is surprisingly good and the ache in my chest when I think about her grows. I also want to tell them I do know what it's like when she gets passionate about something… or someone.

I know what it's like when that someone's me.

It's all I've been able to think about for the past month.

I'd also like to go on record and tell them Casey's mouth can get filthy without ever uttering a dirty word.

Don't even get me started on how X-rated those sounds she makes are.

"Are things working out okay with her working for you?" Charlotte asks after our waitress brings us all a refill. "She doesn't say much about work, but I noticed she's spent quite a few nights at your house. Usually, she goes there in the morning and gets things going, comes back to help me for a few hours, and then goes back to your house for the night." Charlotte pauses and takes a sip of wine and I feel like she wants to ask me something, but instead, she just continues detailing her observations and I soak up everything she's giving me. "I know for a fact when I'm out of town, she stays there. I bet it's nice knowing someone's keeping such a close eye on everything while you're gone."

"Yeah," I tell her, nodding my head as I stare down into my beer, afraid to make eye contact. "It's really helped me focus on Spring Training."

Bo's hand comes down on my shoulder, giving it a squeeze. "It's nice to see you back."

Giving them both a half-smile, I hold up my beer. "To a new season."

CHAPTER 10

Casey

Subject: I'm fine

Ross,

My sister is a worrywart. When I was six and had tonsillitis, she wanted to cancel her show because she thought I was dying. She tends to be overly motherly because our mother is not the most affectionate person and it's my belief that, subconsciously, Charlotte thinks she has to make up for that, and the fact she stole the spotlight for my entire life.

And just to clarify, she did steal the spotlight but I don't care. I've never wanted the spotlight. People always tend to think I'm lying about that, but it's the honest truth.

I digress.

Long story short, I'm fine. Just feeling a little under the weather and going for a check-up. Nothing to worry about.

Thanks for asking, though.

How's everything in sunny Florida?

Casey

P.S. The remodel is so close to being finished. I thought about attaching some pics, but I think it would be better to see it in person for yourself in twelve days. Not that I'm counting.

P.P.S. I'm really going to miss having the run of your house.

Smiling, I shut my laptop and stare at the half-drunk cup of coffee. I was being honest with Ross when I said there's nothing to worry about, regarding my health. I'm positive it's absolutely nothing, but I just want to make sure. Besides, I'm due for a checkup.

Having a visit with Doc Walters is better than a therapy session or a dose of antibiotics. Any time I'm feeling under the weather, usually, all I have to do is walk into his office and I immediately feel better.

He's like the grandpa I've never had and a warm blanket all wrapped up into one.

My sister, on the other hand, is a big blabbermouth.

Those Facetime calls that she and Bo are so fond of tend to run the gamut. They go from being all lovey-dovey to talking about new patio furniture for the pool and what they both had for breakfast… and apparently my well-being. It's annoying.

The best part is they'll literally have those chats anywhere—cars, planes, hotel rooms, the freaking clubhouse. If I were to guess, half of the Revelers know I'm going to the doctor today.

They're worse than little old church ladies running a prayer circle.

Checking my watch, I see I only have about thirty minutes before I need to leave for my appointment so I decide to check in on Phil and take him a refill before I leave. I could use a little fresh air and there's no way I'll be able to finish this pot by myself today.

Coffee just hasn't been settling well lately.

"Hi Casey," Phil says with a big smile. "Brought you more of those homemade ginger snaps."

"Trade you for this piping hot cup of coffee," I tell him with a smile of my own, a genuine one that reaches all the way down to my belly, because those cookies he speaks of are like manna from heaven.

His wife must have them blessed by the pope or use holy water or something.

"What am I going to do when you leave me?" I ask around my first bite of cookie. There's no sense trying to put on airs with Phil. We're past that in our relationship. "Should I follow you to your next job? Do you need a personal assistant?"

He laughs, walking around the side of the house where his crew is finishing up painting the trim around the new windows. "Tell you what," he says, stopping as he assesses the work, "I'll bring you some extra cookies tomorrow to hold you over."

"And then you're going to abandon me? That's it? We're over?"

That gets an even bigger laugh, but I'm not really joking. I'm actually tearing up at the thought of not seeing Phil after tomorrow.

What is wrong with me?

"My wife and I have coffee every Saturday morning at Neutral Grounds in the Quarter," he says with a wink. "You have an open invitation. She'd really love to meet you."

"I'm invited to your breakfast dates?"

"Open invitation," he repeats.

Taking another bite of the cookie, I exhale a contented sigh.

The remodel is basically finished. There haven't been any major issues since Ross has been gone, or at least nothing I couldn't handle. We did have to send back some appliances last week that were the wrong size. Since the ones Ross picked out were no longer in stock, I had to make an executive decision, but I think he's going to be pleased with the replacements.

All of his affairs are in order.

I've made arrangements for interviews when he returns from Spring Training.

The house is in tip-top shape.

Basically, my work here is done, but Ross has asked me to stay on for at least a few more weeks until he has a chance to find someone to hire permanently. I could offer to stay, but the longer I'm here, the harder it will be for me to leave.

I already feel at home here… maybe a little too at home.

But I'll deal with that when the time comes.

"I've gotta run, Phil," I tell him, giving him a departing side hug. "Don't forget I'm making breakfast in the morning for you and the crew."

He tells me his wife is sending a breakfast casserole, which I'm sure will be amazing. The guys all call out their goodbyes and I make my way back into the house to collect my purse and keys.

Fifteen minutes later, I'm walking into Doc Walters's office wondering why I'm even here.

I already feel better.

"To what do I owe this honor?" Doc Walters asks as I perch on the side of the padded table. "You look like you're the picture of health."

He says that with great pride, like he's the reason I'm the picture of health.

"It's probably nothing," I tell him, waving a hand in the air. Taking a deep breath, I exhale. "I've been feeling… off. But now that I'm here, I'm pretty sure it's nothing and I probably just need more sleep or extra vitamins or something."

The truth is I get great sleep, especially when I'm in Ross Davies' bed.

And I've been having those green smoothies he has in his freezer every morning since he's been gone.

"Or maybe it was something I ate?"

Doc Walters gives me an inquisitive look. "So, you've been tired and… experiencing nausea?"

"A little," I say with a nod. "But, per usual, I feel better by just being here."

He smiles and grabs my chart. "Well, it's been about a year since we did any lab work. Let's just cover our bases. Hazel will be in shortly to get everything going."

"I'm not sure…" I start and stop. "I'm fine."

"I'm sure you are," Doc Walters says with a look that tells me I'm not getting out of this. "Humor me, Miss Casey. I'll feel better if I send you out of here with a clean bill of health."

Giving him a smile, I concede. "Okay."

Hazel, his nurse, comes in a few minutes later and draws blood, then hands me a cup to pee in. After I've filled the cup and washed up, I sit back up on the padded table and wait.

"Let's check you over," Doc Walters says when he comes back into the room a few minutes later. "Any other symptoms I should know about? Pains or discomforts?" Using his light, he examines my pupils, takes a peek in my mouth, and then monitors my pulse.

"No," I reply, feeling like I'm wasting both of our time. "Like I said, just a bit tired, but I've been working for a friend while he finds someone to help him full time. And of course, still helping Charlotte when she needs me. So it's probably just that. Plus, I heard there's a bug going around, so maybe my body is just fighting off the germs."

Placing his stethoscope on my back, he instructs me to take a deep breath and listens intently. When he's satisfied with my lungs and heart, he asks me to lie back and begins palpitating my stomach.

"Are you feeling any nausea now?" he asks, moving his hands around on my abdomen.

"No."

"Any pain or discomfort when I push here?" he asks, putting pressure on my right side and then my left.

"No."

Offering me his hand, he helps me back into a sitting position. "Everything looks good, but let's see what the lab results say, okay?"

I nod, giving him a smile.

While he's gone, I occupy myself by checking emails.

Ross hasn't replied to the one I sent earlier, but I didn't expect him to. The Revelers are playing Seattle today and Ross is pitching. I'd love to be there. If Charlotte was still there, I'd make her video it and send it to me like she did last week, but she's back in the studio this week.

Clearing out junk mail, I circle back around to my previous emails with Ross. I have them all saved in their own folder. Sometimes, I go back and read them again. It's crazy how much you can learn about a person when your only ways to communicate are emails and phone calls.

It's almost like we're pen pals.

Who've had sex.

Amazing, mind-blowing sex.

Yeah, definitely not what I want to be thinking about while sitting in the doctor's office.

Clearing my throat, I square my shoulders and skim a few emails to try and distract myself.

I smile as I come across an email from earlier this week. Somehow we got off on a side trip of our favorite childhood memories. And surprisingly enough, even though we had very different family dynamics, we had similar favorite moments.

His was when his mom and dad rented a cabin in Colorado for two weeks. He said his favorite part was he didn't have to share his parents with their jobs or obligations. It was just two weeks of family bonding.

I could totally relate.

My favorite memory is when Charlotte was in between filming and my mom and dad rented a beach house for just the four of us. There weren't any cameras or famous people. It was just us, and it was so easy to forget we had to share Charlotte with the rest of the world.

I'm still scrolling through Ross's emails when the door opens and Doc Walters walks back in.

"Sorry to keep you waiting," he says, the picture of calm, which makes me calm.

Putting my phone back in my purse, I smile. "It's fine."

Walking over, Doc Walters starts to speak again but stops, cocking his head.

The long pause turns my calm into nerves almost instantaneously. "Am I... fine? Or is there—"

"You're pregnant."

I feel my eyes practically pop out of their sockets and my mouth grows drier than the Sahara Desert. Trying to speak, I open my mouth, and then close it, repeating that motion several times as I try to grasp what he said. But he's wrong. He has to be wrong, because there's no way...

"I can't be pregnant."

Doc Walters gives me his signature reassuring smile. "As far as I know there's only one confirmed immaculate conception, so I'm assuming you've recently been sexually active."

"No, I mean, yes, but it was only once... or one night, and I'm on birth control."

He clears his throat and pulls up the rolling stool, having a seat. "Abstinence is the only foolproof method of birth control. Have you missed a pill?"

"Occasionally," I admit, my mind racing as I try to think back about when was the last time I forgot to take one. "But I always... eventually... remember. Are you sure?"

"You're pregnant, Casey."

Letting out a nervous laugh, I fight back the tears pricking my eyes. This can not be happening. Ross and I had sex three times in one night. In the heat of the moment, I didn't even think about a condom. Of course, in hindsight, I realized how stupid that was, but like I told Doc Walters, I'm on birth control. Even though I occasionally forget to take a pill, I always remember and take it as soon as I do. I've been taking birth control for so long, I always assumed that when I wanted to get pregnant, I'd have to be off it for months to make that happen.

The key part of that is when I wanted to get pregnant, which is not now.

Oh, God.

"I can tell you're overwhelmed, which is understandable, and I'm sure you're going through all of the what-ifs and second-guessing your actions," Doc Walters says in the calming tone I've come to love over the years. "Let's take this one step at a time, huh?"

I swallow past the lump in my throat and nod my agreement.

"We'll get you a prescription for some prenatal vitamins and schedule an ultrasound."

Unable to speak, I nod again.

"Is there anything else I can do for you today?"

Shaking my head, I swipe at the tear that falls onto my cheek.

"You're going to be okay," Doc Walters assures me with a pat on my knee.

I try to give him a smile, but it's wobbly and when he quietly exits the room, I let the tears fall.

After Hazel comes in with my prescription, tissues, and a comforting hug, I'm able to pull myself together enough to exit the office and make it to my car. Then I break down again.

A baby?

How am I going to do this?

How am I going to tell Ross?

What is he going to think? What will he say?

My stomach feels sick all over again and it has nothing to do with pregnancy hormones. There is a cesspool of regret, anxiety, and fear stirring. Top that off with the enormous amount of aloneness and I'm a complete mess.

It would make sense to run home to my sister, but I can't go there. Something most people don't know about Charlotte is that she had a baby and gave him up for adoption. She struggled with that decision for years and I'm afraid if I tell her about the baby, it will bring up too many bad memories. I don't want to cause her any undue stress. She's in the middle of producing her next album and can't afford to be distracted.

Besides, I don't know anything except the fact I'm pregnant. A lot of people don't announce their pregnancies until they're out of the first trimester because there are so many things that can go wrong…

What if something goes wrong?

My hand instinctively goes to my flat stomach. Even though there is nothing to feel or see, something deep inside me clicks into place.

It's a moment.

Sitting in my car in the parking lot of my doctor's office, something happens, something that transcends time and space—a connection, a bond, a knowing that I'll do anything in my power to protect this living being… that's part me… and part Ross.

Leaning forward, I rest my forehead on the steering wheel and close my eyes as I let my mind catch up to what my heart has figured out—I'm having a baby.

After driving around for an hour or so, I stop by my favorite cafe for some soup to-go and then head back to Ross's house.

The second I step into the foyer, I immediately feel more at peace.

Stepping into the kitchen, I stand there and stare at the coffee mug from earlier and think about how much my life has changed in a short amount of time. Little did I know that I would walk out of this house one person and walk back into it feeling completely different.

As I perch on the barstool and pull out my soup, my mind continues to process. I think about opening my laptop and sending another email to Ross, but what would I say?

No, he'll be back in a week and I'll tell him then.

Except, that will be the opening game of the Revelers' season. I can't tell him then. I would never want to distract him from the game. And his parents will be here.

Oh, God. His parents will be here.

The soup that tasted so good during my first few bites suddenly sours.

Pushing the container away, I fold my arms and rest my head on the cool granite countertop.

When the doorbell rings, I practically leap from the stool, welcoming the distraction but when I pull the door open, I almost choke on air.

Standing before me is none other than Felicia Davies. The ex-wife. We're acquaintances, but nothing more. When she and Ross were married, she didn't mingle much, unless it was a high-profile event.

She squints her eyes, obviously not expecting me to be the one answering Ross's door.

"Uh, hi," I stammer, holding onto the door for support. My delivery is awkward and I feel my face heat up. I've thought about what it would be like to come face-to-face with her, but never imagined it like this. Ever since she and Ross first split up, I've always wanted to ask her why.

Why on earth would anyone leave Ross Davies?

Why would you not want to be married to a wonderful man like him?

But now, all I can manage are single syllables.

Felicia's scrutinizing gaze drifts past me, like she's expecting someone else to pop out of the foyer.

Taking a fortifying breath, I try again. "Can I help you?"

"I know you," she says, bringing her eyes back to me. "Casey Carradine, right?"

"Yes," I reply, forcing a smile. "That's right."

"What are you doing here?"

I swallow. "I—I'm, um, I work here."

She scoffs and raises a manicured eyebrow in disbelief. "Oh, please."

When my expression doesn't change, hers does. She grows serious and her features harden. What's she doing here? She knows Ross is away at Spring Training, so why is she knocking on his door and who did she expect to open it?

Perhaps she was only knocking out of precaution?

When I think about her barging into Ross's house while he's gone, my hackles raise and it's exactly what I need to find my backbone.

"Can I help you with something?" I ask again.

When she steps forward, like she's going to bypass me and walk into the house, I put my arm out to stop her.

"Excuse me," she huffs, obviously annoyed.

Making direct eye contact with her, I stand my ground. "No, I won't," I say calmly, but it's a front. Between the bomb that was dropped on me today and Felicia's surprise visit, I feel anything but calm, but I won't let her know that. "Ross will be home in a week. If you need something, you can come back then."

She smirks, shaking her head as she rolls her eyes.

There's a brief standoff, but she eventually retreats and turns to walk back to her car. Before she climbs in, she pauses. "Don't be a cliché, Casey. It's never a good look."

I watch her drive away and try not to let her assumptions play into my fears, but it's impossible.

CHAPTER 11

Ross

I'M JUST GETTING OUT OF THE SHOWER WHEN MY PHONE RINGS. TOWELING OFF, I walk into the main room and retrieve it from the nightstand. When I see Casey's name on the display, I quickly swipe my finger across the screen to keep it from going to voicemail.

"Hello?" I answer, unable to control the smile on my face at just the sight of her name.

"Hey." I can tell she's tired from her tone alone, but there's something else there too and it makes my smile fall.

"You okay?"

There's a pause before she answers, "Yeah, I'm fine."

I want to call her out on the bullshit lie she just told, but I don't. This isn't my first rodeo and while I may never fully understand women, I do know that when they say they're fine, they're usually the opposite.

"I just wanted to call and let you know Felicia stopped by today."

"What? Why?" I ask, trying to keep the annoyance out of my tone. Felicia hasn't darkened the doorstep of the house we shared since the day she walked away. Why would she show up now?

Casey sighs. "I don't know. She acted like she was just going to waltz right in, but I didn't let her. I hope that's okay. It just felt wrong for her to be here when you're not."

Her tone is hesitant and I realize she thought I might be mad about it.

I'm not mad at Casey for not letting her in, I'm mad at Felicia for thinking she can still waltz in like it's her house.

"You did the right thing," I assure her.

"You changed the locks, right?" Casey asks. "I mean, it's none of my business, but I got the feeling had I not been here today, she would've walked right in and helped herself to whatever she was after. She was not happy I was here."

"Did she say something to you?"

I'm met with another pause and then she finally replies, "No."

"Would you tell me if she did?" I ask, not believing her because I know Felicia and she can range anywhere from petty to downright rude when things don't go her way. Seeing another woman at the house we once shared would be enough to quickly push her into bitch mode.

"Don't worry about me," Casey says, her tone carrying something that doesn't settle well with me, but I can't put my finger on it. "I can take care of myself."

"Are you sure you're okay?"

Another long pause.

"Yeah, just tired."

It's then I remember the emails we exchanged earlier and that she never let me know how her appointment went today. "What did the doctor say? Are you going to live?" I ask, trying to lighten the mood and get her mind off Felicia. And also hoping she was right and there's nothing to worry about. I hate the thought of Casey being sick.

"Uh, yeah, fine... I'm, uh, good..." She sounds distracted and just as I'm getting ready to ask for more details, she continues. "Hey, I have another call coming in. Can we talk later?"

"Sure, yeah, we'll talk later."

When the line goes dead, I pull the phone away from my ear and look at the screen. I'd give anything to see her right now. If we were face-to-face, I'd be able to truly see if she's as fine as she claims to be.

There was something off in her tone and I'd love to be able to put my concerns to rest, but that'll have to wait until I'm back in New Orleans next week. It's possible Felicia just worked her magic, but my gut tells me it's more than that.

Who was calling?

It's not like me to overthink things like this. I haven't felt jealous of another person in a long damn time. Shit, I didn't even feel jealous when I ran into Felicia with another man. At the time, I just felt numb, like I was living someone else's life. But even now, looking back on it, I feel nothing.

But the thought of another man calling Casey or taking her out... spending time with her... that makes me jealous.

Tossing my towel on the bed, I grab some jeans and a t-shirt. There's no way I can stay in this hotel room tonight. I need a beer. Pressing Bo's name on my phone, I put it on speaker and wait for him to pick up as I finish dressing.

"Dude, are you psychic?" Bo asks with a chuckle. "Mack and I were just getting ready to call you. We're headed to Shorties. You in?"

"That's why I was calling."

"Great. Meet you downstairs."

Twenty minutes later, we're sitting at our usual table at Shortie's. Instead of beer, I opted for a glass of Jack. My mind is too cluttered with thoughts of Casey and phone calls and my ex-wife showing up unannounced for beer.

So, Jack it is.

"Should we be worried?" Mack asks, his eyes trained on my nearly-empty glass. "The last time I saw you drink anything but beer was the week after..."

Draining the last drop, I raise my glass to signal our waitress. "Felicia left," I finish for him. "You can say her name. I'm not a fragile flower. And it's been almost eight months since the divorce."

Bo clears his throat. "Anything you want to talk about?"

The waitress shows up with my refill and I give her a nod of thanks.

"I'd like to circle back around to my original question," Mack says. "Should we be worried?"

Shaking my head, I pick up my glass and give a half-hearted chuckle. "You two are worse than old women."

A hand comes down on my shoulder and I look up to see Bo staring at me. "We just worry about you. Nobody wants to see you back in the dark place you were in last season."

"I'm not going back there," I assure him. "This isn't a setback, it's just..." Part of me thinks it'd be easier to just tell them the truth, but I'd never do that without talking to Casey first. The other part of me likes that no one else knows. Living a life that's often broadcast for the world, I like having something that's just mine. "It's nothing. Just a little tired… and we're coming to the end of Spring Training, which means we're getting ready to start the season and I have a lot to prove. I know y'all have heard me preach about balance."

Taking a healthy drink, I set my glass back on the table. "This is me finding a little balance."

"To a new season and kicking some ass," Mack says, holding his beer in the air.

Bo and I tap our glasses with his and chime in, "To a new season!"

I may never be back to the pre-divorce Ross, but I've come to accept that, and possibly even appreciate it. Felicia and I had been together for so long we'd grown stagnant. And sometimes, I wonder if that leaked over into my professional life too. There is definitely something different about my gameplay.

The new Ross has a clearer view of what he wants and he's not afraid to go out and get it.

A lot of people fear heartbreak after divorce, but not me. I've been there, done that, and survived the aftermath. At this point, there's nothing left to lose.

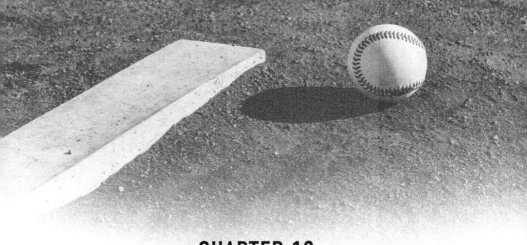

CHAPTER 12

Casey

WITH ONLY THREE DAYS UNTIL ROSS RETURNS FROM SPRING TRAINING, I'M TAKING advantage of the solitude and camping out at his house, avoiding everything and everyone.

As far as Charlotte knows, I'm busy here getting everything ready for when he returns.

It's been a little over a week since I got the news from Doc Walters that I'm pregnant. Later that night, I drove to a pharmacy on the other side of town and bought one of every pregnancy test they had on their shelves. There was still a part of me that hadn't accepted the news.

I needed to see proof.

And every test was positive.

I've spent every day since vacillating between overthinking everything and blankly staring into space. Thankfully, the remodel is finished and I was able to pull myself together for the breakfast I'd promised Phil and his crew. As for the coffee date with him and his wife this past Saturday, I took a rain check.

I also took a raincheck on dinner with Charlotte.

I know I can't hide away forever, but I'm not ready to share this news yet. My ultrasound is scheduled for two weeks from today. Once I see it with my own eyes, hear a heartbeat, and have a due date, maybe it'll be easier.

Oh, God. Just thinking about it makes my stomach queasy and it's not the morning sickness… or rather the all-day sickness. The past few days have been rough.

What will I do when Ross gets home?

How will I face him?

How will I hide this from Charlotte?

I've tried putting myself in Ross's shoes, playing out every scenario over and over in my mind and none of them end well. In one, he's so angry he can't even look at me. In another, he thinks I'm trying to trap him. And in another, the most humiliating, he thinks I'm lying.

Somehow, I feel solely responsible even though I logically know it took both of us to make this baby. He never mentioned using a condom or even asked if I was on birth control. But if he had, I would've told him I was good… covered, protected. I haven't been in a sexually active relationship in over a year. And even though I don't know for certain what Ross's sexual history looks like, I trust him so, I probably wouldn't have thought twice about having sex without a condom.

Visions of that night play back in my mind and my entire body feels flushed. It was the single, most passionate night of my life. I've never felt that way, never been so caught up in my emotions that reality is a fleeting thought. Honestly, until six weeks ago, I thought what Ross and I did was something that only existed in romance novels and movies.

Letting out a wry laugh, I smooth back my hair as I stare out into Ross's pristine backyard with the newly remodeled guest house. It's a little piece of paradise with the pool and garden. I'd love to live here forever, hide away here forever, but I can't.

He'll be home in three days.

I'll be back home in three days.

As I take a deep, cleansing breath and let it out slowly, I give myself a mental pep talk.

I can do this.

I have to do this.

Someone else is depending on me now and I can't let him or her down.

I might not have asked for this, but neither did this baby. I'm going to put my fears aside and put his or her needs above my own. There's no other choice. And when the time is right, I'll tell Ross.

The good news is that if everything goes according to plan and according to the books I've been devouring this past week, I shouldn't go into labor until after the playoffs.

Maybe I'll move to Alaska or something.

Just until after the baby is born.

Wincing at the thought of how cold it is there, I immediately scratch that idea.

What about Mexico?

But then there's that True Crimes story about the girl who went there on vacation and her family never heard from her again.

As much as I'd like to fly under the radar for the next seven months, I know I'll need my family.

I'll need Ross.

Taking another deep breath, I try to calm my heart. I have time. I shouldn't start showing for at least a couple of months. By then, I'll have my own game plan.

WALKING INTO ROSS'S BEDROOM, I PAUSE AND TAKE INVENTORY AND EVERYTHING IS as it should be.

The bed is made with fresh sheets.

The nightstand is tidy.

I took my water glass and crackers back to the kitchen.

My iPad is stowed away in my bag.

The few clothes I'd been leaving here are packed away.

My carbon footprint has been erased and for some reason, that doesn't sit well. I want to be here. More than that—scarier than that—I want to be a part of his life. And not just in a professional or friend capacity. And not because I'm pregnant with his baby.

Even if I wasn't, I'd still want Ross.

Originally, I'd planned on being here when he gets back from Spring Training, but now… I just can't. Not yet.

Alice came yesterday for a clean sweep through the house and to make sure everything is perfect for Ross's return and his parents' arrival. There's a casserole in the oven and all Ross will have to do when he gets home is warm it up and pull the salad and wine from the refrigerator.

I even left some fresh flowers on the dining room table.

His flight is scheduled to land in an hour, so it's time for me to go.

Thankfully, Bo is on the same flight as Ross, which means Charlotte will be preoccupied for the evening and I'll be able to hide away in my room.

I'm dreading facing her. I have no clue how I'm going to get around our normal routine without lying to her. What happens when she asks me to do our weekly movie and wine night?

I never lie to my sister.

The fact I've omitted the truth for the past week or so is enough to make me feel awful.

And although I feel my time of truth coming, I'd like just one more night of keeping this secret to myself.

The hardest part will be knowing that Ross is only a few minutes' drive away, instead of a plane ride. His parents coming for the opener buys me a few more days and, for that, I'm grateful.

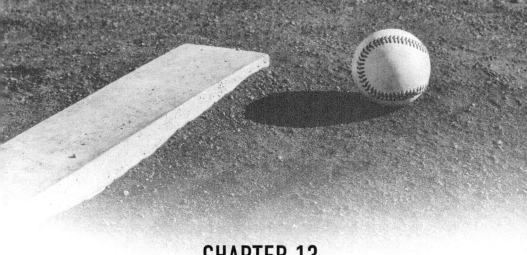

CHAPTER 13

Ross

I DON'T KNOW WHAT I WAS EXPECTING BUT IT WASN'T THIS.

Bo and I just landed in New Orleans and while he gets to run into the arms of Charlotte, I'm left standing here like a chump watching them.

Realistically, I knew Casey wouldn't be greeting me with the kisses I've missed so much while in Florida, but I thought she'd at least be here at the airport. It's a known fact she's working for me right now, so couldn't she play it off as though she's driving her boss home? She could've made up some bullshit story about needing to go over business with me, and I would've gladly played along. Instead, she's a no-show.

"Hey, man, you need us to drive you home?" Bo calls out to me.

I do need a ride but as I see my two friends, hand in hand, ready to make up for lost time, I refuse to be *that guy*. The third wheel, who's always cockblocking, or worse yet, being felt sorry for or pitied.

Fuck that.

"Nah, I'm good." I wave them off, hoping my smile doesn't look as bitter as it feels. "Y'all enjoy your evening and I'll talk to you soon."

As soon as they're out the sliding glass doors leading to the parking garage, I grab my bag and walk outside, waving down a cab.

Thankfully, my driver isn't talkative on the drive to my house, so I pull my baseball cap farther down on my head and sink into my seat. I'm happy to not be behind the wheel because I can appreciate the view of the city as we drive downtown and then into the Garden District.

It's good to be back.

I may not have been born or raised here, but New Orleans has become home to me.

"Have a good night," the driver calls out as I climb out of the car in front of my house.

After closing the door, I wave at him in response and watch him leave before turning and looking at my house.

It seems to be just as I left it on the outside, but I know the inside has been permanently altered, even if only to me. Being with Casey that one night changed me somehow. It relaxed me and reminded me of how good it feels to let go. It made me a better pitcher and teammate and showed me I'm still a man with a lot of passion inside, and I know before I even step through the door, she's left a mark on that house just as she did me.

The sting is even greater when I walk inside and it's empty.

As disappointed as I was when I realized Casey wasn't at the airport with Charlotte, a small piece of me still hoped she'd be here. But, as I look around the entryway and living room, I see there's nothing. No trace of her. I doubt a detective could find a single fingerprint. It's as though she wanted to wipe everything about her and our night together from history.

I hate to break it to her, but all the bleach in the world will never make me forget how she felt in my hands and tasted on my tongue.

What I can't figure out, though, is why the sudden change for her.

Our conversations and emails were great while I was gone. I mean, we never made it to the sexting phase, unfortunately, but I thought we were growing closer and would pick up where we left off once I got home. Casey's been off for the last couple of weeks and I'm going to figure out why. She can't get rid of me that easily. If she wants to go back to only being friends, that's one thing, but I won't let her ghost me out of her life completely. Not without an explanation first.

Walking into the kitchen, I'm surprised and extremely relieved to see my initial observation was wrong. Casey has left me a note, and while it's not exactly what I wanted, it's something at least.

I pick up the piece of paper and hold it to my nose, smelling the sweet scent she left behind, before reading her words.

Welcome home, Ross!

Sorry I'm not here to greet you, but I thought it'd be best for me to let you get reacclimated to your home without any distractions.

Dinner is in the oven and just needs to be warmed up. There's a bottle of wine chilling in the fridge, along with a salad. Enjoy and rest up for the game tomorrow! Your parents will be here tomorrow around noon, don't forget!

Good luck at the game! I'll be there cheering you and the team on. I know it'll be a busy and important day for you and I want you to enjoy your time with your family, so we can chat later about our working relationship going forward.

All my best,

Casey

Disappointment flows through my body and settles deep in my stomach, removing any traces of the hunger I was beginning to feel. Casey's words are all business and I don't like it one bit. I crumple the note and drop it on the counter, not wanting to be rid of it completely, before taking the food out of the oven and placing it in the refrigerator. I bypass the wine and close the door, opting for a bottle of Jack instead. Once I have it, I grab my bag and head straight for my bedroom.

Definitely not how I thought my night would be ending.

WHEN I AWAKE THE NEXT MORNING, I'M SURPRISED AT HOW RESTED I FEEL. JACK AND I only had a brief conversation before I put him away. I might've been a little pissed and a lot frustrated, but I'm not stupid. And I'm no rookie.

Today's the first game and it's time for me to put all my bullshit of the past seven months behind me and get back to being Ross Davies.

Ace pitcher.

Veteran.

Unspoken leader of the New Orleans Revelers.

I also think I must've dreamed about Casey, which is pretty typical nowadays, but there was something different about last night's dreams. They felt more real. Maybe it was because I'm back in my own bed, back to the place where I took her and made her mine, if only for a night.

I swear I can still smell her on my sheets, even though I know they've been freshly laundered.

When I slipped into bed last night, it was so easy to picture her here— her blonde hair splayed on my pillow—and imagine the blanket was her, wrapped tightly around me.

I wished it was her.

Whatever the reason, I think it's safe to say Casey Carradine has completely infiltrated my life.

I just have to figure out what I want to do about it.

But, first, baseball.

Well, third, really. I still have to eat breakfast and go pick up my parents at the airport. Then, it'll be time to put my game face on and kick some ass.

After my game day ritual of eggs, green smoothie, and coffee, I quickly shower and jump in my Rover to head to the airport. It's more practical than the Aston Martin and easier for my parents to ride in. I could've called a driver to do this for me, but that's too impersonal and I have the time. Besides, it's better to stay busy than sit around and overthink things.

When I pull up at arrivals, the first people I spot are my mom and dad standing by the curb. Hopping out, I jog around to help them load their luggage.

"Oh, Darling, look at you!" My mother's voice is caught somewhere between elation and exasperation as she hugs me tightly. "I'll never understand why you boys shave your heads every spring. All that beautiful, thick hair just going to waste!"

"I don't know, Mom, I kind of like it. It might stick around for a while," I tease.

"Don't tempt fate, Son. It'll happen naturally sooner than you think."

My dad rubs his shiny dome and winks. When he pulls me in for a hug, he tells me, "And don't listen to your mother. She loves my bald head; she just won't admit it."

"I can hear you, you know." My mom rolls her eyes. "Yes, I love your bald head but it's because I love you, only God knows why."

This is exactly what I needed. Being with my parents and soaking up their unconditional love and, of course, witnessing their own love for each other. I know things haven't always been sunshine and roses for them but their love has never wavered. They've always been a great example of true partnership, never afraid to show their mutual respect and admiration for each other.

When Felicia and I first broke up, I felt like such a failure… for many reasons but, mainly, because my relationship turned out to be nothing like the one my parents have. I've learned, though, that you can't compare things like that. Each relationship is its own entity and should be treated as such. I've recently come to the realization that, just because one relationship has failed, doesn't mean I can't have something better down the road.

I can thank Casey for that. Even if things don't work out between us, she's given me hope and has helped me see I'm not doomed to be alone forever.

Conversation on the way back to my house is easy as we catch up on anything and everything. Even though I always stay in touch with them and never go more than a few days without a phone call, there's nothing like getting some face time with them, and I don't mean that bullshit that everyone else does.

Actually, my mom tries to get me to Facetime her on a regular basis. She's much more tech-savvy than I am.

"How's the team looking?" my dad asks as we approach the house.

"Good," I tell him, turning into the drive. "Better than we've looked in a few years, actually."

My mom pats my leg and gives me a warm smile. "It's good to have baseball back."

"I agree," I tell her with an exhale, followed by a chuckle. "It's been a long off-season."

Once we're inside the house, I notice my mom's eyes scanning the rooms. She's not one to judge or pry, but I know she was worried about me and how I was handling everything. I can see her relief when she sees everything is clean and in good shape.

"I can't wait to show y'all the guest house," I tell them as I haul their luggage upstairs. "The remodel turned out better than I expected."

"Surprised you were able to pull that off with everything that's been going on," my dad says.

Sighing, I shake my head. "None of this would've been possible if it hadn't been for Casey."

"I hope we'll get to see her while we're in town," my mom says cheerfully as she unzips her suitcase and pulls out her number forty-four jersey.

"Yeah, me too."

After my parents are settled, I leave them to head to the stadium.

Parking in my usual spot, I can't help but smile when I take in the sights of the field and feel the energy of Opening Day. Even though the game won't start for a few hours, there's already a buzz of activity.

Walking into the clubhouse, everyone calls out their greetings as I walk over to my locker and have a seat. My game day jersey is hanging there looking like hope and possibilities and the first jitters hit me.

As I open my locker to organize my gear, I listen in as the guys talk about their first night back home and try not to think about mine.

Or Casey.

Or anything else that's out of my control.

As if on cue, Mack walks up behind me and gives my shoulders a squeeze. "How ya feeling today?"

"Great, man," I tell him with a nod, like I'm trying to convince us both of that fact. "My arm is loose and relaxed, nerves are nice and steady." I know he's not really asking about my arm, specifically, but it's the only answer I'm able to give him right now. He's one of my best friends and he knows me almost better than I know myself, so I have no doubt he understands my underlying message.

I'm only focusing on baseball right now.

"Sounds good. Let's do some good work today."

I like knowing Mack will be behind the plate. There's a level of comfort there because we work so well together. I know he worries about me, or has been worried about me, but I'm hoping to put those worries and fears to rest today.

As soon as he walks off, I take my earbuds from my locker and stick them in, letting the sounds of classical music drown out the chatter. It's something I do before every game and I'm not one to change a ritual if it works, which is why I also help myself to a po'boy and settle into my favorite corner to get ready for the game.

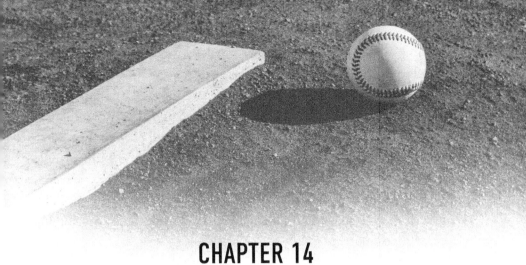

CHAPTER 14

Casey

I'VE BEEN LOOKING FORWARD TO OPENING DAY SINCE THE REVELERS' FINAL GAME last season. I may not know much about baseball, but I love it and I absolutely love being here at the stadium. Seeing the bright purple and gold team colors everywhere, the excited faces of the fans, and my personal favorite… the food.

There's just something about ballpark food and today, I'm wanting it all.

I haven't had any morning sickness the last two days and I'm hoping the trend continues. The last place I want to get sick is a stadium bathroom, that's for darn sure. I'm hoping I can rely on my newly heightened sense of smell to help me determine whether or not something will make me barf.

"Do you want to sit for a while or go ahead and get some snacks?" Charlotte asks as we walk toward our section. She's wearing one of her blonde wigs today and you'd think it'd make us look more alike but no. We could possibly pass as cousins but definitely not sisters.

"It's like you don't know me," I chide. "Food, of course."

When it's our turn to order, Charlotte gets her usual nachos but the strong cheese smell is an instant turn off for me so instead, I order popcorn, a bag of peanuts, and an extra-long hot dog, ignoring the amused look on my sister's face.

"Want a beer to wash all that down?" she asks.

Catching myself before giving my usual answer of the affirmative, I shake my head no. "I'm not really feeling like drinking today. I'll just have water."

I can feel Charlotte's eyes on me as I squirt ketchup and mustard on my hot dog and they don't leave when I add butter and dill pickle seasoning to my popcorn. If she doesn't stop, I'm gonna scream because I can't handle her scrutinizing me so closely, especially when I have such a massive secret.

Maybe coming here today was a bad idea.

She at least has the common decency to allow me to finish my hot dog before the questions start.

"Okay, spill it."

When I don't respond, she tries to grab the bag of popcorn out of my hand but no way is that gonna fly.

Slapping her hand away, I look at her like she's lost her mind. "Leave my food alone! Are you crazy?"

"No," she says in a whisper-shout, in an effort to not draw attention. "But I'm beginning to wonder about you. You're acting weird and I want to know why."

Her demand is heard loud and clear and I wish I could truly spill it, but I can't.

Not here, not today.

"I'm just hungry," I finally reply. "Geez Louise, can't a girl eat her popcorn in peace anymore?"

She lets me take a few more bites before softly reminding me, "We don't keep secrets, Casey."

My stomach begins to sour but it's not because of the hormones. It's the guilt mixed with the nerves and anxiety that has me putting my food aside. When I face Charlotte, I can see the hurt and concern all over her beautiful face and I decide to tell her what I can.

"I'm nervous about working for Ross now that he's home."

Her eyes narrow as she takes in my admission. I never show or admit to any weaknesses when it comes to work. Even though I never planned to be someone's assistant for a living, I've never doubted my ability to get the job done.

"Why would it matter if he's home or not?" she asks. "He was home for the first week you worked for him and that seemed to go okay."

Umm, because now I've had sex with him and I know him intimately and there's no way I can see his gorgeous face and not want to do it all the time. And secrets.

Shrugging, I try to play it off. "I never agreed to stay on permanently and he hasn't asked me to. Besides that, we're… friends… and it's kind of weird working for him. And now he's home for the season and you know how I hate when people hover."

"Casey, he's not going to do that. He'll be so busy now that baseball is back, you probably won't ever see him anyway. Plus, he'll be traveling a lot, too. It sounds like you're overthinking things and worrying for no reason. Ross has told Bo on numerous occasions how much easier you've made his life and how much he appreciates what you've done for him. He credits you with his amazing performances while in Florida, you know."

I have to turn my head to try and hide the blush I feel covering my cheeks and ears. Hearing that Ross has said such nice things about me makes me feel proud of the work I've done and I'm relieved I've helped him in any kind of way. But, I can't help but think how all of it can change— *will change*—once he knows about the baby.

Maybe I'm just trying to protect myself—my heart—for when it all comes crashing down around me. I'll need a Plan B, some way to make a living for myself and my baby.

"I think I know what's going on," Charlotte declares and my stomach gives a small roll. "You're still crushing on him, aren't you?"

"What?" I bark out. Shaking my head, I say, "No, no, definitely not. I mean, I used to have a tiny, baby crush on him but that was before I got to know him. That'd just be weird now."

That sounded convincing, right?

Please, God, let her buy it.

"I think it's natural to feel a little awkward when you start working for someone you used to have a *tiny, baby crush* on, but you're a professional woman and Ross respects you. I know he'd never cross any lines especially because he probably thinks of you as a little sister."

Okay, she can stop talking now.

"Besides," she continues, as I look anywhere but at her, "he may not be ready to date yet, but if he is, you have to be prepared to see him out with other women." She grabs my hand and I pray she can't feel the sweat that's currently coating my palms. "I just don't want you to get hurt."

Why can't the floor just open up and swallow me whole right now?

That'd be better than enduring any more of this conversation, for sure.

I know Charlotte is trying to be helpful and protect me but she has no clue how ironic her words are right now. She'd be so disappointed if she knew I was the one to cross the lines between me and Ross. No, I didn't cross them, I hurdled over those suckers like I was about to win a gold medal. As for preparing myself to see Ross with other women... that's pretty much what my nightmares are made of.

Swallowing, I plaster a smile on my face before waving away her concerns. "I know I'm just being silly. Ignore me and please don't mention any of this to Bo. I don't need him teasing me about this or saying anything to Ross."

"It's our secret." She winks at me causing my fake smile to falter.

Secrets.

I freaking hate that word.

Thankfully, it's time for the game to start and when we stand for the National Anthem, I immediately find Ross standing with the team in front of the Revelers' dugout. It's my first time seeing him in person since I left his bed and I don't even try to deny how it causes my blood to heat up and my heart to pound.

When he walks to the pitcher's mound, I slip my sunglasses on so I can ogle him without being obvious. I can't help it, his butt looks so good in those white baseball pants. Not as good as when he's completely naked, but still great.

And the exact distraction I need to keep my mind off of the *secrets.*

It's odd how much more invested I feel in this game. Maybe it's because Bo made it his mission to educate me in the off-season and some of it stuck? Maybe it's how close I now am with a couple of the players, one in particular?

All I know is that when the freaking ump doesn't call Ross's strikes in the seventh inning, I'm livid.

"Come on!" I yell at the field, arms waving. "Are you freaking blind? That was a strike!"

Charlotte pulls on my shirt, whisper-yelling at me to sit down.

"It was a strike," I repeat, huffing as I pick up my peanuts and crack a few. Shoveling them in my mouth, I continue to mutter about how blind the ump is and wondering if he's getting paid by the opposing team.

Thankfully, despite the bad calls, the Revelers win four to two. And even though Ross was pulled after the seventh inning, he had a great game.

"Let's go down and wait for the guys," Charlotte says, pulling my hand when I freeze with indecision. I realize there's no way she's going to let me leave the stadium alone, but I'm also not ready to face Ross. If he blew me off or pretended like there was nothing going on between us, I think I might die a little inside.

I know I'm going to have to talk to him soon, but I was hoping to get through this three-game homestand, and then they'll be on the road for two weeks. By the time they get back, I'll have had my ultrasound and I'll know a due date… and hopefully, I'll find my courage.

I will.

"Casey," Charlotte says, snapping in my face. "Earth to Casey."

"Sorry, I, uh…" I'm getting ready to lie, but my conscience won't let me. Gritting my teeth, I force a smile. "Yeah, fine, let's go."

Suck it up, Casey.

You're a freaking adult.

You can do this.

Before we make it to the corridor that leads to the clubhouse, two familiar faces pop out of the shadows. "Well, look who it is!"

Ross's mom opens her arms for a hug and Charlotte walks right into them. I love Ross's mom and dad. We sat with them at a few games last year and it was great getting to know them. They're so sweet and it's obvious how much they love their son.

"Casey," Joann coos, pulling me into a warm hug. "We're so happy you were able to help Ross. He's told us how you whipped him and the house into shape and took care of everything while he was gone." She leans back, holding me by the shoulders. "You'll just never know how grateful I am. You were exactly what he needed. Thank you for taking care of him and helping him get everything back in order."

I swear there are tears in her eyes and I don't know if I can take it.

I've always been a sympathy crier and lately, it's been worse. So much worse.

"Don't thank me," I tell her with a nervous chuckle, biting my lip to keep the tears at bay. "I was just doing my job."

That's right, it's a job.

He's paying me.

"But you went above and beyond," she continues, still lovingly squeezing my arms. Then she leans in for a kiss on my cheek, whispering, "Thank you for taking care of my boy."

Oh, God.

"Quit slobbering all over the girl," Jack, Ross's dad, says, stepping up to my side and pulling me into a hug. "But we would love for all of us to get together for dinner before we fly back home."

"Oh, that would be wonderful," Charlotte says, clapping. She loves an excuse for us to cook dinner for everyone. "Tomorrow is a day game, so how about tomorrow night at our house?"

"Well, we weren't trying to invite ourselves over," Jack says with a laugh.

Joann just shakes her head. "Tell us what we can bring."

"Just yourselves," Charlotte assures her. "We'll keep it small."

No. No. Not small. I'll definitely have to talk her into inviting some other players. If it's only the six of us, there's no way I'll be able to blend into the background or avoid having a conversation with Ross.

My heartbeat increases and I start feeling like I might hyperventilate.

"Casey, honey," Joann says, taking my hand. "Are you okay? You look a little pale."

"It's the uh… lighting," I say, shaking my head as I swallow past the lump in my throat. "And the hot dogs. I had a footlong."

"Case," Charlotte says. "You do look pale. Are you going to be sick?"

Wetting my lips, I still feel like I can't catch my breath and also like I might be sick. "I think I need a drink of water… or maybe splash some water on my face… I'll just be…" I motion to the women's bathroom down at the end of the corridor and start walking.

"Could you tell Bo that Casey wasn't feeling well and we went on home?" I hear Charlotte ask. "We'll see y'all tomorrow."

I duck into the bathroom and head straight for a stall.

"You sure you're okay?" Charlotte asks a few minutes later, handing me a wet towel under the door.

"I'm fine," I tell her. "I think something didn't settle well."

When I step out, she inspects me with her eyes. "Ready to go home?"

I nod and she links her arm with mine. As we walk out of the bathroom and down the corridor, I wait for her questions, but they never come. She gives me a respite and by the time our Uber shows up, all conversation of the dinner party is put to rest and we talk about random things until we get home.

Those secrets I hate so much are festering but I need just a little more time.

"I'm headed to bed," I tell her, not waiting around for an inquisition or guilt to overcome me. "Tell Bo congrats on the win."

"Night," Charlotte calls out, concern laced in her tone. "Feel better."

When I make it to my room, I head straight for the bathroom and brush my teeth. Once my face is washed and the stressful day is behind me, I feel my entire body deflate like a balloon. I've been on edge since I woke up this morning, but now, in the sanctuary of my room, I feel like I can breathe freely.

I've never really had much of a desire to live on my own, but I think it's time to find an apartment or something. I've always loved living with my sister. It's easy and comfortable. Plus, with me working for her, I'm never late for the office. But now that she and Bo are together and he's moved in, and I'm splitting my time working for Charlotte and Ross, I'm starting to feel more like a third wheel.

And then there's the baby growing inside me.

Taking a deep breath, I lay back on my bed and stare at the ceiling. As I place a hand on my flat stomach, I try to imagine what it will be like when it starts to grow. This weird sensation takes over and I realize in that moment, my body is no longer just mine… I'm sharing it now with a small roommate.

And we need our own space.

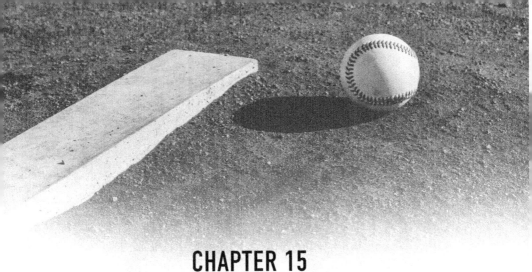

CHAPTER 15

Ross

"YOU WERE ON FIRE TODAY, DAVIES! THOSE SEVEN INNINGS YOU PITCHED WERE DAMN near perfect. Keep up the great work." Our skipper, Buddy Malone, is typically a man of few words unless he's really fired up and after winning our season opener today, he's very fired up.

"Thanks, Skip," I reply as he pats me on the back and makes his way to the rest of the team.

It's another Reveler's tradition to celebrate a win with beignets and beers and once we've all had our fill, things will really start to liven up around here. As much as I love celebrating with my team, I'm ready to get out of here and hopefully, catch Casey before she leaves.

When I see Bo duck out, I think about following him, but just as quickly as he left, he's back.

"Hey, man," he calls, when he sees me looking. "Your parents are waiting for you."

Oh, right.

Not that I forgot they were here, but I can't get Casey out of my damn brain. It's on the tip of my tongue to ask if she was also out there, but then he answers my question for me.

"They said Charlotte and Casey were out there, but they left. I guess Casey isn't feeling well."

My heart sinks, not just because I missed my chance to see her, but also because she's sick. That's like twice in the last month she's not felt well. "Is everything okay?" I ask, feeling the worry set in, but trying to keep it at bay. "I mean, nothing serious?"

Bo shakes his head. "No, I don't think so. It was just something she ate…"

"Good," I say, letting out a breath. "I mean, I'm glad it's nothing serious." I don't want her to be sick at all, but as long as it's something that will pass, it makes me feel better.

"I guess we're having a get-together at our house tomorrow night after the game," he continues. "Charlotte just texted me and said she was talking to your mom and dad and they wanted to have dinner. I guess I'm supposed to invite Mack and a few others."

Dinner at Charlotte and Bo's means Casey will also be there.

"Sounds great," I tell him, giving him a hearty pat on the back. "Tell her we'll be there and to let us know what we can bring."

After I finish up in the clubhouse, imbibing in a beer and a couple of beignets, I excuse myself and find my parents still waiting in the corridor that leads to the player parking lot.

"Sorry guys," I tell them, shouldering my bag and using a card to open the gate. "You know how it is at home games. I wouldn't have cared if you took a car back to the house."

"Nonsense," my mom says, patting my arm. "We had a lovely chat with Charlotte and Casey and saw a few of the other players' significant others. You know how it is, the first game always feels like a family reunion of sorts."

I chuckle, holding a door open for my mom. "I guess it is, huh?"

"Great game tonight, Son," my dad says as we walk toward my Rover. "How's the shoulder?"

"Feels good," I tell him, giving it a roll. "The whole game felt good."

Relief was definitely a predominant feeling tonight. After the way last season ended, I wasn't sure how I'd deliver, but finishing seven innings and only giving up one run was a solid start to the season.

When we pull up to the house, my mind immediately turns back to Casey, wondering how she's feeling and thinking of ways I could see her. With my parents at the house and her living with Charlotte and Bo, it makes it difficult.

Of course, my parents will be gone in two days, but then I'll be prepping to leave for almost two weeks. So, it doesn't leave much time for us to talk and have some privacy.

Have I mentioned how badly I want her back in my bed?

Before I'm able to fall asleep, I crack open my laptop and send Casey an email.

Subject: How are you feeling?

I know it's late, but I couldn't go to sleep without checking on you.

Hope it's nothing serious and you're already feeling better.

Also, I'd like for us to have a chance to talk soon, maybe tomorrow night at dinner?

Ross

I'd like to say so much more, but I'm trying to play it cool. If she's feeling skittish about us, I don't want to completely scare her off. But the truth is I miss her more now that I'm back in New Orleans than I did while I was gone.

WHEN I WAKE THE NEXT MORNING AT OH-DARK-THIRTY, I GROAN A LITTLE AT THE soreness from yesterday's game. Thankfully, I won't be pitching again until our away series, but that doesn't excuse me from my obligations.

On my off days, I'm basically a cheerleader. However, I'll still throw some pitches and play catch with Mack. Unlike the off-season when I train hard, once the season starts I focus on maintaining the growth I made from October to February.

This morning, I also have two interviews. Casey scheduled them for me and even though I'm up a few hours earlier than I'd like to be on an off day, I appreciate her squeezing both interviews into one day. I'd much rather get them over with before we leave for Colorado.

She's so smart and efficient.

And sweet.

And sexy.

Forcing myself out of bed, I head to the shower and jack off to visions of Casey naked.

On the stairs.

Up against the wall in the hallway.

In my bed.

God, what I wouldn't give for a repeat of our night together.

Once I've relieved a little of the tension—cleaned up, dried off, and dressed—I head downstairs.

"Good morning," my mom greets from the breakfast nook. "Can I make you some breakfast before you leave?"

"Just a smoothie for me this morning."

"Coffee?" she asks, getting up from her spot and walking around to the coffee pot.

"Please," I say, pulling the prepared smoothie ingredients out of the freezer and dumping them into the blender with a little milk.

"Charlotte told me not to bring anything tonight, but I was thinking about picking up a couple of bottles of wine and one of those delicious bread puddings from The Crescent Moon."

"Sounds great," I tell her, kissing the top of her head. "We'll drive over together. Since it's an off day and I'm doing these interviews this morning, I should be able to come straight home after the game."

Putting a lid on my smoothie, I turn and collect my to-go coffee and give her one more kiss on her cheek. "Love you," I tell her as I walk out the side door.

"Hope your interviews go well," she calls back, waving from the door.

Having her and my dad here is nice. One thing I learned about myself during the divorce is I don't particularly enjoy being alone. My therapist said it's okay to not like being alone, as long as you *can be* alone.

I can be, but I prefer company. And as much as I enjoy my parents' company, I'd really love to have Casey's.

Half an hour later when I take a seat across from a reporter from a local television station, I feel my pulse begin to race. It's been a while since I've sat down for a formal interview. Back when I was married to Felicia, I'd do them fairly regularly, even when I didn't want to. She thought they were good for my image, but in reality, it was about her image.

How could I have missed that?

In hindsight, the signs were there. Over the past few years, she started making everything about her—*her* charities, *her* speaking engagements, *her* agenda.

"Tell us about the off-season," the woman sitting across the table says, holding a small microphone in my direction. "How did you spend it? Training with your team? Coaches? What was your focus?"

The fact that she jumped immediately into my professional life and didn't start with questions about my failed marriage earns her bonus points in my book.

Clearing my throat, I scratch the back of my head and nod. "Whew, I thought this interview was going to go a lot different."

"Don't worry," she says with a small smile. "Your PA already laid the ground rules about what could and couldn't be asked. We'll be sticking strictly to baseball."

God, I could kiss Casey right now.

And I'm definitely offering her a full-time position. I've already thought about ways to sweeten the deal and make it an offer she can't refuse.

After the interviews are over, I change into warm-up gear and head out to the field to throw some balls and spend some time with my team.

I start with knuckleballs, since that's what I've been working on lately, and then switch it up to some fastballs, which are my bread and butter.

Once I've worked through all my pitches, I jog over to the outfield and play catch with a few guys. The stands start to fill and I can't help looking up to where Casey usually sits.

She's not there yet, but I'm sure she will be. She and Charlotte rarely miss a home game.

At last night's game, I spotted her once and then had to block her out. Since I was on the mound, I needed all of my concentration focused on the game, but tonight is a different story.

"YOU SEEMED DISTRACTED TONIGHT," MACK SAYS AS WE'RE STANDING IN CHARLOTTE'S backyard... well, Charlotte and Bo's backyard, I guess... and Casey's, because she lives here too. But maybe not for long, at least not if I have my way about it.

I take a sip of my beer and try to play off his question. Shit yeah, I was distracted. My thoughts were on Casey the entire night, but I can't tell him that. "No, I was just zoned into the game."

"Really?" Mack says, leveling me with a stare. "Don't bullshit a bullshitter."

Letting out a laugh, I act offended. "What?"

He shakes his head, taking a drink of his beer and glancing around the yard at everyone visiting in small groups. My parents are talking to Charlotte, while Bo is over at their outdoor bar pouring drinks for Phil and Louis...

And Casey just walked out of the house with a tray of appetizers, looking like the whole damn meal.

Mack clears his throat and I look over at him. "What?"

"Nothing," he says, taking another drink of his beer with his eyes glued on Casey. "Except for the fact Charlotte's sister is smoking hot."

In a matter of a millisecond, my body, mind, and soul collide in a response to Mack's observation and I have to remind myself I can't react how I want to—with fists and fury.

"Maybe I'll ask her out," he mutters, still checking out Casey... *my Casey.*

God, what is wrong with me?

I haven't felt this possessive over a human being in... well, forever. I want to pound my chest and yell it from the rooftops—she's mine.

Don't look at her like that and don't even fucking think about touching her.

"She's off-limits," I grit out, swallowing down the rage and sheer jealousy over the mere thought of someone else being with her.

"Says who?" Mack asks with an incredulous look. "Last time I checked she's an adult and this is the fucking twenty-first century where women make decisions for themselves."

Says me, motherfucker.

"It's just that she's basically Bo's little sister, too," I tell him, sounding much calmer than I feel. Maybe this little rant is more for me than Mack, but I'll be damned if he gets to talk to her and I don't. And I'll really be damned if he gets to ask her out.

Over my dead fucking body.

Don't get me wrong, I love Mack like a brother, but I don't care. There's no bro code when it comes to Casey Carradine. My eyes are trained on her, watching her every move.

The way she walks.

The way she laughs.

The way her jeans hug her ass should be a sin.

She's a fucking wet dream—a vixen in denim.

"Well," Mack says, breaking me from my Casey-induced trance. "I guess if I really wanted to ask her out, I'd just be upfront about it and let Bo know what's up, but I still don't see what the big deal is."

When I look back over at him, he's no longer checking her out... he's checking me out, waiting for my reaction. And I realize, he's been bating me this whole time.

"Cut the shit, Davies," he says, lowering his voice so it's just a conversation between the two of us. "I see the way you look at her. And I've seen the way she looks at you."

My entire body feels like it's been lit on fire. If Mack has seen the way we look at each other, who else has seen it?

"If I were you, I'd just walk over and talk to her... you know, like the friends you claim to be."

I'd like to punch him right now. But we're in mixed company and my parents are here, so I'll be an adult. "If I were you, I'd mind my own fucking business."

As I walk away, the only response I get from Mack is a hearty laugh.

My mission to talk to Casey is thwarted by Phil, who wants to shoot the shit about the game today. I appease him for a moment and then excuse myself under the ruse of needing a refill.

When I slip through the backdoor of the house, I see her standing in the kitchen alone.

"Hey."

She seems to startle and then she slowly turns to face me. The look on her face is not one I was expecting. She looks... scared, caged, nauseous... I don't know what description fits best, but it's certainly not desire or hope or longing, which are all the things I've been feeling when I think of her.

"Are you okay?" I ask, wondering if she's still sick. She never responded to the email I sent last night. I made sure to check about a dozen times throughout the day. I thought maybe she was just waiting to speak to me in person. But, so far, our only exchange has been a polite greeting when I arrived with my parents. Since then, she's busied herself with preparing food, serving food, and filling drinks.

"Fine," she says, brushing her hair back off her face and tucking it behind her ear. "I'm good."

There it is, the nervousness that I've never seen from her before now.

Typically, Casey is carefree and collected. She's never riled up about much, even though I've heard she's a spitfire in the stands, which is a hilarious contradiction to her normal demeanor and something I'd love to witness one day.

"You sure?" Taking another slow step toward her, like I'm approaching a frightened animal. "Because it seems like you've been avoiding me since I got back and I'm not sure what happened…"

Because things were going so great between us.

And you made it sound like you wanted to pick back up where we left off.

Casey lets out a sigh, her shoulders falling. "I'm sorry," she says, her head falling into her hands. "It's not you."

"Oh, whoa," I tell her, stepping even closer and forcing her to look up at me. "If you're getting ready to give me the it's-not-you-it's-me line, stop right there."

A small smile pulls at the edges of Casey's gorgeous lips.

And there it is, that instant connection I've always felt between us. The difference is now, there's attraction on top of that and I know it's not just one-sided because when our eyes meet, I see the desire I was hoping for earlier. It's there, but it's buried beneath something I can't put a name to.

"I miss you," I whisper, leaning forward until my lips are at her cheek. Brushing a kiss across her jaw, Casey sighs. "But I don't want to push, so if you want me to back off and we go back to just being friends, that's cool."

When I stand to my full height so I can look down and see her face, there's so much indecision there.

"I don't want…" Casey starts, then stops and causes my heart to fall to my feet, until she continues, "I don't want to go back to just being friends, but I need some time."

Time is fine. I can give her time. I can give her anything she needs, all she has to do is ask.

"Whatever you need," I assure her.

She places her hand on my chest and my entire body responds to her touch. We just stand there in the middle of the kitchen, having a moment until the backdoor opens and closes, causing us both to take a step back.

Thankfully, it's just Phil and he finds what he needs, nodding to both of us before going back outside.

The interruption is enough to clear some of the tension between us and I decide to take this opportunity to talk business, since we probably won't be discussing our relationship any further tonight.

"I want to offer you a permanent position as my personal assistant… life manager… whatever you'd like to call it," I say with a chuckle. Now, it's my turn to be nervous. "I realize we've crossed some lines and this is kind of unconventional, but I can't imagine handing all of my personal information and decision making over to anyone else right now. If you don't think you can do it, I understand, but I'd really love for you to."

Casey's gaze flits from me to the floor and then back.

Worried she's getting ready to turn me down, I decide to sweeten the deal. "Along with the salary we agreed to, I'd also like to offer you the guesthouse, for as long as you want it."

Her eyes grow wide as she chews on her bottom lip. "Well, I… uh," she starts and then blows out a breath. I can see the wheels in her head turning and I hope she's not trying to think of an easy way to let me down.

"I'll accept the permanent position… working for you, that is." She nods as if she's making an agreement with herself. "But I'm going to have to pass on the guesthouse offer… for now."

"Okay," I tell her, wanting to fist pump the air, but refraining. I'd love this even more if she'd agreed to moving into my guesthouse, but I knew that was a moonshot.

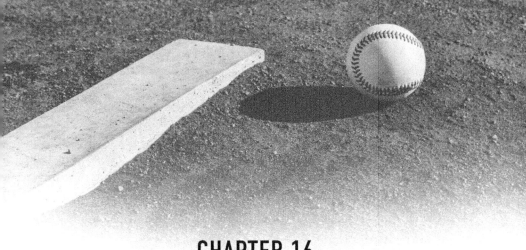

CHAPTER 16

Casey

NEW ORLEANS SWEPT SAN FRANCISCO IN THEIR FIRST HOMESTAND. LAST NIGHT'S game was a nail biter that went into extra innings and ended with Mack hitting a walk-off homerun.

Look at me and all my fancy baseball lingo, I think to myself as I park in front of Ross's house and open the car door.

The team leaves later today for Colorado and will be on the road for ten days.

Since I agreed to a permanent position as Ross's assistant—personal assistant, whatever you want to call me—I figured I should be here to make sure I know everything that needs to be done while he's gone.

His parents flew back home early this morning and I'm officially out of reasons to avoid him.

Knocking on his front door, I feel awkward because for six weeks, this was basically my second home. But since Ross is here, I can't just barge in.

When he doesn't answer, I knock again and after a more than acceptable amount of time, I decide to use the key he gave me and let myself in.

"Ross," I call out as I peek my head into the foyer.

Glancing around, I notice that the house is still in immaculate condition. Not that I thought Ross was throwing ragers in the days I've been gone, but it's nice to see he's staying on top of things. I'm sure his mom did her fair share of chores while she was here.

As I step into the house and close the door behind me, there's a sweet aroma in the air.

Groaning, I close my eyes and inhale.

Cinnamon rolls.

And coffee.

According to the books I've been reading, caffeine is something I'm supposed to be limiting, but I still allow myself one cup in the morning, when I'm feeling up to it.

"Ross," I call out again, stepping into the kitchen and placing my bag on one of the barstools.

The blender he always uses for his green smoothies is drying on the sideboard and I can tell at least one cup of coffee has been drunk from the pot, but there's no other sign of him.

In the middle of the island, there's a note.

Looking over my shoulder and around the corner, I decide to read it. Maybe Ross had to go somewhere and left it for me?

We enjoyed our visit so much!

Give Casey our love and share the cinnamon rolls with her!

Hopefully, we'll see you again in a month or so.

Love,

Mom

Smiling to myself, I place it back on the island and walk over to the cupboard to get a mug for some coffee. The cinnamon rolls are on the stove behind me, calling my name, but that's not what gets my full attention.

Ross Davies is outside the kitchen window, throwing balls into a net.

Shirtless.

And all I can think about is how amazing he felt …

Under me.

On top of me.

The weight of his body on mine.

Being pressed against the wall as he thrust inside me.

His capable hands bringing me to the best orgasms of my life.

Orgasms.

Plural.

That was definitely a first for me. During my other sexual encounters, I was lucky to get one good orgasm. Sometimes, in the past, when my boyfriends would go to dispose of the condom or take a shower, I'd finish myself off.

Of course, I'd never admit that out loud, but it's true.

But with Ross, I never felt more cared for or desired.

And as I stand here and admire the beauty of his long, lean muscles and the way he uses them so precisely, I can't help but want to feel those things all over again. But I can't, at least not until I'm ready to be honest with him.

There's no way I can be in his bed under false pretenses.

I would never taint those memories with lies or secrets.

Which is why I should leave and call in sick or make up an excuse why I can't stay, but just as I'm getting ready to bolt, Ross heads for the backdoor. When he enters the kitchen, I'm frozen in indecision as his eyes lock on mine and a gorgeous smile spreads across his face.

"Good morning."

You can do this.

You're a grown woman.

You're a grown woman who is growing a baby.

HIS baby.

Which is a pretty freaking adult thing to do.

You can handle being in the same house as Ross Davies.

"Hey, good morning," I say, sounding much more in control than I feel. Letting out a deep, cleansing breath, I turn my attention back to the coffee pot and pour some. "Can I get you a cup of coffee?"

I swear I hear him let out a low chuckle behind me, as if he can sense my nervousness, but I don't turn around. I can't. Because he's still not wearing a shirt.

"No, I've had my cup already this morning." Footsteps come up behind me, hesitate for a moment, and then shuffle over to the stove. "But I do think I'll have one of these cinnamon rolls. My mom made them this morning before she left. She must've woken up at two in the morning. But she always loves to leave something behind when she goes."

I swallow and brace myself before turning around to face him. "Yeah,

I saw the note. She's the sweetest." Averting my gaze, I take a sip of my coffee.

"She is and she's totally sweet on you," he says, his tone dripping with honey and making my insides flip. "You've become her new favorite person. I mean, you were always on her good list, but now, you hold the top spot."

I feel my cheeks pinken.

"Nothing to see here, just doing my job," I blurt out, turning back to the sink and busying myself with watering the small plants in Ross's windowsill. They're something I added while he was gone and I'm happy to see he didn't toss them or let them die.

"Thanks for those, by the way," he says, saddling up beside me and invading my space. His smell is intoxicating and I really need him to put on a freaking shirt.

Feeling totally flustered, I dump out my remaining coffee and rinse the mug before opening the dishwasher and putting it in the top rack. "I'm going to the office to get to work. I know you're leaving later today, so if there's anything you need me to work on while you're gone, let me know."

Thankfully, Ross doesn't follow me and once I'm in his office, I flop into the chair and exhale... then inhale slowly... and exhale...

Just a few more hours.

"Knock, knock," Ross says a couple of hours later.

Glancing up from the laptop in front of me, I nearly swallow my tongue.

Ross is no longer naked from the waist up, but the deliciously tailored suit he's wearing is possibly worse. *Good Lord.*

"Hey," I say dumbly, lost for words.

Ross gives me that glorious smile and I'm even more dumbfounded. "I'm packed and thought maybe we could talk for a minute before I have to head out. Mack and Bo are hitching a ride to the airport, so I have to leave a little early."

He's leaving.

I know that's what I've been counting down the hours to, but now that it's here, I already miss him.

And he wants to talk.

I should've seen this coming. Ross is not the kind of man to leave things unattended. He's confident and sure of himself. When he's faced with a problem, he tackles it. And even though I know he sees his divorce as a failure, I don't. Because I know how hard he tried to make it work. I observed it and I've heard Bo talk about it.

"Okay," I finally say, pushing away from the desk as Ross pulls up the leather chair from the corner and sits in it across from me.

"I know we had a brief conversation last night, but I still feel like there's something going on that we need to discuss." His eyes are locked with mine and I love how direct he's being. Even though it makes me uncomfortable, it's really attractive. Any other time, I would be the one to confront the issue. But when I'm the one holding the secret, it's not so easy.

And now would be a good time to tell him, but I can't.

He's getting ready to go on the road and I haven't even had an ultrasound.

"I'm sorry I've been acting so weird," I tell him, letting out a deep breath. "It's just… your parents were here and I'm not sure where we stand or how to do this…"

Ross nods, a serious look on his face. "Yeah, I get it," he says. "And I don't want to put labels on whatever is happening between us, but I do want to see where it goes. If you'd feel more comfortable about it, I'll talk to Bo…"

"Bo?" I ask with a frown. "What does Bo have to do with it?"

He sits back against the chair and cocks his head. "Well, you're basically his little sister and—"

"I'm an adult," I tell him, feeling my hackles rise. "And I make my own decisions."

"Right," he says. "I just thought you were afraid of him and Lola finding out."

Unable to help myself, I bark out a laugh. Oh, God. If only that was it. "Uh, no. I thought maybe you were wanting to keep it quiet because…" I stop, not knowing exactly what to say.

"Because I don't want my private life to be public information," he says sharply. "But that's the only reason. What I do with my time is no one else's business but mine."

Right, okay.

"I want to be with you," he continues, catching me a little off guard. "If you want to be with me too, I'd like to see where this goes."

Swallowing, I nod. "I'd like that too."

His teeth come down on his bottom lip as a slow grin starts to spread. "Good," he says, standing from the chair and adjusting the waist of his slacks that hug his muscular thighs. "We'll pick this up in ten days. I expect you to be here when I get back."

Sir, yes sir.

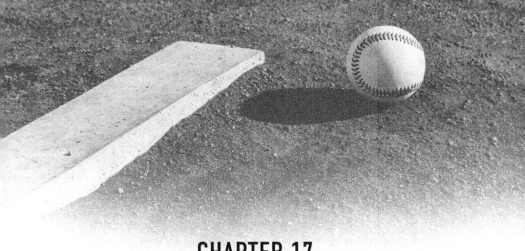

CHAPTER 17

Ross

"WHY DO YOU HAVE THAT GOOFY-ASS GRIN ON YOUR FACE?" MACK ASKS, PLOPPING down in the seat beside me with a groan. I swear I can smell the booze on him. I wouldn't be surprised if he never made it home last night to shower.

Obviously, we spent our off day a little differently.

"Why are you still making rookie mistakes and getting shitfaced before an away game?"

"Why do you sound like my grandpa?"

The pilot comes over the intercom to let us know our flight has been cleared for takeoff. Most of the team will sleep for the three-hour flight. I'm feeling well-rested and thanks to my conversation with Casey before leaving, my mind is quiet. Sure, I wish I could've had more time with her, but I'm happy with how we left things and it makes me hopeful for when I return.

Opening the email app on my phone, I type out a quick message.

Subject: Don't freak out

But I already miss you.

Ross

My thumb hovers over the send button as I stare at the words. I don't know if this is normal. I don't know what the rules are. Shit, I don't even know what game I'm playing. But one thing I know for sure is I miss Casey.

I've been missing her since the day I left for Spring Training which is now approaching the two-month mark. The entire time I was in Florida, I kept telling myself I'd see her when I got back, but now that time has come and gone and I still haven't been able to spend any quality time with her, so the void hasn't been filled.

It helps knowing she's at my house and that she's agreed to see where this thing goes, but it doesn't keep me from missing the shit out of her.

Before I chicken out, I hit send and tuck the phone in the breast pocket of my jacket.

It's tradition for us all to wear suits on our first road trip of the year. The reporters eat it up. Photos from today's departure and arrival will show up on every media outlet that covers Revelers baseball.

"You never answered my question," Mack says, sounding half asleep. "What's up? Did you bang Casey?"

My elbow meets his rib cage and he lets out another groan. "Fuck, man, what'd you do that for? It was a simple question."

"My arm slipped," I smirk, directing my gaze out the window as the plane ascends. I love seeing all the green and blue of the Louisiana landscape. And for every second we're gone, that's a second closer to being back.

"You did, didn't you?" Sitting up straighter in his chair, he leans forward. "What are you not telling me?"

Turning to face him, I exhale and swipe my hand across the scruff filling in on my jaw. Now that we're on a winning streak, I won't be shaving until we lose. My hair is also coming back in quite nicely. "It's none of your business," I tell him.

"You know if you don't come clean I'll make my own assumptions," he deadpans. "Do you really want that?"

"And you know what they say about people who assume," I retort.

Mack laughs, slapping me in the chest. "You are an ass, that's for sure. Now, spill."

"Fine," I say barely above a whisper, hoping everyone around us is asleep. "We… you know." When I wave my hand around in the air, he just gives me an incredulous look.

"Had sex," he offers.

"Yes." Although, I don't like talking about it. What happened between us wasn't just sex. It was different and if I tried to explain it, I know it wouldn't come out right or I'd end up sounding like a pussy-whipped motherfucker.

"Last night?" he asks, resting his elbows on his knees as he leans forward. Thankfully, we're in the first row, so there's no one in front of us.

Shaking my head, I look behind us before answering, "Before Spring Training."

Mack's eyes grow wide. "Are you fucking with me?"

"No, I'm not fucking with you and please keep your voice down. And this stays between us."

When his wide eyes are replaced with an even wider smile, I groan. I was hoping if I gave him a little, he'd be satisfied and leave me alone, but it's obvious all I've done is wet his appetite.

"So, that's why you were in such good form when we showed up in Tampa."

Rolling my eyes, I try to hide my smile, but it's impossible. "I guess."

"You guess?" he asks. "I've been trying to get you laid for the past five months and all I could convince you to do was go on a couple of measly dates. This is huge."

"I told you I wasn't ready and that when I was, I wouldn't need your help."

He settles back into his seat, stretching his legs out in the extra space in front of us. "I can't believe you've been holding out on me. So all that bullshit the other night at Bo's was a front... you lying sack of shit."

Chuckling, I shake my head and lean my head against the seat. "It wasn't a front. She's been acting... off since we got back from Spring Training. While I was gone, we talked every day, usually a few times a day, either on the phone or through email. And then when I got back, it was radio silence."

"But your parents were here."

"Yeah, they were, but it didn't mean she had to freeze me out," I say, sounding like a petulant child. "We'd talked about picking up where we left off and then it's like she got spooked or something. I don't know."

"But you talked before you left?" he asks.

The flight attendant stops by to take our drink order and we both ask for water. Mack probably needs it if he had the night I think he had and I don't usually drink leading up to a game day. We'll both be starting tomorrow and I want to be my best.

"We talked," I finally say. "And she agreed to see where this thing is going."

When I told her I expected her to be there when I got back and her eyes flared with heat, I had to force myself to leave. If I hadn't already been running late, I would've taken her on that desk.

I still plan on taking her on that desk.

I plan on taking her on every viable surface in my house.

"But she's still working for you?" Mack asks, accepting the water from the attendant and passing it to me.

"Thank you," I tell her, and then answer Mack. "Yeah, she's still working for me."

He laughs, shaking his head. "Damn, dude. I can honestly say I didn't see this coming, but I've always noticed a chemistry between you two, so I'm not surprised."

"I really like her," I mutter, partially to him and partially to myself.

My eyes gaze back out the window and I can picture her so clearly sitting at the desk in my office where I left her. Knowing she's there feels right, like she's meant to be there.

"I can tell," Mack says. "And I know you and you wouldn't be trying with someone like her if you weren't serious about it."

He's right, I wouldn't.

I always knew I'd give love another shot. I know there are people who get a divorce and write off marriage, but I've always wanted to be married. Commitment isn't something I'm scared of, never has been and never will be. According to my mom, I was made for monogamy.

Even through high school, I didn't like the idea of playing the field. Once Felicia and I started dating, I was in it for the long haul.

There have been moments I've blamed myself for the divorce and I know I'm not perfect, but I also know I would've done anything Felicia asked of me. That doesn't mean I'm still in love with her or I would go back to her now.

That ship has sailed.

But I want that again.

With someone like Casey.

Maybe it's the fact I've been there and done that or that I'm thirty-one and over the bullshit, but I don't want to waste time on meaningless sex or meaningless relationships. If I didn't see a future with Casey, I wouldn't be pursuing her.

When we touch down in Denver, there are two large buses waiting to take us to the hotel. Game time is in five hours, so we'll have a short turn around once we get there before we head to the field.

"Looking sharp, Davies," Buddy says as he walks by my seat, giving my shoulder a light slap.

"Thanks, Skip."

When he slips into the seat beside me, I'm not going to lie, my heart beats a little faster. After the shit show I put on at the end of last season, I was worried about being traded. Even though I'm on year seven of a ten-year contract, anything is possible. Of course, I'd go wherever I need to continue to play baseball.

But my home is in New Orleans.

"And I don't just mean in that suit," he continues, his eyes focused straight ahead. "I have to say, I was worried about you for a while. I've seen players go through all kinds of shit and never bounce back from it mentally. Sure, they can still throw a ball, hit a ball, catch a ball, but we all know, if your head isn't in the game, you're not going to be the best you can be."

He pauses and I stay quiet, giving him a chance to finish what he sat down here to say.

"You showed up to Spring Training with your head on straight and threw some of your best stuff in that first game. You proved yourself and what a pillar of this organization looks like. We weather the storm and come out stronger on the other side." I can see him nod his head out of the corner of my eye and I feel my shoulders relax and my chest swell with pride. "That's New Orleans… and that's who we are."

My throat feels a little tight, so I stay quiet, letting him finish.

"Looking forward to the season and seeing what you've got for us."

"I appreciate it," I finally say, hoping I don't sound as emotional as I'm feeling. "Thanks for sticking with me and for your support. It means a lot."

Subject: Superstitions

Ross,

I know you baseball players have your superstitions so I don't want to say anything wrong.

What's off limits?

Can I tell you "good game"? You pitched amazing? Nice butt?

Tell me what I can get by with because I don't want to be blamed for anything going wrong.

And I'm guessing you're still not shaving, which I'm totally okay with. You look sexy with or without a beard, but I must confess I've had dreams about the feel of your beard against my skin and would like to experience that again.

Everything is good here. Your house is still standing. Alice came and did a deep clean. Phil hooked me up with a great landscaper who's going to give us a quote on tidying up the backyard. I've already told them they can't touch the pitching mound.

Two people contacted you for interviews, both of them will be done via phone calls and I scheduled them for your off day between Colorado and Arizona.

At your service ;)

Casey

God, I love her smart ass.

Pulling my laptop closer, I start typing my response.

Subject: re: Superstitions

Here're some hard and fast rules:

1.   Never talk about a no-hitter or a perfect game.

2.   If you don't know what a no-hitter is, Google it.

3.   After you win a game, it's perfectly acceptable to say "good game" or "nice butt"

4. Once you start a winning streak, you don't shave.

5. But if you have two at-bats with no hits, you shave it off.

6. Sometimes, we decide not to shave until we hit .500, so it can go either way.

We could be here all night, but I think that covers what you asked about.

Thank you for all you do. I know it's a job and you're getting paid to do it, but you do it well and I'm appreciative. I don't ever want you to think I take it for granted.

About that dream, I'd like to make it a reality.

I've never been one to wish away my life, but I'm counting down the days until I'm back home. And with you.

Wishing I was at your service,

Ross

Our emails are back to what they were before I left Florida, maybe even better than they were in Florida, and I couldn't be happier about it. Relieved is actually more like it. She was pushing me away for whatever reason, but these past few days, things have felt like they're back on track.

The Revelers are also back on track.

The team is gelling and even though we're winning, there are still areas we can improve on. But something about this season reminds me of the last time we went to the playoffs. I have high hopes.

I have high hopes for a few things.

And it feels good.

"SO, HOW DID THE INTERVIEWS GO?" CASEY ASKS, HER VOICE SOUNDING SLEEPY.

Adjusting the pillows behind me, I grab my water and settle in. I've waited to talk to her on the phone for two days. With our schedule, sometimes it's really late before I make it back to my hotel room.

"Great," I tell her after taking a drink. "Thanks for setting those up. Do I have anything else on the schedule?"

"You did have an email from a marketing company who represents a supplement company. They were looking for an endorsement, but I responded for you and told them you don't endorse anything you don't take. Was that okay?"

Chuckling, I smile. "Perfect."

"Oh, we should see if the company who makes those green smoothies wants to use you."

My laugh grows louder.

"Or maybe ESPN wants to do another Body Issue…"

"Shit," I groan, pressing my head into the pillow. "I'm never going to live that down."

"Live it down?" Casey asks, suddenly sounding very awake. "Are you kidding me? That's the best thing since sliced bread. It will live in infamy. Women, and men, will talk about it for years to come."

My laughter dies as I think about Casey checking me out in that magazine. "So, do you have a copy?"

"Not just one," she says too quickly to be a lie.

Actually, I swear I can hear her cover her mouth, like she didn't mean for that little tidbit to come out.

"Are you a closet Ross Davies fan?" I tease.

There's a rustle on the other side of the phone and then Casey answers quietly. "There's no closet about it."

"And where are these copies of the Ross Davies Body Issue?" I ask, growing hard at the thought of her looking at them and pleasuring herself. I know that might be cocky of me, no pun intended, but I can't help it. Does she pleasure herself? Does she think of me when she does?

"Places," she says curtly.

I laugh again, not even hiding my enjoyment of this fact. "Places, huh? And… what might one do with more than one copy?"

"They're going to be collector's items one day," she says. "Because you're, well…"

"I'm what? Old?" I ask, wishing I was with her right now so I could sweep her up and spank her ass for that one.

"I was going to say a legend… or you will be."

"Now you're just sweet talking and backtracking, but I'll let you have it."

The phone line goes quiet and I actually love it when we're like this, just breathing and listening… existing in the same space, even from miles away.

"So, about those magazines…" I finally say, unable to let it go.

"Oh, my God," Casey groans. "I'm never going to live this down."

Nope, not gonna happen.

"Not to change the subject or anything," she adds. "But I was just wondering… does that offer still stand for me to move into the guest house?"

My heart sputters in my chest and then restarts, beating hard.

"Yes, of course," I say, trying to sound calm and like this isn't the best fucking news I've received. "It's yours if you want it."

I mean that quite literally. I'd sign it over to her if she wanted.

Don't ask me the whys of that. It's just the truth.

"Well, I want it," she replies. "I've been looking for a place for the last week and haven't found anything I love that's in my price range and in the right location. I found this great walk-up in the Quarter, but that's a little too far from where I need to be most days. Then there was this garage apartment a few blocks from Charlotte's, but it was more of a studio and the kitchen was so small… and you know how I love to cook."

She's rambling and I love it, so I let her, but she doesn't have to convince me.

"I already told you it's yours and any time you want to cook in my kitchen, you're more than welcome."

That statement was dripping with innuendo and I meant every word of it.

CHAPTER 18

Casey

LYING BACK ON THE PADDED TABLE, THE PAPER CRINKLES BENEATH ME AND I'M chilled. The flimsy gown the nurse gave me to put on isn't giving me any warmth and I'm suddenly feeling very alone.

I've had this feeling wash over me plenty of times in the past few weeks, ever since I found out about the pregnancy, but this is the strongest it's been.

There's an obvious void next to me, where I wish Ross was—standing, holding my hand, experiencing this with me. But I don't get long to dwell on it.

"Good morning, Ms. Carradine," an elderly woman says, walking into the room with a kind smile. "I'm Dr. Campbell." She slides a rolling chair up to the foot of the bed and tilts her head toward me. "Are you ready to hear this baby's heartbeat?"

This is it. This is the moment I've been waiting for—concrete proof of the life growing inside me. But now that I'm here, I don't know if I'm ready.

"Sure," I say, nodding my head nervously. "Okay."

Her warm hand comes down on mine and she gives it a light squeeze. "It's going to be okay, I promise."

Without further ado, she begins typing on a keyboard, then squeezes some warm gel on my stomach. Picking up the wand, she starts to move it around my abdomen.

A moment later, the room is filled with a whoosh, whoosh, whoosh... and tears fill my eyes.

"Baby looks good," she says, looking at the screen before swiveling it in my direction.

That's when I see it, a small blob that's already starting to resemble a real baby.

"Oh, my God," I gasp, my hand coming up to cover my mouth as tears flow freely down my cheeks. "There's a real baby." The chuckle that escapes is half joy and half wonderment. I can see small nubs where his or her arms will be... a head and abdomen... and tiny nubs for feet. It's like a five-year-olds drawing of a baby and it's the most beautiful thing I've ever seen.

"A real baby," Dr. Campbell echoes back. "I'll print out some of these pictures for you to take home... your baby's first pictures."

My baby.

My baby's first pictures.

And the first time I heard its heartbeat.

My heart has been split in two—half still beating in my chest and the other half beating in my belly.

"Baby is measuring about ten weeks and five days, which puts your due date around November tenth."

November tenth.

After the playoffs.

Even if the Revelers make it to the World Series, we should be good.

We.

Me.

Ross.

This baby.

Guilt floods my body as I lay there and realize I've stolen ten and a half weeks from Ross. Well, technically, I've only known about this little peanut for a few weeks. But he should be here today. I know he'd love it, regardless of the circumstances.

There's just something inside me that tells me Ross Davies will be an amazing father. And he'd want to hear his baby's heartbeat and see his or her first picture... know the due date and experience every moment, no matter how small.

I have to tell him.

"Can I record the heartbeat with my phone?" I ask, swiping the tears off my cheeks. "I need to share it with someone."

She gives me an understanding smile and picks up the wand again, pressing it against my belly while I push record on my phone.

Half an hour later, I'm sitting in my car with black and white pictures of the tiny baby growing inside me, a video of his or her heartbeat on my phone, and a new resolve to take back control of my life.

Over the past few weeks, I've kind of lost myself, giving in to fear and uncertainty. But I'm done with that.

Putting my car in reverse, I pull out of the parking lot and head for Charlotte's.

"Char," I call out as I let myself in the backdoor. The entire drive over here, I thought about telling her about the baby. It would be nice to have someone else to share this secret with and since we've always shared our secrets, it would be the natural thing to do. But I need to tell Ross first. I owe him that much. So, this visit is for something else I need to do.

"In the studio," Charlotte calls back.

On my way through the kitchen, I grab two bottles of water and a couple of pieces of fruit. Knowing my sister, she's been living on coffee and donuts. Basically, she's a cop with a smoking hot body and a voice of angels.

"Hey," I say, poking my head in to make sure she's not recording.

Charlotte lifts her head from the notebook in front of her and gives me a huge smile.

"Hey, you." Standing, she stretches and then pulls me into a hug. "I was wondering when you were going to come home. How's work going at Casa de Davies... House of Davies... Davies Corporation, huh?" she asks, wiggling her eyebrows suggestively. "That doesn't sound half bad. Kind of has a CEO-Secretary vibe. Maybe the two of you could..."

"Oh, my God, Charlotte!" I push her away and feel my face heat up. "Here," I say, shoving the bottled water and fruit into her hands. "Drink some water and eat a banana."

"Have you had his banana?"

My eyes grow wide. "What is wrong with you?"

"Why are you such a fuddy-duddy?" She pouts and peels the banana, cramming half of it in her mouth like a child. "If you don't want to talk about sex, what do you want?"

As annoying as she can be, I love her and I'm thankful for her inappropriateness because it worked nicely as an icebreaker.

"I'm moving into Ross's guest house," I say, ripping the band-aid off. "I've been looking for an apartment and nothing has been in my price range or the right location and he offered, so I'm taking him up on it."

"So, you're going to screw your landlord." Nodding, she plops back into her seat. "That could work."

"Are you going to help me pack or what?" I ask, sitting across from her.

Charlotte drops the smile and looks over at me with a serious expression. "Are you sure about this? I know you've made passing comments about finding your own place, but there's no rush."

"I know," I tell her, reaching out to take her hand. "And I love living here, but I really need my own space. It's time." *I'm having a baby.* The confession is on the tip of my tongue, but I swallow it down. I will tell her soon, but not yet. "I need to be on my own and figure things out."

She gives me a soft, sad smile. "My baby sister is growing up."

Tears prick my eyes and I laugh them off, shaking my head.

"Actually, you've always been older than your years," Charlotte continues. "I feel like you've been taking care of me for so long and I depend on you so much…"

"And that doesn't have to change," I assure her. "I'll still be here for you and I'll do whatever you need me to do. None of that will change."

She bites on her lip, her head slowly nodding. "Yeah, it will change, but that's okay. Change is good, right?"

"Yeah, it is," I tell her, hoping she still feels that way when I tell her my other news in a few days.

For the next few hours, Charlotte helps me pack up my bedroom and then goes with me over to Ross's to unload everything into the guest house.

It doesn't take us long to unpack and get things put away and as we're standing in the middle of the great room, Charlotte pulls me into a hug.

"This is a good move for you," she says, her head resting on mine. "I feel it in my bones."

"What no jokes about me boning Ross?" I ask.

"I wouldn't be opposed to it."

For the second time today, I want to tell her everything, but I don't.

And I can only pray that when I do, she's as receptive to it as she has been to me moving into Ross Davies' guest house.

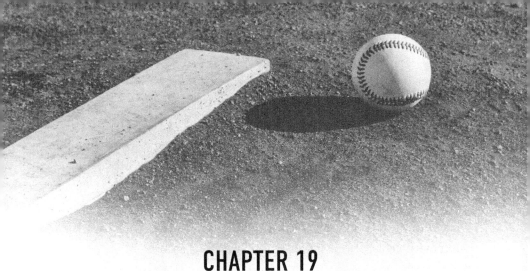

CHAPTER 19

Ross

PULLING UP TO MY GATE, I SIGH IN RELIEF WHEN I SEE CASEY'S CAR PARKED IN THE drive. A small voice in my head said she wouldn't be here and like last time, something would come up or spook her and she'd bail. But she's here and there's also a light on in the living room, which means she's probably inside waiting for me.

I'm so anxious to get to her that I put the code in wrong on the first try. Finally getting it right, I drive up and park next to her car, my eyes glued to the window with the light, willing some sort of x-ray vision to kick in so I can see her.

As I unlock the door and step into the foyer, I can't help the smile and overwhelming sense of rightness I feel when I see her curled up on my couch.

It's always good to be home after a long road trip, but it's so much better with her here.

Setting my duffle bag down, I kick off my shoes and quietly walk over to see she's sleeping.

Her blonde hair is draped over half her face, so I brush it back and tuck it behind her ear. Leaning down, I kiss the top of her head and then her forehead, breathing her in. She stirs a little, but doesn't wake, so I decide to carry her to bed.

I wanted to be inside her tonight, but I'll settle for holding her.

When I scoop her up, I swear she feels lighter than the first night I carried her upstairs, which concerns me a little due to all of her sickness and doctor's appointments. But that's something to worry about another day.

Right now, she's here and she's in my arms and that's good enough.

Her hands grip my shirt as I start to ascend the stairs. "Ross?" she asks, her voice thick with sleep.

"Yeah, baby, it's me."

She mumbles a few noncoherent words against my chest and I smile, kissing her hair.

As I lean down to lay her in my bed, her eyes slowly open. "Ross."

"Yeah."

"You're home."

"Yeah."

"I missed you."

Instead of telling her how much I missed her, I show her, pressing my lips to hers.

At first, the kiss is slow and tender, like we're remembering how good it feels to kiss each other. As Casey opens her mouth, I deepen the kiss and it's like a switch is flipped.

My hands go to the hem of her t-shirt as she pulls me on top of her.

Just like the first time, all thought goes out the window and I just feel… her soft skin, her perfect breasts… "I missed you too," I murmur against her neck as I kiss my way down.

When I get to the waistband of her pants, her body goes stiff and she pushes my hands away, scooting back on the bed.

"What's wrong?" I ask, panting as I catch my breath.

Her hand comes up to her lips which are swollen and red from our kiss, looking even more kissable than usual. I want to taste them, along with the rest of her body, but I don't like the way she's looking at me right now.

"Casey?"

She inhales deeply, her shoulders rising and then falling as she exhales. "I have to tell you something."

My heart drops, along with my stomach. She wouldn't know this, but those are the exact words Felicia said to me the night she told me she wanted a divorce. I get that Casey and I aren't anything official, but like it or not, she does hold power over me and the trepidation at whatever she needs to tell me is still there.

"What?" I ask, sounding a little harsher than I intended.

Her brows pull together and she cocks her head, taking another breath and blowing it out.

"This isn't really how I planned on doing this," she mutters, more to herself than me. "But here goes nothing." Adjusting her shirt, she locks her eyes on mine. "Oh, God… this is way harder than I even imagined and that was… hard."

She blows out another breath and now I'm starting to freak the fuck out. Is this about her? About her doctor's appointments? Is she sick or—

"I'm pregnant."

My heart beat slows.

My breathing stops.

My mind short circuits.

"What?"

"I'm pregnant…eleven weeks tomorrow."

"You're…pregnant." It's not a question. It's a statement. I needed to say it to see if it would help me process the information better. "And I'm…" I look up at her, needing her to finish that statement for me so I know exactly what she's telling me.

"Going to be a dad," she says quietly, swallowing hard.

The night we had sex, I assumed she was on birth control. Everything happened so fast…and I didn't ask…and she didn't say anything…

"Please say something."

When I look back up at her, I see the fear in her eyes. She's worried I'm going to be upset or not want the baby, but that couldn't be farther from the truth. I've always wanted to be a dad.

"We're going to have a baby," I tell her, still wrapping my mind around it.

She nods slowly, pressing her lips together as her eyes fill with tears.

Reaching for her, I pull her into me and cradle her body against mine. "Don't cry," I murmur into her hair. "It's going to be okay… everything is going to be okay."

"Are you mad at me?" she asks, her voice breaking as she falls apart against me. "I swear I didn't know… I've been on the pill for so long. I didn't think I could get pregnant by missing one pill. But I didn't do it on purpose. This isn't one of those Lifetime movies where the girl tries to trap the guy by getting pregnant with his baby and if you don't want to do this thing, I get it… I do… and… I can do it by myself."

The last few words come out as stutters as Casey's sobs take over and she begins to shake.

"Case," I say, trying to calm her. "Don't cry… please don't cry."

For a minute, I just run a hand up and down her back, trying to soothe her as I collect myself and pray I say the right words. *God, please don't let me fuck this up.*

When she settles and her body stills, I take a deep breath like I'm at the plate getting ready to throw a pitch. *Center. Focus. Visualize.* "Casey?"

"Yeah."

"Okay, just making sure you didn't pass out on me."

She laughs and it's sad and still filled with tears, but it's the best damn sound.

"You don't have anything to be sorry for, okay? I've always said it takes two… it takes two people to make a relationship work. It takes two people to make a baby. That night, I should've worn a condom. We should've talked about it. I won't make any excuses for that, but it's just as much, if not more, on me than it is you. So let that shit go."

Swallowing, I close my eyes and inhale her sweet scent because that is what soothes me.

"But I can't say I'm sorry this happened… I'm not."

She stills, her hands gripping my shirt a little tighter.

"I've always wanted to be a dad. Sure, this isn't exactly how I saw it happening, but I'll never be sorry about it…it's not a mistake. You can call it fate or a miracle or an act of God, but it's not a mistake. And it might take me a while to fully wrap my head around the idea of it all, but just know, I'll always be here for you and this baby, okay?"

I feel her sag with relief and I kiss the top of her head.

"How long have you known?"

"A few weeks."

It all makes so much sense now—her being sick while I was at Spring Training, then during our first few games, and her weird behavior when I got back home.

"Are you still getting sick?" I ask, going back to running my hand up and down her back.

"Sometimes… it comes and goes."

"Is there anything I can do for you?"

She sighs, finally letting go of my shirt and wrapping her arms around my torso. "You're doing it."

After a few more minutes of just holding her, I extract myself and discard my jeans and t-shirt on the floor before climbing back in bed and pulling her to me. As I tuck the blankets up around her, she melts into me.

I saw this night going so differently…

A baby.

I'm going to be a dad.

Talk about a fucking curveball.

My mind is still reeling and trying to come to terms with it, but my heart is all in. I wish she would've told me sooner, but I can't change that. All I can do is be here for her—for the baby—going forward and I plan to do that. The rightness inside trumps any anger or resentment.

I can't imagine if I was in her place… who's to say I would've handled it any differently or better?

Surprisingly, sleep comes easily and when I open my eyes again, sunlight is streaming through my bedroom window and Casey is still passed out beside me.

And my first thought is the baby.

Sliding my hand from where it's protectively wrapped around her shoulders, I touch her stomach. It's still flat, so if she hadn't told me there's a baby inside, I wouldn't know.

No one would.

Which brings me to one of many questions: has she told anyone else? Her sister?

The thought of Casey carrying this all by herself makes my insides ache. I can't explain it, but I don't like the idea of her bearing all the burden, not that this baby is a burden, but… shit, I don't know. What the fuck do I know about any of this? Nothing. Absolutely nothing.

I've always heard that a man becomes a father the day his baby is born, but a woman becomes a mother the day she finds out she's pregnant. For her, this has been real from day one… her reality. And I can only imagine what she's been going through… fear of the unknown, anxiety about what she's going to do…

I wonder if she ever considered not having it?

No, that's not Casey.

I don't know how I know that, but I just do. She's always come across as the maternal type. Even though she's younger than Charlotte, she takes care of her.

Shit, she takes care of me.

And I know she's going to be the most amazing mother.

As images of her in all stages of pregnancy flood my mind, I try to imagine her holding a baby, our baby, and then another thought comes at me out of nowhere.

What if something happens?

I mean, I've had friends whose wives and girlfriends have had miscarriages. That happens, probably more frequently than anyone realizes. It could happen to her… to us.

"Your thoughts are very loud this morning," Casey mumbles as she reaches a hand up to rub her face and then brush her hair back.

Chuckling, I forget my hand is still resting on her stomach until her hand comes to rest on top of it and the entire atmosphere shifts.

This is happening.

Me.

And her.

And this baby.

I don't know what it means for us and our relationship, I'd never force Casey into anything she doesn't want, but I need her to know I want her. I want this baby.

Pulling her on top of me, I tip her chin up and force her to look at me.

"Change your mind about anything while you were sleeping?" she asks, her sleepy gaze something I'd love to wake up to every morning. When she traps her bottom lip with her teeth, I brush my thumb against her mouth and then replace it with a kiss.

It's slow and understanding, telling her all the things I want to say, but doing it better.

I'm here.

I'm not going anywhere.

You're not in this alone.

"I need to brush my teeth," she mutters, breaking this kiss and dipping her head.

"I like you just the way you are," I tell her, tipping her chin back up and reclaiming her mouth. "Morning breath and all."

She laughs into my mouth and it causes my dick to stir.

I know when she feels the hardness beneath her because she pulls back again and this time there's nothing but lust and need in her gaze.

Running my hands up her thighs, I realize they're bare.

At some point during the night, she must've kicked off her pants.

The only barrier between us are two thin pieces of fabric.

Without those, all it would take is one thrust and I'd be inside her.

"I want you," I tell her, needing her to know and also giving her the reins. "But I don't want to do anything you're not comfortable with or anything that would…"

Hurt the baby.

Hurt you.

"I want you too," Casey says breathlessly, her hands already pulling at the waistband of my boxers. "So bad… you have no idea."

"Is it okay?" I ask, tugging her closer so I can devour her neck, needing to taste every inch of her. "I mean, with the baby and everything. Is it okay?"

"Yes," she moans as I nip at the sensitive spot behind her ear.

"Tell me if I do anything wrong," I tell her, meaning it for more than just now. "This is all new to me too and I don't want to fuck anything up."

We should be having this conversation with clothes on but I can't stop.

I need her.

Gripping the bottom of her shirt, I pull it over her head and toss it to the floor. Her panties and my boxers follow shortly after and seconds later, Casey is positioning her slick entrance over my hard as steel cock.

From this angle, I can see everything and it's glorious.

With her hand wrapped around my shaft, she guides me inside and I groan at the instant pleasure of being enveloped in her tight heat.

"Fuck, Casey. You feel so good," I groan, my hands going to her hips and she takes every inch of me.

When her hips are flush with mine, I open my eyes to see her gazing down at me, looking like a fucking goddess. Her long blonde hair hangs in curtains around her face. Those soft, perfect breasts are on full display.

"Move, baby, I need you to ride my cock," I command, kneading her pert little ass as I urge her hips forward.

She lets out a moan as her head falls back and her hair brushes my thighs.

Reaching out, I take a handful of one of her breasts and lean up to take it into my mouth, sucking on her nipple.

Casey's high-pitched keen echoes around the room and I smile against her skin, loving the way she completely loses herself when we're together.

"That's it, baby... I want to hear you scream."

Her hips move faster, pressing down harder as she finds the friction she's looking for. I can feel her walls begin to tighten and spasm. Laying back, I reach down between us and rub small circles around her clit until she falls apart... her muscles tensing... her breaths halting... and then she explodes around me.

While she continues to ride out her orgasm, I take over, thrusting up into her.

Another wave hits and I feel her walls spasm again, which sends me careening over the edge.

Cool heat travels up my back as my balls tighten and then I'm releasing into her—claiming her, owning her... and even though she just gave me everything, I want more.

CHAPTER 20

Casey

"DO YOU WANT TO SEE A PICTURE OF THE BABY?" I ASK ROSS AS WE LAY IN HIS BED after a second round of mind-blowing sex. Maybe it's the pregnancy hormones or the fact there aren't any barriers between us, but if I thought our first night together was amazing, then this morning has been otherworldly.

I can't even begin to describe it.

And I might be ruining it by bringing up the baby, but I want to share this with him… if he's interested and I figure there's no time like the present to find out.

"Of course I want to see a picture of the baby," Ross says, sitting up so quickly he pushes me off him onto my side.

Laughing, I look up. "Are you sure? Because if it's too much too soon, we don't have—"

"Casey, show me my baby."

His baby.

Biting down on my lip, I try to hide my grin and also the tears threatening to break free.

Stupid hormones.

"You're really serious about this?" I ask, needing to hear it from him again. Call me needy, but after keeping this secret to myself for three weeks, it feels good to have it out in the open and to know he's onboard. I'm not sure what I expected exactly, but his response was better than I'd hoped for.

"I'm very serious," he says, those gorgeous eyes boring into mine and making me want things I shouldn't. Leaning down, he kisses me, almost making me forget what we're talking about. "Now go get the picture."

Rolling out of bed, I grab my t-shirt off the floor and slip it on as I walk out of his bedroom and down the stairs. As I'm making my way across the dining room to get the ultrasound out of my bag, I hear Ross in the kitchen.

"What can I make you for breakfast?" he calls out as pans clang. "Eggs, bacon, hash browns…"

Bent over, my hand immediately goes to my mouth and I drop the envelope as I run to the bathroom under the stairs. Fortunately, I make it to the toilet. After weeks of dealing with this, I know when it's a false alarm and when it's the real deal.

This was the real deal.

"Casey?" Ross asks from behind me, sounding worried.

Waving him off, I turn my head, hoping he can't see me. "I'm fine. Please go."

"No." Taking a few steps into the bathroom, he pulls a washcloth from the cabinet and turns the water on. I listen while he wets the washcloth and rings it out. Kneeling beside me, he gathers my hair and holds it back. "What can I get for you? Tell me what to do."

The worry is now combined with fear. I can hear it in his voice and it breaks me a little. Ross is such a confident person and even in his most vulnerable moments, I've never seen this side of him.

This raw, unfiltered version who has no clue what to do.

But it's endearing and it surprisingly makes me feel less alone, like I'm not the only one on this ride who's holding on for dear life.

"I'm okay," I tell him as the nausea begins to pass. Sitting back on my heels, I accept the warm washcloth and wipe my mouth, taking a deep, cleansing breath. "You don't have to do this… it's not a big deal, totally normal… and—"

"Casey," Ross says, warning in his tone. He lets my hair go and turns so he's sitting with his back against the wall.

"Ross," I fire back, finally turning to look at him and suddenly I'm hit with an onslaught of unwelcome feelings—fear, uncertainty, guilt. I hate them all, but they're here. I thought it would get better once I told him, but now that I have, I'm not so sure there's not an entire new set of problems coming our way. "You don't have to rearrange your life for me. Neither one of us planned this or asked for this… I don't expect you to jump into the role of expecting father… father-to-be… whatever they call it."

I sigh, sitting down and leaning against the opposing wall, our knees touching.

"What are we doing?" I ask, picking at the edge of my t-shirt. As perfect as Ross has been, I know this can't last forever. At some point, the bubble we've been in for the past twelve hours will be popped.

Ross sighs and I think he's starting to realize the same thing. I can see it on his face. The realness of the situation is sinking in and he has to be wondering what the heck is happening.

"We're going to take it a day at a time," he says, sounding very much the strong, dependable guy I've always known him to be. When he reaches out and takes my hand, linking our fingers together, I swallow down the lump forming in my throat.

"You never even asked me if I was sure this baby is yours." It's barely above a whisper, but it's one of the loudest thoughts in my head. For some reason, deep in the recesses of my mind, I thought Ross might ask for proof this baby is his. I mean, he is Ross Davies and I'm sure there are plenty of women in this town alone who would like to get knocked up by him and trap him in a relationship.

My pulse begins to race as my heart hammers in my chest.

He pulls on my hand, urging me to look at him. "Hey, that never crossed my mind. Okay? I know you, Casey, and I know you'd never do anything like that. So, that's one thing we can just get out of the way and never talk about again."

"Before you, I hadn't been with anyone in over six months," I tell him, feeling the need to bare my soul. "I've only had three sexual partners, you make four. I'm no saint, but I've definitely never slept around. Even though this wasn't planned, I've wanted this baby from the first moment I knew it existed. But I understand things might be different for you and I'd never want you to feel trapped or like you have to do something you don't want to, so don't feel like that okay? And if me living in your guest house is too weird, I can find somewhere else to live."

Swallowing, I take a deep breath and try to keep the tears away. They just come at any time nowadays and it's so annoying.

"Are you done?" Ross asks, his face stoic.

I nod. "Yeah, I guess that's it for now."

"Okay," he says, clearing his throat. "You know what I've been doing with the last eight years of my life. Regardless of what you hear any gossip column or tabloid say, I was always monogamous. There hasn't been anyone since Felicia."

At that, my back goes stiff and I feel like my entire body is on high alert.

Did he just say what I think he said?

I was his first since his divorce?

"And even though this wasn't planned and has definitely shocked the shit out of me, I also want this baby," he continues, nodding his head as his gaze drifts off. "Something you might not know about me is I've always wanted kids. In the beginning, it was something Felicia and I agreed on. We talked about it before I ever proposed, but as time went on, her feelings on the subject changed."

He pauses and I steal glances at his gorgeous side profile, wondering what woman wouldn't want to have babies with this man?

She has to be crazy.

"One other thing I'd like to clear up is how I feel about you."

He turns to look at me, those green eyes staring straight into my soul.

"Just so you know, I was crazy about you before I knew you were carrying my baby."

We just sit there for the longest time—Ross stroking his thumb across my hand, me getting lost in his eyes—before he leans over and pulls an envelope from the counter.

"Want to show me the baby?"

I nod, taking the envelope from him and opening it, pulling out the four grainy black and white photos. Looking down at the tiny blob, I can't help the smile on my face. It's the one where you can see the tiny arms and legs.

"I call it Peanut," I tell him.

Ross is quiet as he holds the picture. I expect questions or comments, but there's nothing, only radio silence.

Just when I think he's getting ready to freak out on me, I see him swallow and then clear his throat. When he reaches up and presses his thumb and forefinger to the corners of his eyes, I realize he's crying... or trying not to.

"Did you have a big head when you were a baby?" I ask, handing him another photo that's of mostly the baby's head. It looks huge, which is normal. I looked it up.

He finally chuckles, and I feel like I can breathe again.

"I did, actually," he says, looking up at me with tears in his eyes. "My mom said she had to buy me those little shirts with the snaps on the collar so she could get them over my gigantic head."

"Oh, God," I say, pressing a hand to my lips.

Just thinking about the end game of pushing a baby out of my hooha makes me cringe.

"But I bet this baby is going to have a perfectly normal sized head," he says, obviously recognizing the pure, unadulterated fear in my eyes.

He looks at all the photos and then looks at them again. Occasionally he looks over at me and I can't say exactly what I see, but at least he's not running for the hills and he's happy. Everything else will work itself out, or at least I have to believe it will.

"Can we not tell anyone for a while?" I ask.

"You haven't told anyone?"

I shake my head. "No, not even Charlotte."

"Okay," he says, handing me the photos back and watching as I put them back into the envelope for safekeeping. "I'll follow your lead... If you want me to make a statement at some point and get ahead of the media, I can do that."

I feel the blood drain from my face at the thought of the whole world knowing I'm pregnant with Ross Davies' baby.

"Or we can send you to a convent or something so you can have the baby in secret."

My eyes grow wide and just when I think he might be serious, he laughs. "Kidding," he says, his green eyes twinkling. "But you should've seen the look on your face."

"I'm not sure what scares me more—nuns or fangirls."

He laughs again and then stands, offering me his hand.

"We'll figure this out," he says, pulling me close and wrapping his big, strong arms around me.

It's then, as I'm tucked close to him—blocking out the rest of the world—I remember something else I can show him, something that will make this a little more real for him… at least it did for me.

"Want to hear the heartbeat?" I ask. "I just remembered I have a video saved to my phone."

Ross sweeps me off my feet and carries me into the kitchen, placing me on the island before grabbing my phone and handing it to me.

He looks like a kid on Christmas morning and I'm holding his more prized gift.

I guess that's a yes.

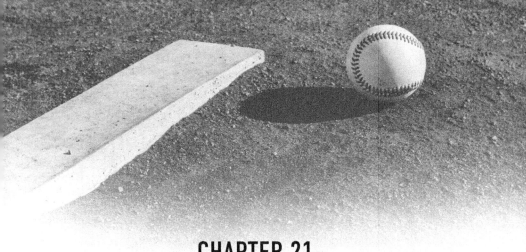

CHAPTER 21

Ross

"FUCK," I MUTTER AS MY CURVEBALL GOES WIDE AND DRAWS A FOURTH BALL. THE batter takes his place on first base, which gives me a few seconds to center myself and try to get my shit together.

I don't know what's going on but this has been my worst pitched game since the beginning of the season and we're only in the fifth inning. Typically, I'm good to go for a full seven but if I keep throwing trash like this, I won't finish the inning.

When I turn and face the next batter, Perez, I see Mack's fist pound his knee twice as he squats into position. That's his sign for "focus, asshole". Pulling the brim of my cap down to signal I heard him loud and clear, I zero in on my target and wait for Mack to call the next pitch. He wants me to greet Perez with my fastball, so I nod my head then, let the ball fly.

Thankfully, the pitch does its job—*a strike down the middle.*

The second pitch, though, zips close enough to Perez's shoulder that he has to jump out of the way to avoid being hit. The crowd immediately starts booing and I don't blame them one bit. For a second, I wonder how Casey is reacting. She didn't feel up to being here tonight but I hope she's still watching on TV. Then again, maybe I don't.

Glancing up to home plate, I see Mack coming for me, which means my time is almost up if I don't get these next two outs soon.

"Dude, what the hell is going on?"

Hiding my mouth behind my glove, I answer, "I don't fucking know but I'm working on it."

"Well, work harder so we can get off the field." He starts to walk away but pauses, glancing back to me. "And this better not be about your new lady-friend, either. Keep that shit at home."

Before I can respond, Mack takes off jogging back behind the plate. I don't like him putting the blame on Casey in any way but he's right about me needing to get my head in the game so we can finish this.

I wait for his next sign then throw my pitch. This time, my expletive is loud and clear as I stand helplessly, watching the ball being crushed out of the park and into the stands behind me.

That's the third home run I've allowed in this game and when I see Buddy coming my way, I know I'm done.

Thankfully, we end up scraping by to win, no thanks to me. The bullpen deserves that win.

I avoid everyone I can after the game and head straight for the showers.

I don't need advice and I sure as hell don't want any pep talks.

I just want to be home.

With Casey.

We've fallen into a pretty great routine lately and I miss her when I'm not home. I'm still trying to wrap my head around the two of us having a baby but regardless, it's happening and I'll be by her side for every step.

It's a relief when I make it to my car with minimal interactions from my teammates but it's an even bigger one when I step inside my living room and see Casey sleeping on the couch. Again. She's always tired, thanks to the pregnancy, but I don't mind. I think it's fucking adorable, especially when I find her sleeping in unexpected places.

Yesterday, I found her in my game room, passed out with the TV on and the video game controller still in her hand. She'd been playing Call of Duty and not gonna lie, I think I fell a little in love with her in that moment.

I have to remind myself it's way too soon to be having thoughts like that but when I kneel down beside her and gently brush the hair off her gorgeous face, I know it'd be so easy to love her.

But I can't rush things.

There are just too many variables, things that could change in an instant.

I'm not an idiot. The fact Casey holds all the power here is very evident. And even though I trust her, there's still a nagging voice in my head. It's constantly reminding me that she could leave tomorrow—just walk out like Felicia did—and I'd be left picking up the pieces all over again.

We've both avoided having any kind of real conversation about us and our future. For all I know, she doesn't want a real relationship with me. Do I want one with her? I think I do but things are happening so fast. And, yet, we haven't even been on a fucking date.

How do you woo someone you've already knocked up?

Casey rolls onto her side, facing me, and opens her eyes. She doesn't seem startled or surprised to see me watching her so closely, just… happy.

"Off game, huh?" Her voice is raspy and sexy as hell.

I nod my head in response while picking up a section of her long hair and letting the strands glide through my fingers.

"Want to talk about it?" she asks.

"No, I want to talk about you. How are you feeling?"

"Well, I didn't throw up today, so I'd say I'm pretty great." I watch as she sits up and stretches her arms above her head. I don't think she realizes how sexy she is, which only makes her more attractive. "Sit with me," she beckons, holding her hand out to me.

I follow her command and as soon as I'm settled on the couch, Casey straddles my lap. This seems to be a favorite position of hers and you'll never hear me complain.

No fucking way.

"I'm sorry the game didn't go well." My eyes close but it's not because of her words. Her fingers have found their way into my hair and are currently massaging my scalp. If I was a cat, I'd be fucking purring. "Is there anything I can do to make you feel better?"

"You're doing it," I say with a groan. I had no idea how good being touched like this could feel.

"Surely, there's something else I can do for you," Casey murmurs before leaning forward and sucking my earlobe into her mouth.

My eyes fly open and find her watching me. She's as full of desire as I now feel.

"Case—" I start but I honestly don't know what to say. All I know is I want her right here, right now. In any way she wants me.

"Shhh," she whispers, her voice deep and husky. "Let me take care of you."

She tugs at my t-shirt and I sit up and help her remove it. As soon as I lean back, her lips are on me, kissing my mouth before traveling down my neck and stopping at my nipples. Before Casey, I never realized a guy's nipples can be as sensitive as a woman's but now, it's one of my favorite forms of foreplay. When her teeth graze my sensitive skin, my hips buck, thrusting my hardening cock against her body. Not one to rush, she lazily kisses her way to my other nipple and swirls her tongue around it.

How can she be so calm right now when I need her like I need my next breath?

"I want you," I grunt.

"I want you, too," she says, unbuckling my belt and slipping the leather out of the loops before throwing it on the floor. "In my mouth."

Oh, hell yes.

Casey slides onto the floor in front of me, pulling my jeans and boxer briefs down at the same time. My dick is standing at full attention now and when she grasps it firmly while licking her lips, it twitches in her hand. I start to chuckle but quickly swallow it when I feel Casey's tongue lap at my tip.

She licks down my shaft and back up again and it's the best kind of torture as I wait for her to take me in completely. She doesn't make me wait for long, thank God, and I let out a deep moan when she wraps her mouth around me and slides all the way down.

I slide my fingers through her long hair, keeping it out of her face while allowing her to set and keep her own pace. After she pumps me in and out of her mouth a few times, I'm surprised when she pulls my dick out all the way.

"I need to be naked. Like, right now," she explains.

I gladly help her out of her dress and am thrilled to discover she's not wearing a bra. My hand reaches out and cups one of her breasts before bending down and sucking a firm nipple into my mouth. Casey gasps before admonishing me. "Oh, no, you don't. It's still my turn."

Chuckling, I hold my hands up in surrender and allow her to pick up where she left off.

She sucks me more eagerly now and I absolutely love watching her go down on me. I'm so close to coming but when I see her slip her hand into her panties, I pull myself out of her mouth.

"What's wrong?" she asks.

"As much I love watching you get me off while touching yourself," I say, standing her up and sliding her panties off. "I need to be inside you."

When I guide her back to my lap, she wastes no time sliding me into her wet heat and it takes every ounce of strength I have not to come on contact.

"Damn, baby. You're so wet. Did you get that wet just from sucking my cock?"

"Yes," she says on an exhale, a look of relief covering her face as we're finally connected the way we're supposed to be. "I've been thinking about doing this all day. I love having you in my mouth but I love this even more." She bounces on my lap a few times, tilting her head back in pleasure before looking back up at me. "I want you on top, though."

"Say no more." I immediately roll her onto her back, raising one of her legs and draping it over my shoulder. I love how she's not afraid to tell me what she wants and the fact she's been thinking about this...wanting this, *me*, all day has me burning for her.

"Mmm, that's it. I love to feel your weight on me." Her pussy clenches around me and I begin to thrust. When I'm inside Casey like this, it's as though the rest of the world doesn't exist. All that matters is us, our connection, and how we make each other feel.

And we feel fucking amazing.

Too soon, we're both gasping and clutching each other tightly as our orgasms take over, leaving us sweaty, sticky, and sated.

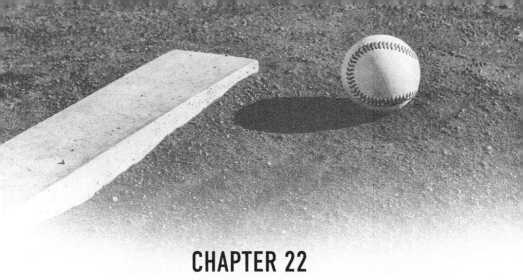

CHAPTER 22

Casey

"STOP PACING," ROSS SAYS FOR THE FIFTH TIME IN THE LAST FIVE MINUTES.

Halting my steps in front of the large window in his living room, I mutter, "I can't."

"It's going to be okay."

"How do you know?"

He walks up behind me, wrapping his arms around me. "Because we're in this together and because I know your sister and Bo. They're going to be supportive."

My stomach drops again at the thought of what we're getting ready to tell them. I know Ross is right. I know Charlotte and Bo will be supportive. Even if they're not at first, they will be eventually. But it's the in-between that freaks me out and also the unknown. How will my sister handle this news? Will it bring up unwanted feelings about her own pregnancy?

Ross dips down and presses his lips against my cheek and I relax into him.

He's my soothing balm.

Anytime I start to get anxious or nervous about anything to do with the baby, I think of him or go to him and he makes it better.

After my appointment yesterday, which I went to alone, because I don't want to risk Ross Davies being seen leaving an OB/GYN office, he insisted that we tell Charlotte and Bo. This way, I can at least have my sister with me at future appointments.

He's been really great about not pushing too hard. And he understands my reservations about going public with the pregnancy. But I'm almost fifteen weeks along and I'm starting to show. My stomach is still small, like I ate too many tacos, but it's there, and in a few more weeks, I won't be able to hide it.

Which brings me to my next hurdle—telling my parents.

Ross has been frothing at the bit to share the news with his parents, who desperately want grandchildren, but I've been dragging my feet with mine.

They've been through this before, and even though Charlotte was younger than me, I'm still worried about how they'll react. On our weekly phone calls, I've played it safe and avoided all conversation about Ross and living in his guest house because they weren't happy about it.

We don't understand why you'd move out of your sister's house.

It doesn't look good to live in some guy's guest house.

Ross isn't *some guy*, but tell that to parents who are surrounded by Hollywood's elite.

"They're here," Ross says, kissing the top of my head and walking to the foyer to open the door.

Taking a deep, fortifying breath, I put on a smile and join him.

Something about this moment feels a lot like playing house, which doesn't settle well with me, but I put it out of my mind for now and focus on the task at hand.

"Hey, man," Bo says, walking up and clasping Ross's hand and pulling him in for a manly hug. "Thanks for having us over."

Bo leans down and kisses my cheek. "Charlotte brought her famous buffalo chicken dip."

"I've got chicken and steaks for the grill," Ross says, taking the dish from my sister as she makes her way up onto the porch. "And Casey made a delicious looking salad."

"A salad is all we get from you?" my sister teases, giving me a wink. "I'm disappointed. I came for the twice-baked potatoes."

"You know we've gotta stick to the protein," Ross says, covering for me, because the truth is I was so sick this morning he finished making the salad.

Charlotte rolls her eyes. "Just because the two of you have a figure to keep doesn't mean we have to follow suit. Isn't that right, Case? The Carradine girls need their carbs."

"I'll make it up to you and bring you a special batch next weekend when the guys are on the road." I smile and bring her in for a hug. "We'll make an entire meal out of twice-baked potatoes."

"And wine," she adds, moving into the kitchen and helping herself to some veggies Ross cut up. "Speaking of…"

Ross answers her question without her finishing it by grabbing a bottle out of the fridge and uncorking it for her.

"Case?" she asks, holding up a glass.

I swallow, realizing now is probably as good a time as any to tell her I'm on a no-wine diet for the next five months… or longer, since I've decided to breastfeed the baby.

Clearing my throat, I lick my lips and look up at Ross who nods encouragingly.

"I have something to tell you," I begin, glancing back up at Ross. "We have something to tell you."

My heart is literally trying to bust its way out of my chest as I try to control my breathing.

God, this is harder than telling Ross.

At least with Ross, I knew he was partially to blame, but Charlotte and Bo are outsiders… they're not part of the Casey-Ross-Baby trio… and that scares me.

Like with Ross, I decide the quicker the better. "I'm pregnant." My eyes flick from Ross to Charlotte and then over to Bo, before settling back on Ross. "*We're* pregnant."

Charlotte's wineglass slips, but thankfully doesn't break. Ross hadn't poured her any wine yet, so she didn't spill anything either, but the sound echoes around the kitchen as everyone holds their breath.

Ross's eyes are on me.

Bo's are on Charlotte.

Charlotte is staring at the wineglass.

"Char," I urge, trying to decipher her reaction and gauge my response accordingly. Is she mad at me? Sad?

Her head snaps up and her blank expression freaks me out.

"Please say something."

Righting the wineglass, she picks it up and holds it out to Ross, who takes her silent plea and fills the glass... nearly to the top. Bringing it to her lips, she tips it up and practically drinks the entire glass. When she sets it back down, swiping a hand across her mouth, she levels me with a stare.

"Please say that again."

Breathing deeply, I fill my lungs with air and then exhale. "I'm pregnant... Ross is the father... It happened after we were together one night. To save you from doing the math, because I know how much you hate it, I'm fifteen and a half weeks pregnant and due the second week of November."

"So..." she starts, then stops. Her eyes drift from me to Ross, then back to me. "Are the two of you... together?"

My palms feel sweaty, so I rub them down the front of my yoga pants and then clasp them together to keep from fidgeting. "We're taking it one day at a time," I tell her. "It was just as much of a shock to us as it is to you."

"No," Charlotte says with a humorless chuckle. "No, I doubt that, because I didn't know that *you*," she says, pointing to Ross, "were fucking my sister."

"Charlotte!" My eyes grow wide and I look to Bo for some help, but he just throws his hands in the air and shakes his head. Turning back to Charlotte, I go to Ross's defense because I know he won't. He'd take all the blame if I'd let him. "It's not like he seduced me, okay? I'm just as much responsible for this as he is... actually, more. I'm more to blame. I seduced him—"

"Casey," Ross says, trying to stop me, but I keep going.

"No, listen," I say, walking around the counter and taking Charlotte's hands in mine. "We'd been working together and you know I had a crush on Ross." She looks at me, her expression softening a little. "Actually, when you basically forced me into working for him, I thought you were setting us up or something, but that's not how it was. We kept things as professional as possible."

I look to Ross and he just smirks.

"Until one night before he left for Spring Training... we had a little too much wine... a lot too much wine... and I attacked him. Right here in this kitchen... literally just went for it."

At that, Charlotte chuckles and rolls her eyes. "So, the one time you just *go for it*, you get knocked up?"

"I know, right?" I reply, laughing as a few tears prick my eyes. "And I'd forgotten to take a pill here and there… totally not responsible, I know, but I wasn't… you know." I widen my eyes, trying to convey that I hadn't been with anyone for quite a while before Ross.

Charlotte nods because she understands my silent communication, so I continue.

"And that night was…" Filling up my cheeks with air, I blow it out and look behind me, realizing we still have an audience. "Well, it was… intense."

"And we made a baby," Ross says matter-of-factly. "End of story time. Who wants steaks?"

Everyone laughs at his attempt to ease the tension and even though I know we're not finished with this conversation, Charlotte nods. "Yeah, I could eat."

"Me too," I tell him, giving him a reassuring look as he and Bo walk out of the kitchen to fire up the grill, leaving me and Charlotte alone. "I'm sorry I didn't tell you sooner… I freaked out and didn't even tell Ross until a month ago. Since then, I've been trying to figure out a good time to tell you, but every time I'd work up the courage, I'd think about…"

I drift off, not wanting to bring up her pregnancy or the baby if she doesn't want to talk about it.

"The baby," she offers.

Nodding, I walk around the counter and push myself up onto a barstool, while Charlotte pours herself another glass of wine. This time, she takes a sip—not a guzzle—and I'm hopeful this conversation will go better than I'd feared.

"Yeah, the baby… you don't talk about it much anymore and I didn't want to bring up bad memories or hurt you in any way."

She gives me a sad smile. "You're not, Case." Reaching across the counter, she grabs for my hand and I give it to her. "I've come to terms with all of that. I just worry about you. Even though you've always taken care of me, I'm still your big sister and I worry about you. To hear some guy, even if it was Ross Davies, knocked you up—"

"Stop saying that." I close my eyes, letting out a laugh of exasperation. "You make it sound like we're fifteen-year-olds in high school. And it wasn't just him… he didn't get me anything. I helped. It was me too."

This time, her smile is wider and I see her swallow hard, like she's fighting back emotions.

"That's a very mature, adult thing to say." Nodding, she glances down at the counter and then back up to me, and this time, there are tears in her eyes. "When you were standing there telling me you were pregnant, it was like I was looking at my twelve-year-old little sister all over again. I know you're an adult and more than capable of raising a baby. Shit, you've practically raised me. And I don't know what your relationship with Ross is like or what it will be, but I know he'll be a good father."

I know all of those things too, but to hear her say it makes me feel better. It's the encouragement I've needed to know I can do this.

She's been the missing link.

I know I have Ross's support and that is enough… I could make it be enough, but Charlotte and I have had each other's backs through everything. She's been my best friend and confidante, my voice of reason, and also the person who tells me it's okay to take a risk.

"Tell me this is going to be okay," I whisper, needing to hear it from her.

Her hands grip mine tighter. "It's going to be more than okay… you're going to kick motherhood's ass and I'm going to be the best fucking aunt ever."

"Please don't use that language around my baby."

Charlotte breaks out into a fit of laughter as Ross and Bo walk back into the kitchen. I can see the relief on Bo's face. He was worried about her too, but now that he sees she's okay, he seems to be also.

I love that about them. They're each other's biggest fans and biggest protectors. Bo would slay dragons for Charlotte and she'd burn the world down for him.

I want that.

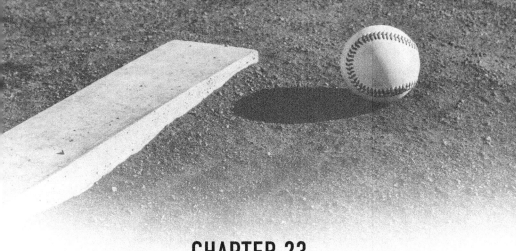

CHAPTER 23

Ross

"DAVIES," BUDDY SAYS, POKING HIS HEAD OUT OF HIS OFFICE. "CAN I SEE YOU FOR A minute?"

It's still a couple of hours before game time. Most of the guys are in their own little world, playing video games or listening to music. Since it's an off day for me, I was just shooting the shit with Mack.

He looks at me, giving me an eyebrow raise. "Good luck with that."

"Yeah," I reply, standing up and heading toward Buddy's office.

I hope this doesn't have anything to do with my last few starts. To say I've been off my game is putting it mildly. I'm basically in a slump, which can happen during the season, but it's too early for that and my arm feels great, which means it's exactly what Mack accused me of.

It's Casey.

Well, not her exactly. This isn't her fault. It's mine and my overactive brain. I can't shut it off. All I do nowadays when I'm not with her is think about her and everything that could go wrong.

With the baby.

With her.

With us.

After Felicia told me she wanted a divorce, my world felt like it was spinning out of control. I didn't get a choice in the matter. One day we were married and doing everything we could to make it work, or so I thought, and the next minute she needed to talk to me… and it was over.

Something about now is reminiscent of that, like there are all of these moving parts and I'm not in control of any of them.

"What's up, Skip?" I ask, stepping into Buddy's office.

"Close the door," he says, not looking up from the stack of papers in front of him. "Have a seat."

Okay.

Feeling like a kid called to the principal's office, I shut the door and sit in the leather chair, waiting for the hammer to fall.

"I'm assuming you've heard about the trade with New York," he starts, finally looking up at me and making my stomach drop.

Of course, I've heard about the trade with New York, but what exactly does that have to do with me? As far as I know, it's a done deal. But I don't like my name and trade used in the same sentence.

"Yeah, I know about it."

Buddy nods. "Good," he says, gathering his papers and tapping them into a neat stack. "Along with Malcolm Malone, we also acquired a closer. He's been sent down several times, but I think, with good coaching and someone to help him work through his shit, he could be a valuable asset to our bullpen."

Immediate relief rushes through me and the fog clears as I let out a deep breath. Buddy smirks, like he knew I was sweating it for a minute and I kind of want to punch him for it. Except for the fact he's more like a second dad to me and I'd never hurt an old man.

Smirking back at him, I shake my head. "And you want me to help this guy work through his shit?"

"Yeah," he says, pushing away from his desk and grabbing a file. "I think it'd do you both some good."

He's such a sneaky bastard sometimes and he knows I'd never turn down a chance to help another player. This is also his way of letting me know he knows I'm also working through some shit.

"And who is this guy?" I ask, trying to run through New York's roster and think about who they'd trade this early in the season.

"Owen Thatcher."

Owen Thatcher.

"I haven't seen that guy since we both played in Detroit." I shake my head. "We go way back."

Buddy huffs a laugh. "I know, which is why I think you could help him. Plus, he went through a nasty break-up not too long ago and has two kids… single dad. It's gotta be hard on him, but with what you went through at the end of last season, I thought you'd be able to help him. And I've seen how you are with the guys in the clubhouse. They look up to you and listen to you."

"I don't know about that," I say, feeling a little unworthy of the praise. I'm not sure I've really been filling the leader role as of late.

"I do," Buddy says, setting his pen down and lacing his fingers behind his head as he leans back in his chair. "Even when you think you're not on your game, you're still better than most."

Shaking my head, I start to argue with him, but he gives me his signature glare and I shut my mouth. If Buddy Malone says it, you listen.

"Fine," I tell him. "I'll do what I can."

"Good, he'll be here in two days."

THATCH AND I FALL INTO AN OLD CADENCE AS WE THROW BALLS INTO A NET IN MY backyard.

"Can't believe we're here," he says, bending down and grabbing another ball out of the bucket. "Who'd have thought the two of us would end up on the same team again?"

Chuckling, I throw a knuckleball, appreciating how it felt as I released it. "Nothing surprises me anymore."

"That's the fucking truth," he says, winding up and throwing a nice fastball. He definitely has some heat.

"Buddy mentioned you had a nasty breakup," I say, trying to sound casual. I don't want to pressure him into talking, but if he needs to get some shit off his chest, I want him to know I'm here to listen.

Thatch blows out a breath, shaking his head. "If by nasty he means feeling like I've had my life flipped upside down, yeah, I guess you could say that."

I think he's going to stop there, but then he continues.

"Lisa and I were together for six years. She never wanted to get married but we had two kids together. I thought we were good, you know? Then one day, I come home and the nanny told me she'd left me a note. It basically said she wasn't cut out for this life and knew I could give the kids a better life than she could and she bailed."

We stand there for a minute, just letting that settle between us. I wasn't sure what to say and he was obviously reeling in memories or still trying to wrap his mind around it.

I can't imagine.

"Just fucking bailed… our daughter is five and she asks me every night when she's coming home. It kills me. Our son is three and he knows she's gone, but he's easily distracted."

"I'm sorry," I tell him, rubbing my chest as my thoughts drift from Felicia to Casey to this baby… I've been battling thoughts of Casey leaving me like Felicia did and even though I know they are two completely different people, it doesn't quiet the noise in my head.

"Who watches the kids while you're at games and on the road?" I ask, wondering how you handle logistics for something like that. Shit, I need Casey to run my everyday life. If by some crazy chance she decided she didn't want to be a mother or be with me and upped and left, I'd be so fucking screwed.

He sighs, running a hand through his hair. "My mom came down here with us. She's going to help me set up the house and find a good nanny, but it's hard knowing who I can trust with my kids when I'm thousands of miles away. But I've got to figure out my shit or I'm going to get sent down and I can't let that happen."

Of course, he can't let that happen.

He's now the sole provider for two children.

"I'm here for you if you need anything… the whole team will be," I assure him. "But I also have a great therapist, if you want someone professional to talk to. It really helped me after Felicia left."

"I can't believe the two of you got divorced," he says with true incredulity in his tone. "I thought you were the perfect couple."

My laugh holds no humor. "Yeah, well, so did I… for a while, but things aren't always as perfect as they seem."

"I know what you mean," he says. "I think I'm done, man."

At first, I think he's talking about throwing balls, but then I realize he means more.

He's done with relationships.

"I'm so done with women," he continues. "They're all the fucking same."

The Owen Thatcher I knew from college was a fun-loving guy who was easy going and willing to do anything for anyone, but this version is harder, and I can see the thick layer of protection he's built around himself.

There's something about it that's familiar, like seeing myself from a different angle. I remember a time not too long ago when I thought it would be easier to not get attached to anyone else after Felicia.

No heartache.

No betrayal.

No disappointment.

Then I met Casey.

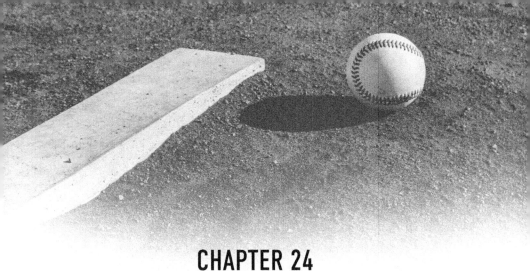

CHAPTER 24

Casey

THANKS TO MY LACK OF ENERGY DURING THE DAY, I END UP TAKING QUITE A FEW NAPS and that often leads to bouts of insomnia.

It's not just the naps keeping me up tonight, though.

Ross and I went to bed over three hours ago, he made me come twice, and then we showered and he went to sleep. I, on the other hand, have been staring at the ceiling, tossing and turning for over two hours thinking about the fact I have to call my parents tomorrow and tell them about the baby. We have our big ultrasound in two days and it's time. I can't hide it from them any longer.

Ross has wanted to tell his parents for a while. He claims they will be beside themselves with excitement and I believe him. But I can't help feeling the opposite about mine.

It's not that my mom and dad are horrible people. I love them. We talk on a pretty regular basis, but it's about mundane topics. My mom tells me about her friends she lunches with and business in LA. My dad always inquires about my safety and how Charlotte is really doing. As much as they love us, they also love their lifestyle of the rich and famous.

To most people, it probably looks cold and uninviting, but they do care about us and want what's best for us. And when push comes to shove, they have our backs… mostly.

One thing I've never approved of is how they handled Charlotte's pregnancy. It was like they didn't know how to handle it so they let people who cared more about her career than her life do it for them. I was a kid, but I could see the mistakes they were making.

Of course, hindsight is twenty-twenty and I think they eventually saw the error of their ways, but I'm not sure I've ever let that go. It's not that I'm holding a grudge or unforgiveness, I just don't trust them as much as I should.

And now that I'm pregnant, those old feelings have resurfaced and I'm struggling to tell them.

When I try to roll over for the fifteenth time, Ross stirs and I decide it's time to give it up and get out of bed. Besides, I'm craving something sweet and I know I won't be able to sleep until it's satisfied.

Slipping out from under Ross's arm, I inch off the bed and tiptoe my way downstairs.

Ross told me I should wake him when I can't sleep, but just because I can't sleep doesn't mean he shouldn't. Besides, he pitches tomorrow night and needs his rest.

To say he hasn't been on his game lately would be an understatement. At the start of the season, he was on fire, retiring batters right and left, but lately he's lucky if he pitches enough innings to claim the win… or loss, which has been the case lately.

The Revelers are on somewhat of a losing streak and I can tell it's getting to him.

And Bo.

And all the other players I see on a regular basis.

They're all now growing out beards until they win again… or hit five-hundred… or whatever. I don't really know. All I know is that I feel like I'm to blame for Ross's slump and I want to do anything I can to help him.

Allowing him to sleep is one thing I can do for him.

Unfortunately, as I'm bent over, rummaging through the refrigerator, I hear a creak on the stairs.

"Sorry," I whisper, as he stumbles into the kitchen, feeling bad for waking him.

He yawns and runs a hand through his hair, messing it up even more than it already was… making him even sexier. Delicious. Maybe I'm not hungry for food after all.

These second trimester pregnancy hormones are no joke... I want sex all the time.

"It's okay," he says, coming up behind me and placing his hands on my stomach. "Is the baby hungry?"

I nod. "The baby is starving and keeping me up. It needs something sweet."

Oreo ice cream is my usual go-to, but it doesn't sound good tonight. Neither do the Thin Mint cookies Ross special ordered for me from some Girl Scout stash he found online.

"I need beignets," I tell him, suddenly hit with a very specific craving for puffed pastry and powdered sugar. Realizing it's the middle of the night and we don't have the ingredients to make any, I'm sure I'll figure something else out to satisfy it... for now. But first thing tomorrow—

"Let's go get beignets, then," Ross says, interrupting my thoughts.

Turning in his arms, I frown up at him. "It's after midnight."

"Cafe du Monde is open twenty-four hours a day."

He's right. But Ross and I never go anywhere together, at least not in public. We've driven over to Charlotte and Bo's for pizza and to pick up dinner to-go, but that's pretty much been the extent of our outings.

"But you're pitching tomorrow and you need your sleep."

Bending down, he brushes his lips against mine and then over to my cheek, whispering in my ear, "If my girl wants beignets, I'm getting her some beignets."

Ross's use of *my girl* sends tingles down my spine. Cupping his cheeks, I pull his mouth to mine and show him how much I love that he claims me for his own and caters to my cravings.

"I'll take that as a yes," he says, his voice low and husky and doing things to my body.

"It's that or sex," I tell him, going back for another kiss.

He chuckles into my mouth. "How about beignets and then sex."

"I love your bargaining skills."

Twenty minutes later, I'm waiting by the front door, dressed in yoga pants and an oversized t-shirt, with a cardigan to cover my bump and my hair in a messy bun.

Ross comes jogging down the stairs wearing jeans and a hoodie, looking delectable. But when you're as beautiful as Ross Davies, it doesn't matter what you wear… or don't wear.

"Ready?" he asks, pulling a cap down low, covering his eyes.

When I get a good look at it, I pull back in disgust. "What the heck are you wearing?"

He smirks. "It's my decoy."

"It's a Dodgers hat."

"Exactly," he says, opening the door as our Uber driver appears at the gate. With a hand on my back, Ross ushers me out of the house. "I can't really go out in Revelers attire, so I keep this handy for when I want to go out and not be recognized."

Rolling my eyes, I snort. "How many people expect to run into Ross Davies at Cafe du Monde at one in the morning?"

"I'm not taking any chances."

I can appreciate that, so I take his hand and follow him to the car.

When the driver pulls up in front of Cafe du Monde, I'm pleased to see that while there are quite a few people at the tables, there isn't a line.

As we walk up and find a table in one of the corners, I breathe in the sweet aroma, my craving already being somewhat satisfied just by being here. Maybe it's the warm breeze or being in the Quarter or the guys playing jazz on the street corner, but it makes me feel… good.

"I haven't been here in forever," I tell Ross as he pulls out a chair for me.

"I haven't either," he says, sounding distracted.

I'm getting ready to ask him if something's wrong, but then I realize what he's doing. He's scanning the restaurant to see if anyone has noticed him, which causes me to do the same, but it seems like we've managed to slip in undetected.

"Does that get old?" I ask.

He finally looks over at me and furrows his eyebrows. "What?"

"Checking around to see if you've been noticed."

"I do it without even thinking," he admits. "When it first started happening, it always caught me off guard. I remember Felicia loved it at first, then after a while, she hated it, like it interrupted her life or something. So, I got to where I'd do what I call a perimeter check every time we'd go somewhere and try to get ahead of any situation."

Shaking his head, he adjusts his hat. "Sorry, I shouldn't bring her up."

"Don't be sorry," I tell him. Reaching across the table, I place my hand on his and he flips his palm over, lacing our fingers together. "She was a part of your life for a long time. I don't expect you to just not ever bring her up."

"Hey," I say, wanting to change the topic because talk of Felicia always puts Ross in a bad mood and I want to enjoy our time together. "This is kind of our first official date."

That earns me a smile.

"Maybe you could buy me a t-shirt," I continue. "You know, to commemorate the occasion… nothing says first date with your baby mama like a t-shirt from a beignet joint." I waggle my eyebrows, making him laugh.

Ross's laugh is one of my favorite sounds and it eases my worry a little.

When a waiter comes over to our table, I order two beignets and a chocolate milk. Ross orders four with a cafe au lait, earning him a raise of my eyebrows. Guess I'm not the only one craving something sweet.

As the waiter starts to walk away to turn our order in, Ross stops him. "Could we also get one of your t-shirts?"

"In a large, please," I add with a huge smile. I was kidding about the shirt, but I really have always wanted one. And since I'm living in t-shirts these days, I'll happily add a new one to my collection.

"Thank you," I tell Ross as he pulls out his wallet and counts out some bills for when the waiter returns.

He tucks his wallet back into his pocket and looks over at me. "I should've taken you on a dozen dates by now… so don't thank me for this."

"This," I tell him, wishing I could do more than hold his hand, "is perfect."

When the beignets arrive, Ross and I both dig in.

If you've lived in New Orleans for long or been to Cafe du Monde more than once, you know the rules: don't inhale or exhale, just hold your breath and take a bite.

Which brings me to something I've been wanting to ask him. "I know that with baseball, it's impossible to know how long you'll be in one place," I start, hoping this doesn't sound like I'm asking him for his five-year plan or anything. "But do you plan on staying in New Orleans?"

He finishes his bite and wipes some of the powdered sugar off, missing a little, but I don't say anything because it's pretty dang cute.

"I love it here," he says. "I mean, if I'm ever traded, I'd obviously go wherever, but..." He shrugs, looking out at the street as the musicians change tunes. "I have three more years on my contract and I'm hoping to stick around even after that. This was a brand-new organization when I came here and I'd love to finish out my career here, but it's hard to see that far into the future."

I know what he means. I'm struggling to see another five months into the future. I've been repeating my mantra—*one day at a time*—over and over in my head for so long, I tend to forget to look much further. But the last week or so, I've been thinking about what happens after the baby is born? Where does Ross see us in six months? A year? Where do I?

It's a lot and not really the kind of conversation you have at Cafe du Monde at two o'clock in the morning, so I shelve those thoughts for another day.

"What about you?" he asks. "Did you ever consider living in LA, closer to your parents?"

I vehemently shake my head, as my mouth is full of pastry. "Never," I finally say. "I hate LA. I know that probably sounds harsh, but I saw what Hollywood did to my sister and I know moving back here was the best thing to ever happen to her... and to me."

Ross's eyes find mine and he holds my stare.

After a minute or so passes and he doesn't say anything, I have to ask. "Is there something you want to talk about?"

His expression shifts, but I can decipher it, then he looks down at his plate. "No, why?"

I shrug and then shake my head, brushing it off. "You just seem like you have something on your mind."

That earns me a noncommittal grunt and like the few times before this, I know he's not going to say anything. Ross is an open book on so many topics. He never shuts me down when we talk about his parents or baseball. He's usually even pretty forthcoming about Felicia, even though I can tell he doesn't want to talk about her. But there's something else... something that makes him look at me in a certain way that makes me feel like he wants to say something, but can't or won't.

Not wanting to push, I try changing the subject. "Tell me more about the new guy."

"Thatch?" Ross asks, his brows furrow as he uses a corner piece of a beignet to sweep up some powdered sugar and shrugs. "He's a good guy and we go way back, but he's been through some rough times lately."

"With being traded?" I ask.

Ross shakes his head. "No, he's good with that. Actually, that's probably the best thing that's happened to him in a while. Buddy has high hopes for him and we need what he has to offer. I think he'll end up making a great set-up pitcher."

He pauses, licking his fingers.

The action causes my mind to go to dirty places... like Ross's head between my legs. Actually, I think he's done that exact thing before he—

"Do you know what a set-up pitcher is?" he asks, looking up at me.

Whatever he sees makes him smirk and it's borderlining on pornography.

I honestly don't know what's wrong with me these days. Charlotte's always called me a closet whore and holy crap, I think she's right. It's the only way to explain how him licking his fingers and smirking can make my panties wet.

And just thinking that makes me blush.

I shake my head and take another bite so I won't have to speak.

A low, rumbly laughter shakes his chest and I hope he's not getting ready to call me out on my blatant ogling and obvious train of thought. Thankfully, he just continues his mini-lesson on baseball.

"He's the guy who comes in before the closer, usually around the seventh inning."

That thought makes Ross pause and I know he's thinking about his recent starts and the fact he's not made it to the seventh inning. I see a change in his demeanor, but he tries to recover and continues talking about Owen.

"If he's good at his job, he'll eventually be promoted to a closer, but every team needs a good set-up man."

"What about the other stuff you were talking about?" I like when he discusses things with me and sometimes I think it helps him too. He has his teammates and I know they're close, but surely having someone outside of the game to talk about stuff with is a good thing. Even though there's an eight-year difference between us, we usually seem to be on the same page.

Ross shrugs, popping his last bite into his mouth and chewing for a moment while he thinks about what he wants to say. "His girlfriend left him and their two kids."

"Oh, my God." My hand covers my mouth as I try to process the thought. "She just left?"

He nods and his eyes are back to roaming the restaurant, not making contact with mine.

"Yep, she told him it was too much for her and she couldn't do it anymore." When he sighs, I wonder if what Owen is going through makes him think about Felicia. It sounds similar to what she told him, but I think her reasons for leaving were a bit different. To me, it sounds like Owen's girlfriend didn't want the lifestyle, where Felicia wanted it, but she wanted the spotlight for herself.

"What's he going to do?" I ask, suddenly worried for his children. Baseball players have a rigorous schedule. Unlike other professional sports, their season lasts for half the year, one-hundred-and-eighty-seven days, to be exact, and that doesn't include Spring Training and postseason play. Half of their season is on the road, which means three months out of the year, he's gone.

"I mean, his kids are young, I'm guessing."

"Five and three," Ross says, and there's something unreadable in his tone. "But his mom came to stay with him for a while to help them get settled and be with the kids until he finds someone."

"Like a nanny or something?"

He shrugs again, adopting that closed-off attitude that's been bothering me lately. It's like he flips a switch and shuts down, then in another breath, he's back on.

"Yeah, I guess… he had one in New York, but she was an older woman and couldn't relocate with him. So, he's looking for someone like that. He'll probably go through an agency or something."

I nod, still thinking about those kids and how a mother could just leave like that.

Charlotte gave up her baby, but she was eighteen and felt like it was the best thing she could do for both the baby and herself. I have to agree with her. Eighteen-year-old Charlotte was still finding herself, and even though I know she would've found her way and been a good mother, I believe she did the right thing.

But once you have a baby and you're a part of its life, how do you walk away?

Placing my hand on my stomach, I rub a small circle, silently promising I'll never do that. I couldn't. I already love this baby too much.

Our waiter from earlier shows back up with a bag, pulling me out of my thoughts.

"Almost forgot your shirt," he says with an apologetic expression. "Sorry about that."

"Oh, thanks," I say, taking the bag. "I did too."

He shifts awkwardly on his feet and for a second, I think he's waiting to be paid, but then I remember Ross paid him earlier when he brought out our beignets. Leaning down closer to the table, he drops his voice to a whisper, like he's making a drug deal. "This is probably a stupid question, but are you Ross Davies?"

Ross clears his throat, keeping his head down and giving a small nod.

"Can you sign my order pad?" the waiter asks, sliding it and a pen over to Ross. "I promise I won't say anything until y'all are gone. But I'm a huge fan… huge."

Taking the pad, Ross signs his name to the top page, then flips it and signs a few more.

"Thanks for not saying anything," Ross says, handing it back to the waiter. "And thanks for supporting the Revelers. We appreciate it."

The waiter beams as he puts the pad back in his apron pocket. "Thanks for being so cool, man. And I hope y'all kick Tampa Bay's ass this week."

To his credit, he doesn't even look back as he walks away… or break into a happy dance.

I can't help but smile as I glance back over at Ross. "You just made that guy's night."

Ross chuckles, shaking his head. "Let's get out of here."

Taking my hand as we walk out, he lifts it to his lips and kisses the back of it before tucking it close to his chest. Like earlier, I feel like he wants to say something, but he doesn't. We walk in silence to a bench that's down the sidewalk as Ross pulls out his phone.

"The Uber will be here in three minutes," he says as we stand on the outskirts of Jackson Square.

I lean into his arm, think about how much I love the way I feel when I'm with him—wanted, needed, cherished. Closing my eyes, I try to commit this night to memory. The warm New Orleans night and just the two of us.

"Thanks for our first date," I tell him, squeezing a little tighter as he rests his chin on the top of my head, pulling me closer.

I hope what I'm feeling is real.

And I hope, one day soon, he lets down his walls and allows me inside, completely.

Because when I let down mine, I can see forever with him.

THE DRIVE BACK TO HIS HOUSE IS QUIET. I THINK, NOW THAT MY CRAVING HAS BEEN satisfied, the exhaustion is setting in. Ross has the driver let us out at the small gate for foot traffic and we walk hand-in-hand up the sidewalk.

As he's putting in the code to the gate, I can't help the huge yawn.

"How many naps will this require for full recovery?" he asks, looking down at me with a smile I've come to love. It's one he doesn't give to anyone else but me... it's soft and sincere, a hint of teasing, but packed with so much warmth it makes my insides melt.

I bite my lip, like I'm calculating. "Depends. Is that after-beignet sex still on the table?"

Ross's gaze turns from playful and light to heated and needy. "Sex with you is always on the table... speaking of, how do you feel about literal sex on the table?"

Feeling a blush creep up my neck and spread to my cheeks, I swallow.

"Sex... on the table... that could be good."

Who am I kidding? Sex on any surface with Ross would be amazing.

He chuckles, kissing the top of my head as we make our way to the front door. Unlocking it, he ushers me inside and relocks the door behind us, setting the alarm. When he turns and finds me watching him, his eyes drop to my lips and the next thing I know I'm pushed up against the wall in the foyer. Ross's hands are in my hair, pulling at the messy bun until it falls around us. His mouth is devouring mine, like he's a starving man... tasting of sugar and a hint of coffee.

"God, Case." He moans my name, sending a bolt of need to my core.

"I've been wanting to do that ever since we left the house." When his lips begin to trail down my neck, I tangle my fingers in his hair, loving the way I can feel his hardness pressed against me.

"Take me to bed."

CHAPTER 25

Ross

"HEY, BABE, I HAVE THE LAPTOP SET UP. YOU READY TO CHAT WITH MY PARENTS?"

The use of an endearment, like babe, just rolling off my tongue kind of catches me off guard. But when Casey walks into the living room carrying coffee mugs for us, she doesn't seem bothered by it. I probably shouldn't either. It feels right. Everything with her feels right, even though my brain is still trying to find the warning signs—anything that flashes in bright red, telling me this is going to end badly.

Did I miss those with Felicia?

Did our relationship have red flags I ignored?

Glancing back over at Casey, she gives me a small, nervous smile, and the only thing I see is the woman I'm starting to fall so hard for… and the mother of my unborn child. She doesn't know about these thoughts I've been having for the past few weeks. The ones where I picture her leaving me… taking the baby… leaving me and the baby. I have Owen Thatcher to thank for this new train of thought. Ever since he showed up and we had our heart-to-heart, I can't help but think about all of these new what-ifs.

"Are you sure you want to do this over Skype?" Casey asks, pulling one of the decorative pillows into her lap, probably as a decoy.

Telling my parents in person would be my preferred method, but since that can't happen, this is the next best option. At least it's better than a phone call.

While I'm adjusting the laptop and connecting the call, Casey picks up her coffee and takes a sip, savoring it like it's a lifeline.

"It's going to be fine, trust me," I tell her, squeezing her hand.

She gazes at me with those deep brown eyes of hers and I realize how ironic those last two words are coming out of my mouth. Here I am telling her to trust me, *wanting her to trust me*, when I can't even offer her the same courtesy.

I'm an asshole.

An asshole who wants to fix it and make it all better, but before I get a chance, my mom and dad's faces appear on the screen. They both give us a big smile and wave and I notice something. They're sitting next to each other on the couch, coffee mugs in hand, just like Casey and I are. It's a small thing but somehow it feels like a sign from the universe.

You're not screwing up.

This is right.

She's the one.

"Good morning," I say, reaching an arm behind Casey's back and pulling her a little closer.

If my mom and dad notice our proximity, they don't say anything.

"Good morning, Honey," my mom says with a warm smile. "And, Casey, it's so good to see you. How are you, dear?"

"I'm good, thanks." I feel her relax a bit, like she's reminded that my parents love her and this is going to be okay. "How are you?"

"Oh, good," my mom says. "Just happy to see your two smiling faces this morning. I was just telling Jack I can't remember the last time we Skyped. Ross tends to hate technology, so this must've been your influence."

She and my dad laugh like they're sharing an inside joke and I roll my eyes.

If they only knew.

"No," Casey says quickly, picking up her coffee mug and taking a sip as she settles into the conversation. "It actually wasn't my idea. It's all Ross. He said since the two of you couldn't come this month like you'd planned, this is the next best thing."

My dad leans a little closer to the camera, like he's telling a secret. "Well, just so you know, you're a good influence on him."

Casey chuckles nervously and covers it with another sip of coffee.

My dad reaches over to a side table and comes back on screen with a few sheets of paper.

"Something I meant to talk to you two about is hurricane season," he says, sliding his readers down to his nose as he peruses the papers, which if I had to guess have all sorts of information about hurricane preparedness printed on them. "I know it's in full swing down there and I just want to make sure you have all the supplies you may need, as well as, an evacuation plan if one hits."

He pauses long enough to push his glasses back to the top of his head, then continues. "If you need help with this, you just let me know. Those storms are nothing to play with."

Leave it to my dad to consider himself an expert on a weather condition he's never experienced before.

"We're covered, Jack," Casey says, elbowing me slightly when I start to laugh. "But we appreciate your concern. Hurricanes are no joke."

She's so good with my parents and it's all genuine, so I don't know why I'm still struggling with trust issues when it comes to her... *us*.

According to my therapist, who I've been seeing quite a bit lately, it's still normal to have reservations about starting a new relationship after a failed marriage. I want to be able to know Casey, inside and out, open myself up to her completely and have her do the same, but I just can't seem to make that final leap. I know we don't have to be in a committed relationship just because we're having a baby; the baby is coming regardless, but it's what I want. I want monogamy and intimacy.

I want what my parents have.

I want unconditional acceptance and love and I'm pretty sure I want it with Casey and that she wants it too.

But once your heart has been trampled to shit, it's hard to give it away again, knowing the outcome could be the same a second time.

"We do appreciate you taking such good care of our boy," my mom says, looping her arm around my dad's and leaning into his shoulder. "It helps us not worry so much about him."

"I've told y'all not to worry—"

"That's just what parents do," my dad says, giving me the look. "One of these days, you'll be one and you'll realize no matter how old or successful your kid gets, you still worry about them." This thought makes him laugh and shake his head. "One of these days, you'll be paying for your raising and I'll be sitting back pulling the grandpa card."

Maybe it's the fact the color has drained from my face or the way Casey has gone still as a statue, but my mom swats at my dad.

"Oh, Jack. Knock it off. You know he was a good kid." Now it's her turn to lean in, closer to the computer. "Don't listen to your dad, Honey. He's just giving you a hard time."

Clearing my throat, I swallow and let out a deep breath. "So, uh…" I pause and cough again, feeling like a lump is lodged in my throat. "Yeah, that's actually kind of why we called…"

I drift off, trying to think of a more eloquent way to say what I need to say but come up empty-handed. Casey tenses a bit, like she's bracing herself for the worst, so I put my arm around her and kiss the top of her head.

My mom's sighs of admiration let me know that little gesture didn't go unnoticed.

Keeping my eyes trained on Casey, I exhale. "We're having a baby… Casey and I are having a baby."

There's a moment when it's just us, me and Casey, and no parents are on the other end of the line. It's the first time I've said those words out loud and it's hitting me like a ton of bricks. I see the tears pooling, turning Casey's brown eyes into pools of amber.

"We're having a baby," I repeat. "In November."

When my mom screams, followed by, "I'm gonna be a grandma," the bubble bursts, and Casey and I both jump.

"A baby?" my dad asks, bringing my focus back to the screen. His expression is a bit confused, but not angry or upset, just needing clarification. "I didn't know you two are…" He waves his hand around in front of the screen, unsure of what to say. "Are you together?"

"We're still, um, testing it out," I say, turning to see Casey wipe under her eyes. She's letting me take the reins on this revelation but I'm floundering all of a sudden, unsure of what to say or how to explain to my parents exactly what's going on here. Maybe it's because I'm struggling to define it myself… or afraid of giving it the label it deserves.

"Testing it out?" Mom repeats. "That's the silliest thing you've said in a long time, Ross Samuel. If the two of you are having a baby together, I'd say you're more than testing it out."

Her look of exasperation mixed with confusion almost makes me want to laugh… almost, if it weren't for my heart that's practically beating out of my chest. When I look at my dad, he seems to still be reeling from the revelation.

"I know it's not conventional," Casey says, finally recovering enough to join in on the conversation. She always seems to come to my rescue exactly when I need it. "But as excited as we are about the baby, it was a complete surprise… definitely not planned. And we just don't want to rush into anything. No matter what becomes of our personal relationship, Ross and I are one hundred percent committed to this baby and being the best parents we can be."

She's amazing.

In this moment, I want to say *fuck it all*.

Fuck the fears and reservations.

Fuck the stupid nagging in the back of my brain telling me this could all blow up in my face.

Fuck testing the waters.

But I'm just not that guy. I don't make rash decisions. I don't fly by the seat of my pants. And, again, I have no clue what Casey's response would be. Would she laugh at me and say I'm crazy or would she want to jump feet-first with me?

"I can't say I understand," my mom continues, reaching across and taking my dad's hand for support, which he freely gives. "But you're both adults and you've made me a grandma, so I'll let that be good enough. I'll let you two figure it out and just pray for the best."

My dad nods. "You know if you need anything, we're here for you… both of you."

"Thank you," Casey says, reaching for my hand the same way my mom did my dad's.

And like him, I give it… freely.

"Congratulations, Son," my dad says. When I see the emotion in his eyes, I have to choke back my own. I'm not one of those people who haven't ever seen their father cry, but the few times I have, it's always made me emotional in response.

"Thanks, Dad."

"Thank you," Casey says, relief evident in her tone and posture.

"We'll call you after the ultrasound tomorrow, okay?" I tell them, kissing Casey's temple.

"You'd better," she says, sitting up straighter. "We need another Skype session."

"Or Facetime," my dad chimes in.

Casey lets out a laugh, nodding her head. "I'll make sure you get more of these."

"Good," my mom says, looking happier than I've seen her in a long time. "I need to dust off my vinyl cutter machine." The excitement in her voice is palpable.

My dad just rolls his eyes, shaking his head. "You've created a monster. You know that, right?"

"What will the baby call me?" she asks, off in her own little world. "I need to know before too long so I can personalize my things. I can make the baby things too… I can do some cute little onesies… and burp cloths."

"That would be really sweet, thank you," Casey says, sounding tired, but content.

Glancing at the clock on the screen, I see it's past noon and more than past the time Casey usually takes a nap.

"A baby," my mom says, still reeling. "I can't believe it."

"We'll call you again soon," I tell them. "Definitely after the ultrasound."

My dad nods, squeezing my mom a little closer. "Looking forward to it."

"Love you… both of you," my mom says, waving at the screen. "All three of you."

"Love you too," I tell them.

My mom blows a kiss and then the computer screen goes dark.

"We did it," I say, feeling like I pitched an entire game instead of talking to my parents over Skype. Slumping down on the couch, I pull Casey back with me and kiss her head.

"It wasn't so bad."

When my phone vibrates in my pocket, I assume it's my mom or dad sending more congratulations or wanting more information. It will be an ongoing thing for the next few months. I won't be surprised if my mom finds a way to fly out here soon.

But looking at the screen I see it's not them.

In fact, it's no one I want to hear from. Ever.

Felicia.

This is the third or fourth time she's called in the last month or so and I'm tired of it. I never answer or respond in any way and yet, she keeps calling. This is the most she's reached out to me in almost a year, so I can't imagine what she could want to talk about.

I know I should text her and say anything she wants to say to me, she can say to my lawyer, but I don't. I just let the call go to voicemail then delete it, not listening to it first, before tossing my phone onto the coffee table.

"Who was that?" she asks, looking up at me.

I shake my head, not wanting to lie to her, but also not wanting to bring Felicia into this moment or into our lives period. "No one," I tell her, shoving the phone back in my pocket and then pulling her closer.

Turning so I can stretch my legs out, I guide Casey to lay back against my chest. When she's nestled between my legs, I place my hands on her stomach. It's my new favorite position to lay in with her. She has a tiny yet very round bump now and it's the cutest thing.

It's also fucking sexy as hell.

"How is the peanut?" I ask.

Casey hums contentedly. "The peanut is great. I love how I can feel him flutter… or her, I guess it could be a girl too. Hopefully, we'll get our first kick soon. I was reading in one of my books last week that you usually start feeling kicks by twenty-five weeks, so I'm not quite there yet… but soon."

Her voice starts to trail off and I know a nap is on its way.

As I stroke small circles on her belly, I can't help but smile as I think about what it will be like to feel him or her kick. It's all getting so real. Tomorrow, we're learning the baby's sex.

I'm equal parts excited and terrified.

My thoughts are momentarily distracted by Casey's soft snores. Wrapping a protective arm around her, I settle deeper into the couch and decide to catch a few minutes of sleep too before I have to leave for the stadium.

As I drift off, I wonder if this will be how it is once the baby gets here… will we still be sneaking naps together?

YOU WOULD THINK, SINCE I THROW BALLS FOR A LIVING IN FRONT OF THOUSANDS OF people with very minimal jitters, a doctor's appointment would be a piece of cake.

But you'd be wrong. So very wrong.

My stomach is in knots and has been for hours and I'm not even the one the doctor will be examining.

We finally get to find out if Peanut is a he or a she.

It's a big day for me and Casey.

But, I've also been reading the baby books Casey has stacked on every nightstand and end table in my house. So, now, there's also the part of me that knows, if something's wrong, this will be the appointment that will tell us.

Who knew all the things that could go wrong?

Typically, I'm a very positive person, glass half-full and all that, but the thought of something going wrong and causing Casey or the baby any kind of distress has me feeling like I'm going to throw up.

Lord knows we don't need anyone else throwing up around here. Thanks to Casey, there's been enough vomit in my house to last a lifetime. But I'm not complaining. According to the books, morning sickness, or all day sickness where Casey is concerned, is a good sign. It's an indicator that a woman's pregnancy hormones are high and the pregnancy is stable.

Stable is good.

While Casey and I wait in the lobby, I can't stop my leg from bouncing up and down.

Thankfully, she's much calmer and is quietly reading a magazine.

"Are you like this before a game?" she asks.

"Like what?" I reply, knowing damn well what she's getting at.

"You're going to bounce a bald spot into the carpet under your foot."

Letting out a laugh, I shake my head. "I'm the complete opposite, actually. But it's different. I know what to expect before and during a game. I have no fucking clue what's going to happen today when we go back there." I nod my head toward the hallway leading to the exam rooms.

Casey places her hand on my thigh and squeezes, causing my attention to move from my nerves to how close her hand is to my dick.

It's an innocent touch but a decent distraction.

Before I get a chance to shift back to bouncing my leg, a nurse pokes her head out a door and calls Casey's name.

We follow her to a room at the end of the hallway, where she instructs Casey to disrobe from the waist up and put on a gown that's provided.

Needing more of a distraction, I ogle her as she undresses and smile at the sight of her belly. When she winces as she's climbing up onto the exam table, I lurch forward.

"Are you okay?" I ask, concern flooding my body in a hot wave. "Is it the baby?"

She huffs out a laugh. "No, it's my bladder. I had to drink a ton of water before the appointment to ensure the technician can see everything and now I have to pee."

Letting out a sigh, I lean against the table beside her.

"Relax, okay?" she says, placing her hand on my arm. "It's going to be okay."

When she looks at me like that, it's so easy to get lost in her gaze and let the world fall away. And once again, I'm reminded of the power she wields over me. So much power.

"Hello," a voice calls from the door, giving it a light tap.

"Come in," Casey calls out, lifting her head a little to see past me.

The tech introduces herself and briefly explains what she'll be doing before beginning the ultrasound. I watch as she squirts some lubricant onto Casey's bump and then starts rubbing a wand around on her stomach.

For a moment, it's quiet enough to hear a pin drop and then there's a whooshing sound that fills the room.

"Do you hear that?" Casey asks, her voice full of excitement.

"Is that the heartbeat?" I ask, feeling my own begin to race.

"It is," she says with a giggle. "Look at the screen."

I move to where I'm standing next to Casey and look at the computer screen the tech is pointing to. "Here's your baby," she says.

I'm not really sure what I'm seeing but every now and then, I recognize random body parts. A leg, some fingers, a head... and then I see the heartbeat... on the screen, it's literally beating.

And so, so real.

I don't know why, but seeing that tiny beating blip on the screen takes my breath away. My mouth is dry but my eyes are most certainly not.

We really did it.

We really made another human.

As I allow this reality to settle over me, I look at Casey in awe. She's been growing our baby all this time and obviously, I knew it but now it's so fucking... real.

Ten minutes ago, I was ready to throw up my lunch and now I feel like I can move mountains.

I'm going to be a dad and I can't wait.

Casey tugs on my arm, bringing my attention from the screen back to her. "Are you okay?"

"I've never been better." I give her a watery smile before whispering, "Thank you for bringing me today."

Before she can respond, the tech turns and asks if we'd like to know the sex of the baby. I know I sure as hell do but I look at Casey to let her know, it's her call. She nods excitedly and we both look back at the screen waiting for the magic to happen.

I watch as black and white swirls and blobs fade in and out on the screen until something catches my eye. And then two smaller somethings underneath it.

"Is that a..."

"Penis and testicles?" The tech finishes for me. "Sure is. Congratulations, you're having a boy!"

A boy.

A son.

Our son.

I, honestly, didn't care if it was a boy or a girl, as long as it was healthy, but there's something special about knowing for sure and I couldn't be happier.

Leaning down, I kiss Casey as tears roll down my face. When I pull away, I see she's crying too. As I wipe her tears away, I cup her cheeks and kiss her again, needing the connection and some way to convey how grateful I am to her for this moment.

"We have a son," I whisper, feeling more complete than I have in a very long time.

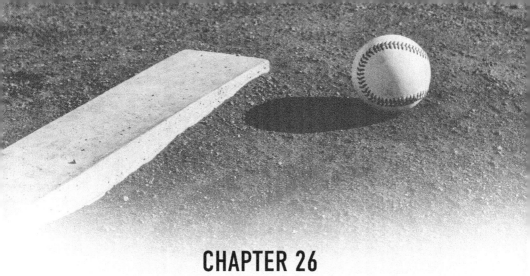

CHAPTER 26

Casey

I'M HAVING A BABY BOY.

Ross and I are having a baby boy.

Dirt and bugs and burps and toots and I cannot wait.

I know nothing about raising a boy but I'm so excited I can hardly stand it. Of course, I want him to stay inside as long as possible but I can't wait for him to be here so I can hold him and sniff him. Is there anything better than the way a baby smells? I don't think so. I already love him more than I've ever loved another person.

Ross is quickly becoming my number two, though.

I'm not ready to admit any serious feelings and I know Ross isn't ready to hear them but I feel myself falling for him more and more each day. There are times I think he's falling too, but then his demeanor changes, like he's pulling away and putting up barriers between us.

Frankly, it makes me mad. But I don't want to push him. I know his heart is still healing and I'd never want him to feel like I'm pressuring him in any way. The day Ross Davies admits his feelings for me, I want it to be because they're real, true, and freely given.

Sighing, I start at the top of the page and begin sorting through Ross's e-mails, again, for the third time today, vowing to pay closer attention this time.

Get it together, Casey.

The Revelers are in Atlanta, so I'm staying in Ross's house instead of the guesthouse, like I always do when he's on a road trip. And I can't help feeling like I'm playing house—like this is our house and Ross is mine and this baby is going to complete our family.

For a girl who never daydreamed or fantasized about things like this while growing up, I've quickly reached pro-levels. I can't help but love the idea of the *three* of us being here together. Always. I didn't even realize how much I wanted a life like this until it fell into my lap.

When the doorbell rings, it snaps me out of my reverie and I quickly make my way to the front door. I'm not expecting anyone and I'm so caught off guard, I don't think to look through the peephole before opening the door.

Big mistake, Casey. Huge.

Standing before me is Felicia and she looks about as happy to see me as I am to see her.

"Yes?" is the only greeting I can manage.

"You're still here?" is her response and this conversation isn't going to go well, I can already tell.

Trying another tactic, I ask, "Can I help you?"

"I need to speak with Ross."

"He's not here. Maybe you should try calling next time so you don't waste a drive over here for no reason."

"Oh, I've been calling," she says, raising her eyebrows. "I just didn't know he wouldn't be here."

She's been calling? As in she and Ross have been talking on the phone? That's new information.

"Okay, then next time, call before you come so we can avoid this." I go to close the door but stop when I hear a gasp escape Felicia's mouth and her hand stops the door.

Shoot.

"You're...pregnant?" I can't tell if she's horrified or disgusted, but whatever she's feeling, it isn't good. If she was going to find out about the baby, I'd rather Ross have been the one to tell her.

Then she laughs. Loudly.

"Wow, Casey." She throws her hands up in the air, dramatically. "First, you live in your famous sister's shadow and now, you're trying to replace me while playing house with my husband. You've got some fucking nerve…Is it even his baby?"

With my heart pounding in my chest, I square my shoulders and try to stay calm.

"My relationship with Ross is none of your business," I tell her. I'm not one to look for a fight or argument, but I've never been one to back down either. I just don't think an altercation with Felicia Davies is a good idea, regardless of the fact I'm five and a half months pregnant. "You need to leave."

"I guess you really will do whatever necessary to sink your claws into Ross." She pauses, shaking her head as so many emotions pass over her face… her beautiful, but hateful face.

She smirks, squinting her eyes at me.

How can someone so pretty be so mean?

"But," she continues. "Getting knocked up is a pretty desperate and bold move."

"Leave." I feel my face heat as my chest heaves.

"Well," she says, placing a manicured hand on her slim hip. "Enjoy it now because Ross will come to his senses soon and he'll see what a fucking gold digger you are and kick you to the curb where you belong."

I want to cuss so badly, I'm shaking but I don't want her to know her words hit their target, like a freaking bullseye. Instead, I slam the door in her face and lean into it while I try to catch my breath.

Turning, I put my back to the cool wood and listen to the slam of a car door and then tires peeling out of the drive.

Ross really needs to change the code to the gate.

And I need to get away from this house for a while.

I need to clear my head of all the daydreams and fantasies and ex-wife and figure out what's real and what's not. Taking calculated steps, I walk upstairs and begin collecting my things from Ross's room.

Leaving most of the books, I only take the few I read the most.

Before I walk out, I look around and see how easy it was to remove myself from his life. The lack of permanence hits me like a ton of bricks. Instead of hiding away in the guesthouse, which hasn't even had a chance to feel like home because of all the time I've spent in Ross's main house, I go to the one place I always feel safe.

Pulling up in front of Charlotte's I exhale, finally breathing a little easier.

She's coming out of the side door before I can even get out of my car. Thanks to my growing belly, simple daily tasks are becoming harder. I don't get a chance to explain why I'm there.

The tears begin falling and then I'm being wrapped in a hug. Charlotte's arms hold me tight, while she speaks hushed words that comfort me in a way only she can.

Once she's emptied the contents of my car into my old bedroom, she gets our favorite blankets from downstairs and we snuggle into the mound of pillows.

"Tell me what happened," Charlotte finally says, opening a package of Thin Mints and offering me one.

Sniffling back some lingering tears, I take the cookie. "Where did you get these?"

"Ross brought a few boxes over here for safekeeping."

I can't help the laugh that escapes, but it's followed quickly by a sob.

"What is wrong with me?" I ask, eating the cookie even though the tears are back. "I can't quit crying and I'm not even sure what's wrong… it's probably just me and that freaks me out because I'm never like this. You know me. I'm usually the calm and collected one. I don't get to freak out and break down over nothing."

Huge, wracking sobs kick in and I feel out of breath.

Charlotte sits me up and begins rubbing soothing circles on my back. "Slow, easy breaths," she whispers. "In and out…deep breaths."

I try to do what she says and eventually, I begin to calm. "Felicia stopped by the house again," I tell her, my eyes feeling as raw as my heart. "She said she and Ross have been talking. What does that mean? What if she wants to reconcile with him…or worse, what if he wants to reconcile with her?"

My words come out monotone as a numbness takes over.

"Have you talked to Ross about this?" Charlotte asks.

Shaking my head, I feel a lump reappear in my throat, making it difficult to speak. "No."

"Let's not jump to any conclusions without you speaking to him first, okay?" Her arm wraps around my shoulder and she pulls me to her until her head rests against mine.

"I've felt like he's been hiding something from me for a while now," I confess. "Sometimes when he looks at me, I can just feel it. And I ask him what he's thinking about and he says nothing…or changes the subject." Feeling as dejected as my words sound, I continue, "What if it's been about her this whole time. Maybe she's why he pulls away."

I feel Charlotte's mood change. She goes from worried to mad in a matter of a few seconds.

"Well," she starts, grabbing my shoulders and forcing me to face her, "we'll figure this out. And if for some ridiculous fucking reason Ross wants that bitch back, we'll go from there."

My eyes lock with hers and I see the solidarity there. The same solidarity I've given her for so many years is shining back at me and I realize that even if my worst-case scenario comes to pass, I'll be okay.

Charlotte will always be there for me.

I'm not alone.

"I think you need to tell mom and dad about the baby," she says after a few minutes of silence. "I think it would take one thing off your plate and give you less to worry about."

Sighing, I take in a deep breath and exhale. "I know."

"Maybe just get some sleep tonight and we'll tackle that one tomorrow, okay?"

I nod, needing that. My body feels even more tired than usual. Maybe it's the third trimester looming and this is what I have to look forward to for the next three months, but I literally feel like I can't keep my eyes open.

"The guys are probably at the field by now," Charlotte says, climbing off the bed. "I'll send Bo a text and let him know you're here and ask him to tell Ross, unless you want to text him."

"No," I tell her, knowing I should talk to him, but I don't know exactly what I want to say and I know the conversation we're destined for should be done face-to-face. Besides, he's pitching tomorrow and I don't want to worry him. "Ross hates texting. Just tell Bo we were having a girl's night and I fell asleep."

Ross will believe that. He might try to call, but I can put him off until tomorrow. By then, I'll be better rested and have a clearer head.

Surprisingly, sleep actually comes easy. Maybe I'd cried and worried myself into exhaustion or maybe it's the baby sucking the life out of me, regardless, I sleep so soundly that when my phone rings, it scares me so bad I forget where I am.

Forcing my scratchy eyes open, I groan at the accosting sunlight filtering through the sheer fabric on the windows and I remember where I am.

Not Ross's house.

Not Ross's bed.

My old bed.

Charlotte's.

My phone stops ringing and then immediately begins again.

Rolling over as far as I can, thanks to my growing belly, I stretch until I reach my phone on the nightstand. Unplugging it, I pull it to my face, expecting to see Ross's name on the screen, but it's not.

Swiping my thumb across the screen, I reluctantly place it to my ear. "Hi, Mom."

"Casey Marie Carradine," her tone is all too familiar and I inwardly cringe.

"Good morning to you too," I reply, hoping I'm not in too much trouble. I have been a bit more lax about my weekly calls, sometimes going a week and a half or so between them. She hates that, but like I've told her before, the phone lines run both ways and I don't always have to be the one to make the call.

She lets out a laugh that holds no humor and it causes me to be a bit more alert.

"Would you like to explain to me why you're on the front page of *The Daily Dish*?"

That question has me straining to sit up in bed. "What?"

Surely, she means Charlotte and not me. Maybe she forgot who she called—

"Casey Carradine, younger sister of popstar princess, Lola Carradine, was seen leaving an appointment last Monday morning. It seems as though Baby Carradine is having a baby herself."

Oh, God.

Swallowing, I close my eyes and nearly drop the phone, but her words keep me hanging on.

"She was accompanied by Ross Davies, ace pitcher for the New Orleans Revelers. Sources tell us Davies separated from his wife last year and now speculations are circulating that Ms. Carradine is the reason for the split from his college sweetheart, Felicia Davies. The two had been married for seven years and it's been unknown why they called it quits, until now."

No.

No, no, no.

"Casey," my mom's tone brooks no argument. "Please tell me this is false information."

New tears prick my eyes as I try to wrap my head around what she just read. Licking my lips, I swallow. "It's not…well, I mean…"

"Are you a homewrecker, Casey?" She audibly huffs and I can picture her pacing the pristine marble floor in her expensive shoes. I bet she's already called an attorney to get ahead of this and save the Carradine name from being drug through the mud. "Because that's what this article is painting you out to be and I just need to know what we're up against here."

*We're…*what *we're* up against.

I've seen this scenario play out so many times throughout my life with Charlotte, but never with me as a focal point. I don't even know what to say.

"I was going to tell you…about the baby," I finally manage to get out. "But the other stuff…"

Pausing, I try to collect myself, but fail.

What happens when Ross reads this… what if it's partially true?

Did I come into Ross's life in the middle of a reconciliation with his wife?

Have I been wrong about his feelings for me?

Is this just a fantasy in my head and in reality, Ross is trying to make lemonade out of lemons…?

Panic begins to set in and the next thing I know I'm practically hyperventilating.

As I gasp for air, my vision starts going dark, like an old movie coming into focus.

Dropping the phone, I try to get off the bed, but get tangled in the sheets and stumble, falling to the floor and taking the lamp from the nightstand with me.

"Casey?" Charlotte's voice is distant and I hear heavy footsteps.

A few seconds later, or maybe minutes, the door flies open and she's beside me on the floor.

"Casey!"

Between the searing pain in my chest and head, I can't respond or focus.

It's too much.

And then everything goes dark.

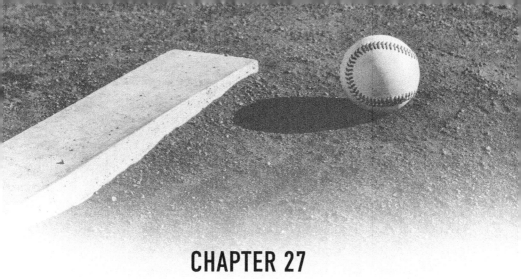

CHAPTER 27

Ross

AFTER GETTING MY SHOULDER ICED DOWN, I SHOWER AND THEN DIG OUT MY PHONE.

When I tried calling Casey before the game, she didn't answer. Bo relayed a message for her last night, saying she was at Charlotte's having a girl's night, so I tried not to bother her. I know Casey misses spending quality time with Charlotte and I'm glad they're taking advantage of this time while we're away. But something about not talking to her last night and then not hearing from her this morning doesn't sit well with me.

Since I was pitching today, I tried to stay focused and not think too much about it. Now that the game is over and I managed to make it through six innings without fucking it up completely, I need to talk to her.

"Good game," Mack says, taking a seat beside me.

I huff, shaking my head. "Not good enough."

"You threw some good stuff. Don't be too hard on yourself."

That's easier said than done and he knows it.

What was nice was seeing Thatch come in during the seventh inning and finish strong. He shut down four consecutive batters and only gave up one run in the eighth.

"Thatch saved my ass."

Mack nods. "He's good…getting better," he says, watching me.

When Bo walks by, I stop him. "Hey, have you talked to Charlotte?"

He frowns, shaking his head. "No, I was going to ask if you'd talked to

Casey, but I'm guessing that'd be a no."

"No," I tell him, that heaviness from earlier settling in my gut. "She didn't answer my call this morning and I don't have any missed calls, but I'm getting ready to head out and try her again before we leave."

If Mack knows something is up, he's being respectful of my privacy and I couldn't be more grateful. The last thing I need is my team breathing down my neck.

Stepping outside the main doors of the clubhouse, I find a quiet alcove and tap Casey's name on my phone. It rings a few times and just when I think it's going to voicemail, Charlotte picks up.

"Hey, Ross," she says, sounding tired and putting me even more on edge than I already was.

"Where's Casey?" I ask, raking a hand through my hair.

She sighs. "Don't freak out, okay?"

Don't freak out?

Is she serious?

She can't start a conversation like that and expect me not to freak out.

"Charlotte," I warn, feeling like I'm about to come unglued if she doesn't tell me what the fuck is going on right now. My words come out like sandpaper as I grit my teeth together, "Where's Casey and why are you answering her phone and asking me not to freak out?"

"She's okay," she starts and it only makes me feel marginally better. "But I took her to the hospital earlier this morning—"

"The hospital? Are you fucking kidding me? Why didn't you call me?"

Now, I'm pacing like a caged animal as I picture Casey in the hospital and my mind goes to all those fucking baby books and the scary shit that can happen.

"I said don't freak out." Her tone is firmer, making me check my attitude a bit. "I didn't think about anything at first except getting her checked out. Then, once I knew she was okay, she asked me not to call you because she knew you pitched today and she didn't want to mess up your game."

I sigh, squeezing my eyes together and pressing my head into the concrete wall in front of me.

"She had a panic attack," Charlotte continues. "It's a long story but the important part is she's okay. The doctor said her blood pressure was a little high and he wants her to take it easy. He suggested she go on modified bed rest for a few weeks."

"What does that mean?" I ask, feeling helpless. I'm hours away and Casey was in the hospital and I wasn't there... "What about the baby?"

"The baby is fine and so is she," Charlotte assures me. "Modified bed rest is basically just her resting as much as possible and not doing any heavy lifting or exerting herself too much. She can sit, stand, take short walks... stuff like that."

My heartbeat slowly starts to regain a normal rhythm.

She's okay.

The baby is okay.

"What caused the panic attack?" I ask. As long as I've known Casey, I've never known her to suffer from any type of panic or anxiety disorder. She's typically calm and collected, in charge.

Another loud sigh greets me from the other end of the line. "This is really a conversation you should be having with Casey, but I know you'll just worry yourself sick over it..." She pauses, taking another breath. "Felicia showed up at your house again and her and Casey kind of got into it. Felicia said some things that really shook Casey up. I'm hoping they're not true, but she's going to need to hear that from you."

The line goes silent for a moment and I take the opportunity to reign in my anger.

Fucking Felicia.

I knew I should've just called her and found out what she wanted. She showed up at my house back during Spring Training and I shouldn't have put it past her to do it again.

"I'm only going to say this once," Charlotte continues. "If you're fucking around with my sister or leading her on in any way, I will cut your balls off and feed them to you."

Swallowing, I wince at the visual she just painted for me, knowing it's not an empty threat.

"Now, I'm going to guess that your ex-wife is full of hot air and wanted to get a dig in at Casey once she noticed she's pregnant. So, I'm going to give you the benefit of the doubt...innocent until proven guilty and all that."

Oh, shit.

Felicia learning about the baby like this is not good. She has a vindictive streak a mile long. When she feels like she's been wronged, her claws come out and she goes for blood.

"But that's not all," Charlotte says. "I need you to brace yourself for this one…and also be prepared for a call from your agent, since you don't have a publicist—"

"What the fuck?" I growl out, not sure I can take much more than what's already been dumped in my lap.

"There have been some pictures leaked to a few media outlets of you and Casey. One of them was from when you were on your way into the doctor's appointment and a few from the past year or so… there was even a photo of the four of us when we were all out for dinner after a home game…They're basically painting Casey out to be some sort of homewrecker, linking her to the demise of your marriage."

"That's fucking crazy," I yell, forgetting where I am and practically losing my mind at the idea of anyone speaking like that about Casey. Lowering my voice, I grit out between clenched teeth, "You know that's a fucking lie, Charlotte."

"I know the photos of all of us are innocent, but they're using them out of context and we both know how the media can manipulate information to meet their needs…"

For a second, I think about punching the wall in front of me, but I know that wouldn't do anyone any good. It wouldn't help Casey and it sure as fuck wouldn't help me.

"What should I do?" I ask, sounding as desperate as I feel.

She's quiet for a moment and I'm worried she's going to tell me to go fuck myself.

I'm kind of leaning toward that response when she finally says, "If it was me, I would talk to the team publicist and see if they can do anything. You should probably also call your agent. You have a good relationship with him, right?"

I nod. "Yeah, I do."

"Good, use the resources you have and get as far ahead of this as you can."

"What about Casey?" I ask, wishing I was there right now. I need to see her and know for myself that she's okay. I want to talk to her and hold her.

"Give her some space…she has a lot to think about and she needs to take care of herself…and the baby." Charlotte's voice drops to barely above a whisper. "She's safe here."

She's safe there, but not with me, that's what she's trying to say. But I can't just *not* see her. She has to know that.

"I'll stop by when we get back to town," I tell her.

"I'll call if anything comes up," she promises. "She's going to be fine."

When I hang up, I lean into the wall, letting it hold me up for a minute while I get my shit together.

BY THE TIME WE MAKE IT TO THE AIRPORT, I'VE ALREADY CONTACTED MY AGENT AND talked to the team publicist.

There's not a lot we can do, but it was agreed I'd make a statement to clear things up. According to them, in cases like this, it's better to be upfront and honest. The basic gist of what will be released is this:

One, my marriage ended because my wife didn't want to be married anymore. End of story. I've taken the high road as much as I can when it comes to the divorce, but I'm done with that.

Two, Casey and I didn't start a relationship until February, long after the divorce was finalized.

And three, we are in fact having a baby.

This secret we've held onto so tightly for the past few months has gone public. I'm guessing by the time we land back in New Orleans, everyone and their dog will know. Which means, things are going to be crazy for a while and all I can think about is how to protect Casey from the media shit storm that's brewing.

"You okay?" I hear Bo ask as he slides into the seat beside me.

Opening my eyes, I keep them trained on the seatback in front of me. We're somewhere in the air between Atlanta and New Orleans and if I could make this plane fly faster, I would. The anxiety and anticipation of needing to see and be with Casey are overwhelming.

"I'm fine," I tell him, but we both know that's a lie.

He lets out a deep sigh and kicks his legs out in front of him. From my peripheral, I can see him adjust and readjust his head on the seat, like he's trying to get comfortable, but if I had to guess, there's something on his mind and he's not wanting to say it.

"Just fucking say whatever you need to say," I tell him. My voice sounds gruff and much harsher than my normal delivery, but I can't help it.

Bo clears his throat. "Don't take this the wrong way," he starts, making my body tense at his words. "But Charlotte asked me to talk to you and tell you she thinks you need to give Casey some space... and time to think things through."

"I know," I bite out. "She told me."

"Yeah," he says, running a hand through his hair. "Well, she wanted me to reiterate it and make sure you're not going to come there when we get home. She said cars have been lingering out at the gate and she thinks they're probably reporters looking for a story. If you come, it'll just make things worse."

Fuck.

Fuck, fuck, fuck.

"Since we're only going to be home for a few days," he continues. "Maybe it'd be good to let all this blow over and then by the time we get back, the two of you can talk and figure things out."

"There's nothing to figure out," I tell him.

He's quiet for a minute, but I can tell the conversation isn't over.

"Maybe not for you," he says, a finality to his tone. "Casey needs rest and she doesn't need any stress. I know you want what's best for her and the baby. This is what's best."

Growling, I clench my fists tight. "I'm what's best for her."

I'm not sure who I'm trying to convince more, him or me.

"I don't doubt that," Bo says, leaning forward. "Listen, man, I know how you're feeling...I mean, I know it's different with the two of you and you have a baby on the way to think about, but I remember what it was like when I had to walk away from Charlotte. It was the hardest fucking thing I'd ever done...but it was worth it. In the end, everything worked out and now she's mine forever...and I don't ever plan on leaving her again."

I look at him, seeing the rookie who was so focused on the game he couldn't see two feet in front of him, but also seeing the man he's become. He's right, he did have to walk away from Charlotte. I was there and I saw what it did to him, but also saw the way he came out on the other end and they're both stronger for it.

"I'll do whatever I have to do to make her safe and happy," I tell him. The selfish part of me wants to go claim my girl and take her home with me. But the realistic part of me knows that's not what's best.

Not for her.

Not for the baby.

And not for me.

Because as much as I want Casey, I need to know she wants me too.

So, I'll give her some space and I'll pray for the best.

Hopefully, when all this blows over, we'll find ourselves still standing—stronger, together.

When the plane lands in New Orleans, I take the back exit they offer us. Pulling my hat down low, I drown out the reporters standing vigil and jump into the back of a car.

The drive to my house is quiet, even my thoughts have died down. It's been such a fucking rollercoaster of a day, from finding out Casey went to the hospital, to Felicia's bullshit, and the tabloids. I feel like I've crammed a week into the last twelve hours.

All I really want to do is reclaim the bubble Casey and I have lived in for the past few months. I want her curled up against me in my bed… our bed. I want to smell her sweet smell and hear her soft snores. I want to eat Oreo ice cream at the kitchen counter in the middle of the night. I want to rest with my hand on her stomach and dream about the baby growing in there.

Instead, the driver rolls up to my house. It's not dark because I always leave the perimeter lit up for security purposes. And thankfully, none of the reporters followed us here, at least not that I can see. But it is empty. Casey's car isn't in the drive.

As I unlock the door and close it behind me, I immediately feel her loss.

I'm reminded of when I came home from Spring Training and experienced the same thing but this time is worse. Much worse.

Her shoes aren't by the door.

Her bag isn't on the hook in the hallway.

Walking into my bedroom, I notice the books she always reads aren't on the nightstand. The clothes she'd started leaving in one of the drawers of my dresser are gone. There's not a second toothbrush in the bathroom… it's like she was never here.

And the thing I hate about it the most is how easily she was able to erase herself from my life.

But I did that.

As much as I've wanted her close, I've also needed to keep her at arm's length. It was self-preservation and fear of the unknown, but I realize now, it was stupid because she's worth it.

She's worth the risk and possible heartache.

She's worth putting myself out there again and not knowing what the final outcome will be.

She's worth it all.

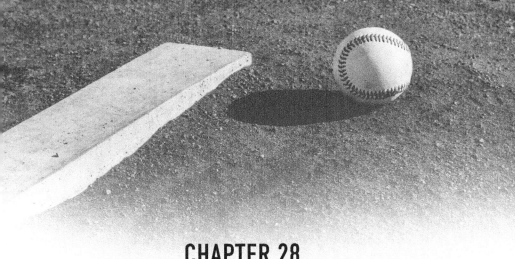

CHAPTER 28

Casey

"HOW ARE YOU FEELING?" CHARLOTTE ASKS FROM THE DOORWAY.

Closing the book I've been reading—which I would like to point out is not a book about babies or pregnancy—I adjust the pillows behind me.

Charlotte insisted I shift gears and go for an escape read, so contemporary romance it is.

And even though it is getting my mind off worrying about the baby and whether or not I'm going to have another panic attack, it isn't doing anything for my heart. In fact, I miss Ross more and more with every page.

"Useless," I say, tossing the blanket off. "I feel like I should be up doing something."

Charlotte shakes her head. "Nope, doctor's orders."

I think she's letting her role of caretaker go to her head. Typically, this is reversed and I'm the one forcing her to take care of herself. I like that better. I'm not used to letting other people take care of me or my business.

"Ross stopped by."

My head snaps up. "What? When?"

She looks down at the floor and toes the thick carpet. "Just a few minutes ago. He wanted to see you, but said something about it being easier this way…so he dropped off more Thin Mints and this."

Walking over, she hands me a letter.

Seeing Ross's handwriting makes my heart clench. A letter is so old school, so Ross, and it makes me miss him even more. Holding it up to my nose, I inhale, catching a hint of his manly scent—earthy and woodsy. It reminds me of the t-shirt I've been sleeping in that I stole from his room when I left four days ago.

"They're leaving for the airport later today," Charlotte says quietly. "He said he'll see you when he gets back."

I nod, feeling tears prick at my eyes.

"Thank you," I tell her as she turns to walk out, closing the door behind her.

I want to wallow in my sadness, in how much I miss Ross and wish he was with me right now, but it was my choice to remove myself from what felt like an out-of-control, stressful situation.

When I passed out from a panic attack earlier this week and Charlotte drove me to the hospital, it was a wake-up call. I was scared… not for me, but for my baby. Then the doctor said my blood pressure was high and that it could lead to preeclampsia, which I know from all the books I've read is bad. It could mean premature labor, but so could panic and anxiety.

So, until I feel in control of my emotions and have a better grip on my life, I need this time away.

Also, Charlotte and I have talked quite a bit about the media coverage and she feels like things will die down in a week or two. Once it's no longer news, they'll find something else to talk about.

Ross made a statement, which was very direct and seemed to clear up misconceptions about me and our relationship, or tried to. Even if they didn't help with the media, it helped me realize how serious he's taking this and it did my heart good. I know from experience the gossip blogs can still spin things any way they want, so I'm not delusional in thinking this will all just go away.

I'm just trying to take this time to rest and really think about what I want. In just a few short months, I'll have a small life depending on me. He'll depend on Ross too, but what I need to figure out between now and then is what our family will look like. Will it be two parents who support each other and love him unconditionally? Or will it be two parents who love each other and him unconditionally?

I know what I want, but I need to talk to Ross.

Opening the small envelope, I pull out the note and unfold it.

Casey,

I want you to know that just because we're not physically to-gether doesn't mean I'm not thinking about you every second of every day. But your health and safety, and the health and safety of our son, is my biggest priority, so I'm giving you the time and space you need.

There are so many things I want and need to say to you, but I'll be patient.

I hope you're resting and doing everything the doctor told you to do. If you need anything, I'm just a phone call away. Even if you're up in the middle of the night eating Oreo ice cream and don't want to eat it alone, call me. If you're feeling anxious, call me. If you just want to say hello...I'm here for that too.

You're fully stocked with Thin Mints.

At your service,

Ross

There're no declarations of love or feelings, but I didn't expect that. His sign off, however, makes me smile and takes me back to our emails. On one hand, it feels like forever ago that we were navigating our new working relationship, but on the other, it feels like everything has happened so fast.

Bringing the note back up to my nose, I inhale again and close my eyes, picturing Ross at his house and wishing, not for the first time, I was there with him. I could be… I could go to him, but I want to make sure this isn't a fantasy and that Ross and I can exist outside of the bubble we'd created.

When my phone rings, I have to dig through the piles of blankets on the bed until I finally find it.

Pulling it out, I feel my heart deflate when it's not Ross's name on the screen.

"Hi, Mom," I say, trying not to sound too disappointed.

She huffs out a laugh. "Well, hello to you too."

"Sorry," I tell her, holding Ross's letter back up and reading it again.

"How are you feeling?" she asks. "Are you doing everything the doctor told you?"

She and my dad have come around a little in the past few days. According to Charlotte, they were both really freaked out after the whole panic attack and my mom felt guilty, like she'd caused it. Sure, she was part of it, but it wasn't her fault. Now that I look back on it, I realize it was a lot of things that combined into the perfect storm—Ross's distant behavior, Felicia playing on my fears, a little exhaustion, and then my mom dropped the gossip bomb on me and everything detonated.

"Charlotte hasn't let me out of bed for more than bathroom trips and mandatory showers for the past three days."

"Good," she says, letting out a deep sigh. "Your father and I were thinking about flying out there."

Shaking my head, I'm thankful this isn't a FaceTime call because there's no way I could hide my expression. "That's really not necessary," I tell her, trying to keep my tone light and happy. "I know you and Dad are busy and there really isn't anything you'd be able to do."

"Are you sure?"

Even when Charlotte and I were younger, our mother wasn't the most nurturing person, so the fact she wants to come out here and check on me is touching. But honestly, it feels like more than I can handle right now. I'd really like a chance to figure things out on my own without their intervention.

"I'm sure," I tell her, hoping I'm convincing enough. "Charlotte mentioned you were thinking about coming out here for the holidays… that would be nice."

I'll give birth to this baby by the holidays.

That thought equally delights me and terrifies me, but it's happening regardless.

"It will be nice," she says and I wonder if she's also thinking about the fact there will be a baby by then and she'll be a grandmother, like it or not.

After we say our goodbyes and I end the call, I pull up Ross's number and hover over it for a minute. I think about texting him, even though he hates it, but decide an email would be better.

Subject: Thank you for your service

Ross,

It's like you have a sixth sense and knew I was running low on fuel, aka Thin Mints. I don't know how you continue to keep me in supply, but I couldn't be more grateful.

I know this has been a long week for you and I'm sorry if it's caused you undue stress, that was never my intent. Actually, that's what I was trying to avoid for both of us. But let's face it, this is a stressful situation... but I'm hoping in a few more days, some of the craziness will quiet down and we can have a chance to talk.

In the meantime, I am resting and feeling much better.

Peanut is good. I can feel him move and that helps me feel calmer, knowing he's still growing and thriving. That's crazy, being able to call him a he without thinking he could also be a she. LOL.

Hope the Revelers have a great road trip. I know you'll be pitching again tomorrow night, so good luck out there.

I pause, thinking for a minute about how I want to end the email. Something inside me tells me to take a chance… go out on a limb and put myself out there. I think Ross needs it. I think he needs to know I can meet him halfway and he's not the only one who's scared of being hurt or left. I feel that too. It's scary and uncertain, but I'd rather go through this with him than anyone else in the entire world.

Placing my hands back on the keyboard, I go with the only thing that feels right.

Yours,

Casey

CHAPTER 29

Ross

LEAVING CHARLOTTE'S HOUSE WITHOUT SEEING CASEY WAS ONE OF THE HARDEST things I've had to do in a while.

I know it's what Casey wants and needs right now, but it doesn't mean I have to like it. Of course, I'm on board with whatever keeps her and the baby safe, but I feel like the other half of my heart is missing and it fucking hurts.

It's obvious to me now how my feelings for Casey have only grown over the last few months, so being away from her… not being able to see her and touch her… is harder than I thought it'd be. Not to mention missing out on the small moments with the baby, talking to it, and feeling her round belly… it's my only connection to him and I fucking miss it.

I want my family together—Casey and this baby, they're my family.

Without them, I now feel like something is missing.

At least I was able to leave her some of those Thin Mints she loves so much. She's one of the most selfless people I've ever known and if all it takes are those cookies to keep her happy, then I'll place a lifetime order right the hell now.

Stopping at a red light, I quickly glance at my phone to make sure I haven't received any new messages from Felicia. Thankfully, there are none, so I continue driving, ready to get this over and done with.

Yesterday, she texted me yet again, asking if we can meet somewhere and talk. I debated all night on the best way to respond because I want this to be the last time I talk to Felicia. She was fine on her own until she saw Casey was a bigger part of my life and now, her harassment has gone too far. This shit ends now.

Not wanting to seem eager, I waited until this morning to reply and told her to meet me in Jackson Square at noon. Meeting her in public is risky, I know, but I'll be damned if I let her in my house ever again. At least with us meeting there, we should blend in and be able to find a semi-private bench.

I'm just hoping there won't be too many people around and she doesn't cause a scene.

She does love an audience.

After I find a parking spot and pay, I quickly cross Decatur Street and head for St. Peter. There are plenty of tourists milling around, as usual, so I pull the brim of my cap—an Atlanta Braves one this time—down low and make my way inside the gated area. Walking along the paved path, I see a bench sitting under one of the large trees on the perimeter of the square unoccupied, so I claim it and wait.

Thankfully, Felicia is right on time and spots me without much effort.

Her bright smile seems so authentic that it catches me off guard. I honestly have no idea why she's so happy to see me.

She's the one who left.

She's the one who wanted a divorce.

So, why does she want to talk to me at all?

That's just one of the many questions I have for her today.

"Hey, Ross!" She walks up to where I'm sitting, like she doesn't have a care in the world.

I can tell she expects me to stand and hug her or greet her in some kind of warm way, but I don't budge. It goes against every bit of manners that have been so deeply ingrained in me, but I remain in my seat.

This isn't a social call for me; this is me taking care of business.

"Have a seat," I tell her, motioning to the open spot next to me and sit up straight, making sure to put as much distance between us as possible.

"Someone's a Grumpy Gus today," she says with a giggle as she sits. "You must be tired from your trip back home."

It's weird to hear her speak as though she still knows me, knows my work schedule and my typical behaviors. The way I see it, I'm practically speaking with a stranger. I know nothing about the woman next to me and I don't plan on changing that.

"I think we both know there are some things we need to discuss, so let's not waste our time with small talk and get down to it," I begin, wanting to set the tone for this meet-up.

She laughs again, shaking her head like I just told the funniest joke. "What has gotten into you?" Leaning forward she pinches my cheek and I pull away from her, pressing my back into the bench. "What happened to my fun-loving guy?"

"First, I'm not *your* anything," I deadpan, leveling her with my stare. "And second, I'm not feeling very fun-loving, especially after the way you spoke to Casey the other day. That's unacceptable. You had no right being at my house, you gave that up in the divorce. If I remember correctly, *it didn't bring you any happiness*…and I believe that's a direct quote."

She was very adamant in the divorce that she didn't want anything from our life together, except cold hard cash, which she got her fair share of.

I watch her eyes as she registers my mood, probably realizing for the first time that I can't be manipulated by her anymore and this isn't a conversation she can dominate. This new Ross is over her and he's done playing games.

"The accusations you made toward her were ridiculous and completely out of line," I continue, wanting to say so much more, but trying to keep my cool and make it through this without drawing attention. "That's the last time you talk to her. I don't want you stepping foot on my property again and I never want you talking to her again, period."

She has the audacity to look shocked that I called her out. Or maybe it's because I'm taking Casey's side over hers? Regardless, I've managed to shake her up, which is surprising.

"Ross," she starts, her mouth agape. "It's obvious she's just trying to trap you. And even though we're divorced, I still care about you and I'm just looking out for your best interests."

When her face falls like she's going to get emotional, it takes all my power not to roll my eyes.

"Why should you care, Felicia?" I want to stand and pace, needing an outlet for the pent-up anger and frustration I'm feeling, but I force myself to stay seated. "You're not a part of my life anymore, so you have zero say in how I spend my time and who I spend it with. That's what divorce means."

"I made a mistake."

"Yeah, you did and I don't want it to happen again, so leave Casey alone."

"No, I mean, about us."

Her words shut me up and I try to school my reaction, but fail. The incredulity has to be written all over my face because Felicia's nostrils flare and she huffs out her own frustration.

When all I do is stare at her, dumbfounded, she continues.

"I was wrong… I thought I was doing the right thing. I felt trapped and stifled and I thought a new life would make me happy, but I should've listened to you. I should've stayed and worked things out. I should've given you… *us*… another chance."

Felicia grabs my hand with both of hers and has tears in her eyes when she says, "I miss you, Ross. Please give us another chance. Because I still love you and I think deep down, you still love me too… I mean, we were together for ten years. You can't just turn those feelings off."

Yanking my hand from hers, I stand. "Yes, I can," I grit out, pulling at my hair in an effort to ease the tension rolling through my body. "When the person you love walks out on you and claims you can't make them happy any more, you find a way to turn off those feelings… We're done. *I'm* done. It killed me when you left, but I figured out how to survive without you… I've moved on and there's no turning back."

"But I'm ready now," she says, a little too loudly with desperation dripping from her words.

"Ready for what?"

"Ready to try for a baby," she says, with full-blown tears streaming down her cheeks. "It's what you wanted, right? I thought I couldn't do it and that I didn't want that kind of life, but I know now that I do and I'm willing to give it a try… to give you what you want."

She stands, her hands clasped at her chest as she begins to plead. "Please, Ross… I know this was what drove us apart… and you do too. Without that in our way, we can be together… you can't tell me you're not tempted."

"I'm not tempted," I reply, faster than my brain can process. "Not in the slightest. I've found someone who loves me for me and we're starting a family together. That's what I've always wanted… Casey is who I want."

Just mentioning her name makes my chest tighten.

I wish she was here right now instead of Felicia.

I wish I was telling her this—*I want you… you're it for me.*

"You don't really mean that," Felicia practically shrieks. Her tears dry as anger takes their place. "I know you Ross Davies… I know what you need. I know how to make you happy."

Her words are coming faster and louder and she encroaches on my personal space and I back away from her.

With a finger pointed at my chest, she continues. "You've had your fun with the little trollop. Point made. If you were trying to make me jealous, it worked and I forgive you. So, let's put our errors behind us and move forward."

Dropping her hand, she closes in on me faster than I can deflect. Her arms wrap around my neck and she tries to pull me closer, like she's going to kiss me.

The next few seconds happen in slow motion and almost simultaneously.

As I'm attempting to extract myself from her embrace, I see her eyes cut to the side. Following her gaze, everything becomes so clear.

Only a few feet away, stepping out from behind another tree, is a photographer with his camera poised directly at us, ready to capture the moment.

The bastard has probably been here the entire time, waiting to catch me in an uncompromising position but I refuse to be played like that.

Grabbing Felicia's arms, I step out of her embrace.

Before I can speak, memories flash through my mind and my anger builds.

The pictures of me and Casey from last year…

The ones of the two of us leaving the ultrasound appointment…

And now, today.

It was all a set-up.

"What the fuck is wrong with you?" I growl, backing even further away from her. "You hired that fucking photographer, didn't you? And you were behind the leaked photos of me and Casey."

I've known the woman standing before me for a large portion of my life, but I don't recognize her at all. Never in a million years would I expect her to stoop so low.

"I don't get it," I continue, needing some answers. "Why the sudden change? Why am I all of a sudden good enough for you again? Is it because I'm with Casey? Or is it because I'm truly happy and you can't stand it because you're not? Please explain it to me."

"I thought I wanted something else… something more, but you know as well as I do the grass isn't always greener on the other side. During the past year, I've realized how great we were together and I want it back."

I take another step back and shrug.

Moments ago, I was raging inside but now when I look at my ex-wife, I just feel sorry for her.

"It's not going to happen. The sooner you accept that, the better off you'll be."

"You can't mean that—"

"Felicia, I'm done with this conversation," I tell her, feeling like we're at an impasse, but wanting to bring this to an end. "I'm with Casey and happier than I've been in a long time. I should thank you, really. If you wouldn't have left me, I wouldn't have been free to be with Casey and discover what a true partnership is."

I pause, feeling the weight of this moment and the realization that comes with it—I'm in love with Casey and the only thing I feel for Felicia is sorry. "I hope you can find that for yourself one day but believe me when I say, it won't be with me."

Turning on my heels, I walk out of the park and out of Felicia's life for good.

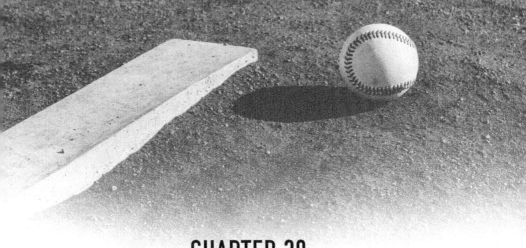

CHAPTER 30

Casey

"MOM," I BREATHE INTO THE PHONE, PINCHING THE BRIDGE OF MY NOSE. "I DON'T need you putting a tracker on Ross. Besides, you know as well as I do that tabloids and gossip columns cannot be trusted."

About that time, Charlotte walks into the living room, where I've been promoted to. After my doctor's appointment yesterday, that she insisted on accompanying me to, she has relaxed some and allowed me to move around more freely.

Last night, we called in pizza and watched movies.

Today, she's planning on calling Frank and asking him to come and pick us up and take us to the French Market to get a sno-ball.

I need it.

Even though I haven't been doing much outside of being at Ross's house or the guest house, something about being cooped up at Charlotte's without Ross is making me go stir crazy. At least when I'm at Ross's, I feel like I have work to do and it gives me purpose. And when I'm at the guesthouse, I feel like it's my own space. But here, I just feel like I'm under a very watchful eye and in some sort of weird limbo.

"I'm just worried about you, Casey," my mom finally replies. I can hear the click of a mouse in the background and I know she's on a witch hunt for information about Ross and these new pictures she claims have surfaced.

"I'm fine," I say as calmly as possible.

Looking up, I find Charlotte's eyes on me from the other side of the room.

"What does she want?" she mouths.

I shake my head, not wanting to get into it, especially while our mother is still on the other end of the line.

"Well, I don't want to cause you any stress," she continues. "We definitely don't need another episode like last week, but being ahead of the game is a preemptive strike. You don't want to be caught off guard because that gives them the power…"

"Them?" I ask, feeling my frustration grow. "Who's them, mom? And this isn't some tabloid war. It's my life and I'd appreciate it if I could handle it on my own… in my own way."

Closing my eyes, I place a hand on my belly and exhale. *Calm. Calm, calm, calm.*

"I'm not Charlotte," I add, glancing over at my sister apologetically. "This isn't something a publicist needs to handle. When they figure out that I'm the least exciting person on the face of the planet, they'll get bored. Next week, someone else will be the weekly scandal and they'll forget all about me."

I hope. Not just for my sake, but for Ross's too.

"Well, I hope next week's news isn't the father of your baby getting back together with his ex-wife."

She drops the bomb so coldly, I feel a chill creep up my spine.

That wasn't a nice thing to say to a stranger, let alone your own daughter, but that's my mother. She's a real talker and she doesn't beat around the bush or soften the blow.

"I'm sorry," she says when the line grows quiet. "I shouldn't have said that, but I don't want you to get your heart broken. You're a good person Casey and you deserve to be treated with respect."

When I still don't say anything, she fills the silence. "If you don't want to look at the photos I sent over, don't. You're right, this is your life and you should be able to handle it how you see fit. I'll try to stay out of it, but if you need anything, your father and I are just a phone call and a plane ride away."

"Thank you," I tell her, feeling a bit raw from her accusation and tired of the constant back and forth.

Is he?

Isn't he?

Are we?

Aren't we?

"I'll call and check in tomorrow."

"Okay, talk to you then."

When the line goes dead, I lean my head against the back of the couch.

Charlotte gets up and comes to sit beside me. "What was that all about?"

Handing her my phone, I can't look at her as I relay the message. "She sent over more photos of Ross and Felicia and she said they look like they're new and they're… *romantic.*"

Just saying the words makes me feel sick to my stomach, and it's not morning sickness.

Thankfully, since I've entered my third trimester, I've felt much better. It kind of went away overnight. Now, I'm just dealing with anxiety and high blood pressure, and what a joy that's been. One thing is for sure, pregnancy is not for wusses.

However, the blood pressure was much better at my appointment yesterday. My doctor told me to continue to rest and relieve as much stress as possible.

I doubt new photos of Ross and Felicia are what he had in mind.

"Want me to look?" she asks, still holding my phone. "Or we can pretend they don't exist and you can wait and talk to Ross when he gets home."

I nod, glancing out the window. We could do that. But something my mom said strikes a chord inside me—it's better to know. I've always been one to be prepared… tests, road trips, hurricanes, holidays, birthdays… you name it, I'm prepared.

"Let me see them," I say, turning back to her. I'm not a chicken. And even though everyone around me has handled me with kid gloves lately, I'm not fragile. I might've had a mental breakdown, but everyone has their breaking point, and it doesn't make me weak.

She scoots closer until we're side by side, then she pulls up my email and opens the latest one from our mother. When she clicks on the link and the page loads, the first thing I see is Ross, wearing an Atlanta Braves baseball cap. He might think he's disguised, but I could recognize that gorgeous profile anywhere… and God, I miss him.

But then, my eyes drift across the photo to Felicia.

They're sitting on a bench in what looks like Jackson Square and Felicia is laughing. With her head thrown back, she looks gorgeous in the afternoon light. The way her body is angled toward Ross's makes them appear… intimate.

When Charlotte scrolls down, the second photo seems even more incriminating. They're standing in this one and her arms are around Ross's neck. It looks like a kiss in motion… her head is angled and his is tilted down.

My stomach lurches and I push the phone away.

I can't.

Shaking my head. "I don't want to see anymore."

To Charlotte's credit, she doesn't say anything… she doesn't try to tell me that what I'm seeing is fake news, but she also doesn't jump to conclusions about Ross or speak badly of him.

Instead, she takes the phone from me and sets it on the coffee table, then stands.

"I'm calling Frank and having him come pick us up," she announces as she walks out of the room. "We need sno-balls sooner rather than later."

An hour later, we're in the backseat while Frank drives us to the French Market. As I watch the city go by, my mind drifts to Ross… not that my mind is ever far from him, but something about this ride reminds me of our date to Cafe du Monde.

As much as I'd like to go back to that night, when we were still in our bubble and everything was still our secret to keep, I'm glad the past week has happened. It forced me to really look at my life and what I want out of it. For so long, I've felt like I was drifting, not necessarily on a path, but just floating through life.

My parents were always very driven people, striving for success and more success. They always knew where they were going in life and they've always had back-up plans for their back-up plans.

Charlotte basically had her life planned out for her, and even when she was being used by the industry, she still had an end game. She knew what she wanted. And now, after years of playing other people's games, she's finally living life on her own terms.

Me, however, I don't know, I just never really had a clear direction of what I wanted to do. I enjoy helping people and I like giving things order, which makes me good at what I've been doing. But Charlotte needs me less and less and I don't want to be Ross's paid employee anymore.

I want to be in his life, but under much different stipulations.

"Do you want Frank to get our sno-balls?" Charlotte asks, bringing me out of my thoughts.

Turning to her, I frown. "No, why?"

She shrugs. "You just haven't been out much and I didn't know if—"

"I'm okay," I tell her. "I need to get out... I've been subconsciously sequestering myself for the past few months. Outside of a couple of times, I haven't been anywhere. But I'm done with that. I don't want to hide and everyone knows about the baby, so what does it matter anyway?"

Charlotte smiles and she looks proud. "Good for you," she says, squaring her shoulders and nodding her approval. "It took me years to make that leap. But I've always known you were way smarter than me and it's showing."

Shaking my head, I laugh. "I'm not smarter than you, but I have learned from watching you. You're way more courageous than you give yourself credit for... I admire that. I've also always loved the way you've been unapologetic about being yourself."

"I hid behind a label and a rock-and-roll lifestyle for years," she says with a snort. "That's not courageous."

"But you're not anymore and that is."

Reaching across the seat, she grabs my hand. "Can you let us out and make the block a few times, Frank?"

"Sure thing, Ms. Carradine," he replies from the driver's seat as he slows down beside the entrance to the French Market.

When we step out of the car, I inhale the familiar scents of the Quarter—some good, some not so good, but the combination is distinctly New Orleans.

"Maybe we should grab a po'boy before we get a sno-ball?" I suggest.

Walking down the sunlit sidewalk on a summer afternoon with my sister—no disguises, no secrets hanging over my head—it makes me feel alive and free.

After we grab two po'boys—crawfish for Charlotte and cochon de lait for me—we stroll while we eat and talk about nothing and everything— the fact we're not melting from humidity today, a woman's killer shoes, predictions for today's game, plans for starting on a nursery for the baby… but that brings me back to that feeling of limbo.

Where will the nursery be?

Ross's guesthouse?

That seems weird.

"I feel like we're avoiding the elephant in the room," Charlotte says as we walk through the French Market toward our favorite sno-ball stand. "How are you feeling about Ross and the photos? You don't have to talk about it if you don't want to but I don't want you to feel like you have to bottle it all up. That's not good for anyone and definitely not you… or the baby."

She pauses. "And I'll listen without prejudice, so you don't have to worry about that."

"I know," I tell her, looping my arm through hers. "And I appreciate everything you've done for me over the past week… giving me a safe place to land and being a buffer to the media and Ross. I needed this time to think and soul search. So, I just wanted to say thank you for that."

Pulling her arm from mine, she wraps it around my shoulder and hugs me as we continue to walk. "You never have to thank me for that… or anything else. We're family and we've always got each other's backs… it's me and you, always."

I nod, feeling a lump forming and not wanting to turn on the waterworks in public.

When we get to the stand, Charlotte orders for both of us, choosing our favorites, and places a twenty on the counter.

"I don't like the photos," I tell her, my eyes traveling to the people milling around and back to the guy making our frozen treats. "They make me sick, actually. But they also helped me realize I'm in love with him. I wouldn't feel so strongly about those photos if I didn't… I want to fight for him. I want to tell him how I feel… take the risk and let the chips fall where they may."

She turns to me with a knowing look. "That's what I thought you were going to say."

Of course she did. She's my sister and even though we're two completely different people, we've always been on the same wavelength and usually know what the other needs or wants before they do. And she's always been on my side, regardless of the situation and I can't even begin to tell her how much that means to me.

"Thanks for this," I tell her, holding up my sno-ball. "Not just for treating me, but for getting me out of the house and always giving me a safe place to talk."

Charlotte gives me a smile, bumping my shoulder with hers as we walk back through the market. "I love you and I just want you to be happy, you know that."

"I love you too," I tell her, leaning my head over as she pulls out her phone.

After she lets Frank know we're ready to be picked up, telling him our location, we start toward the crosswalk.

"Ms. Carradine," a man says, coming out of nowhere and invading our personal space, immediately putting me on high alert.

Out of instinct, I step in front of my sister, putting a hand out. "Please leave her alone—"

"Is it true you're pregnant with Ross Davies' baby?" he asks, louder than necessary and making my spine go rigid.

My heart begins to race as I realize he's not after a photo of Charlotte or a comment about her latest project…it's me he's after. As my hand goes protectively to my belly, I start to reply, but Charlotte beats me to it.

"Move out of our way or you'll be talking to my lawyer."

"I just want a statement…" he says, following us as Charlotte pushes me toward the corner.

"No comment," I tell him, keeping my head down.

"Have you seen the new photos of Ross and his ex-wife?" he calls out, drawing attention from bystanders who are now watching with great interest.

Charlotte's hand clasps my wrist. "Just keep walking."

When Frank's car pulls up at the curb, I feel relief wash over me. He steps out, immediately taking charge of the situation. Opening the back door, he ushers both of us inside before closing it and telling the reporter to fuck off.

His words, not mine, but I concur.

With adrenaline pumping, I glance out the back window as we drive off and watch the reporter fade into the background. I'm sure he got a photo and I have no doubt it will resurface in some form or fashion, but I know from experience it's futile to worry about stuff like that.

"Shit," Charlotte says, blowing out a loud exhale. "I didn't see that coming."

"Me either." But I should have. I just haven't reconciled the fact that I'm now linked to Ross Davies and he's been known to have his face grace the covers of magazines across the board, from sports publications to gossip magazines. When you're as gorgeous and talented as he is, that's going to happen. If I want to be a part of his life, it's something I'm going to have to come to terms with.

"Are you okay?"

Inhaling and exhaling until I feel my heartbeat go back to normal, I nod. "Yeah, I'm good."

"Frank, can you take the scenic route?" she asks.

"You got it."

After a few minutes, we both realize we still have sno-balls to eat and make quick work of them before they melt. The coolness alleviating any lingering tension.

Frank drives us out of the French Quarter and instead of going directly to the Garden District, he turns the opposite way and gets on I-10. We drive for a good fifteen minutes before he gets off on an exit and starts taking roads I've never been on before.

As we drive, the only thing I can think of is needing to see Ross.

I need to talk to him.

I want to feel close to him.

I miss him.

"Can you take me to Ross's house?" I call out, loud enough for Frank to hear me.

"Are you sure?" Charlotte asks. "I don't know if you should be alone—"

"I'm fine," I say, cutting her off. "I know you're concerned, but I'm not fragile or breakable. And I want to be there when he gets home. His house is well-protected and since I haven't been seen there in a week, I doubt anyone will be camped out, knowing he's on the road. Besides, if Frank drops me off, my car won't even be there."

She sighs, leaning back against the seat. "And you'll be there without any transportation."

"You're not far and I know how to dial 9-1-1."

Huffing out a laugh, she shakes her head. "You're so freaking stubborn."

"I learned from the best."

A few minutes later, Frank pulls up at Ross's and I put in the code to let us into his drive. Charlotte insists on following me inside to make sure there aren't any boogie men or crazy paparazzi hiding out. Once she's satisfied the place is safe, she leaves, making me promise I'll call and check in frequently. Of course, I do. I appreciate her concern and I love knowing she's readily available if I need her, but this is where I want to be.

Standing in the space between the kitchen and living room, I turn in place, taking everything in. Even though Ross isn't here, he's still everywhere… in the coffee mug draining on the sideboard of the sink, in the bucket of baseballs by the backdoor of the kitchen, in the stack of sports magazines on the end table in the living room… with a baby book laying on top.

As I walk over and pick it up, I see he's dog-eared a page, so I turn to it.

How to Support Your Soon-To-Be Mom

Smiling, I run a hand over the cover before placing it back in its spot.

Even though it feels good to be here, it's too quiet. So, I go over and turn on the television, cueing it to ESPN. The Revelers game will be on soon, so I go into the kitchen to start a pot of decaf coffee. Just smelling the beans puts me in a good mood and fills the house with a familiarity that does my soul good.

Once that's going, I walk down the hall to the office and flip on the light. Nothing looks like it's been touched, which isn't a surprise. During my time here, this became my domain. Even though it's all of Ross's personal business and effects, he allowed me to take it over.

Sitting down at the desk, I pop the laptop open and realize I haven't checked my email today.

The last one Ross and I exchanged was from the day before last when he was on his way out of town. Hoping there might be something to set my mind at ease, I log in, but am met with a virtually empty inbox.

There are a few things that need to be dealt with, but nothing from Ross and nothing that needs immediate attention.

Sighing, I close it down and walk back into the kitchen to pour a mug of coffee, then settle on the couch. At least I'll get to see him on the television for the next few hours. That'll have to be enough to tide me over until he's back home.

Home.

With me.

As much as I love this house, it isn't home...he is.

Right before the game starts, my phone vibrates. Thinking it'll be Charlotte checking in on me, I roll my eyes and then nearly drop the phone when I realize it's not her name that pops up on my screen.

It's Ross's.

If you're wondering how much I miss you, this is how much.

Holy cannoli, he actually texted me.

Swallowing, my thumb hovers over the screen. I want to touch the words, like they're an extension of the man. He has no idea how much I needed that... those words, the connection... a life raft in a sea of uncertainty.

Not wanting to distract him from the game, I stall on a response. Do I respond? Do I wait? Unable to ignore it, I reply quickly, keeping it short and sweet.

I miss you too.

I wait for the text to be read, but as far as I can tell, it hasn't been.

But Ross comes out on the field, looking like a man on a mission. He's more focused than I've seen him in a long time. He makes it through the first two innings with only eighteen pitches, allowing no hits.

There's no celebration or fanfare, just him out there on the mound taking care of business.

In the third inning, Mack comes out to the mound when Ross walks a batter. Part of me thinks this is where his game will shift and I worry he'll fall back into the slump he's still been trying to dig himself out of. But instead, he throws three consecutive strikes and finishes the inning strong.

During the fourth and fifth inning, it's a mixed bag of strikeouts and pop flies, but still not one runner makes it to first base.

Even for someone like me, who's not that great with the rules of baseball, I know this has the potential to be something great.

As Ross takes the mound in the sixth inning, the commentators begin discussing the possibility of a no-hitter and it spikes my anxiety and nervousness. I also am taken back to a conversation Ross and I had about how players don't talk about no-hitters, especially not during a game.

In solidarity, I mute the television and watch the next two innings without any sound, except my own. The further the game goes, the more vocal I become. At some point, I shed the blanket I'd been hunkered down in and I'm no longer curled up on the couch, but pacing in front of the television.

In the eighth inning, the Revelers are up to bat and Ross hits a double, putting them up by six runs.

"Yes! Go, baby," I yell.

And that's when I feel it, a significantly noticeable kick to my abdomen.

Freezing mid-fist punch, I look down at my belly, willing it to happen again. After half a minute or so, when there's no action, I start to walk around the living room, keeping an eye on the game as Ross comes up to pitch.

"Come on, baby," I urge, to the one in my belly and the one on the television. Rubbing my round basketball that seems to be growing every day, I wait patiently for him to give me another kick so I know that's what I felt.

When the umpire makes a crap call, I yell again, throwing my hands in the air. "You've got to be kidding me!"

Kick.

That one gets me, I can't help it, I start laughing and then he does it again.

This baby likes it when I yell at the umpire.

He's totally my kid.

I wish I could jump through the screen and tell Ross to feel it… I'm in awe of the life growing inside me.

We did this.

And I want to share every moment with him.

As I look back up at the game, I catch it just in time to see a batter crush one of Ross's pitches into left field. Holding my breath, I will the outfielder, Ramirez, to catch the ball, but it's just out of his reach. He slides to the ground and the ball rolls away from him. The centerfielder scoops it up and launches it to second base, halting the runner, but he still makes it to base.

Dang it.

The camera goes back to Ross and the disappointment is evident on his face and the way his shoulders slump. I watch as he shakes his head, wiping the sweat from his brow. To his credit, he strikes out the next batter to end the inning. And even with the hit, this is still the best game he's pitched all year.

The crowd cheers for him as he walks to the dugout. When they continue, he steps back out and takes off his cap again, waving in gratitude.

I can't help the swell of pride I feel inside.

He's amazing, not just because he's so freaking talented, but because he's quiet in his confidence and gracious in his achievements.

There are so many things about Ross Davies the fans never see. They don't see the way he cares for people around him. They don't see how he'll go out of his way to help someone else. They don't know how respectful he is of his parents and how grateful he is for everything in his life, never taking anything for granted.

That's the kind of person I want my son to have as a father.

Just as I'm getting ready to turn the television off and find a book to read, the camera zooms in on Ross as he puts on a headset. Turning the volume back up, I soak him in—messy hair from working his ass off, chiseled jaw hidden by a few days' worth of scruff, those eyes that see my soul… lips that I miss kissing.

"Ross, tell us what was going through your mind during tonight's game," the reporter says from behind the camera.

Ross shakes his head, eyes darting to the ground. "I was just out there trying to throw some good pitches and hoping for a good game."

"I'd say you did more than throw some good pitches," he replies. "After you hit that double in the eighth, it seemed like tonight was your night. I know I speak for everyone in the stands, but we thought we were going to witness your first no-hitter."

"A no-hitter is kind of like Fight Club… we don't talk about it," Ross says with a grin.

"Fair enough," the reporter says. "So, let's switch gears. I always like to ask players what they miss about their home field when they're away. Besides the fans, what's something you miss when you're on the road?"

Ross pauses, bringing his hand up to his mouth and pinching his lips in thought. "I'd have to say the peanuts," he finally answers, glancing up and meeting the lens of the camera with those bright green eyes.

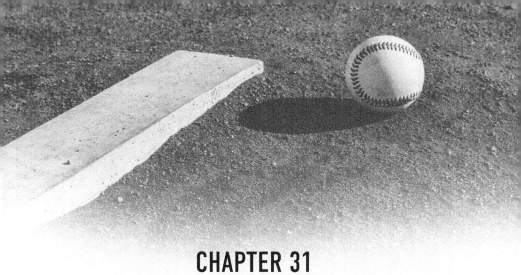

CHAPTER 31

Ross

PULLING UP TO MY GATE, I EXHALE A HUGE BREATH.

It might be after midnight and I may be exhausted… and it might seem dark and lonely, but it's still good to be home, more so tonight than usual because it brings me one step closer to being with Casey.

Tomorrow morning, when I wake up, I'm going straight to Charlotte and Bo's house.

Casey and I are going to talk and I'm going to lay it all on the line for her.

The need to tell her how I feel—how much I love her and want to be with her—is overwhelming. It's been building up inside me for days now, like a bomb about to detonate, and I can't wait much longer. Regardless of how she feels for me, I have to tell her I want a life with her and our son. I'll be as patient as she needs me to be, take this as slow as she needs, but I want her to know I'm committed.

After I open the door and toss my bag down in the foyer, I reset the house alarm and toss my keys onto the table. Bypassing the kitchen, I head straight for the stairs. My bed is calling my name.

Walking into the room, I lean down to turn a lamp on and I'm momentarily startled by the lump in my bed. Then that rush of fear turns to a ball of emotions I find hard to describe—exhilaration, relief, gratefulness…

As I kneel down beside the bed, I'm greeted with the sweetest sounds—Casey's deep breaths, followed by the cutest snores I've ever heard.

My heart races as I realize she's really fucking here. And she's in my bed. *Our* bed.

So many questions flood my brain.

How long has she been here?

Where's her car?

Did she watch the game?

More importantly, did she see my interview?

Even more importantly, does she love me as much as I love her?

I should let her sleep, I know I should, but I can't. I need to see her beautiful eyes, to talk to her, feel her skin against mine, and I need it right fucking now.

Standing, I quickly undress—only leaving on my boxer briefs—and turn back to her, realizing she's kicked the blanket down to the end and is tangled in the sheets, taking up more than half the bed.

I can't help but chuckle at how freaking cute she is.

And she's here.

Exactly where I need her to be.

When I slip into bed behind her, I drape my arm over her hip and place my hand on top of her belly, pulling her as close as I can get her.

Our Peanut.

I know it's only been a little over a week since I saw her last, but she's gotten bigger, which both delights and angers me. I love seeing her body change as our son grows and I don't want to miss any of it, regardless of how small. I want Casey with me all the time. If I didn't think it would be too tiring for her, I'd ask her to travel with me.

As I begin rubbing small circles on her stomach with my thumb, she lets out a deep sigh, almost as though even while sleeping, she knows I'm here and she's relieved. I hope that's true.

Not able to help myself any longer, I place my lips above her ear and kiss her hair, inhaling her sweet scent as I do. When I feel her body tense, I know she's awake.

"Ross?" she whispers, her voice thick with sleep.

"Yeah, baby. I'm home."

"I'm glad." She snuggles into me and laces her fingers through mine, still on top of her stomach. Her ass pushes against my dick and I try not to groan at the contact. I'd love nothing more than to take her right the fuck now, but first, we have to talk.

"Case, are you awake?"

"Kinda."

"I need to talk to you."

She lets go of my hand and rolls onto her back, a look of apprehension clouding her face. I rub my thumb over her forehead and down her cheek and jaw, hoping to reassure her before I say anything more. When I give her a small smile, she relaxes a bit and the squeeze around my heart eases as well.

"First of all, Bo told me you saw the photos of me and Felicia from the other day and I just want you to know I'm sorry about that. The whole thing was a set-up…and the pictures don't tell the true story."

"What is the true story?" she asks and I can tell she's open to hearing me out and not jumping to conclusions. I love that about her, that she wants my side of things and trusts me enough to be here after everything she's seen.

Leaning in, I place a small kiss on her cheek and then her lips, before giving her the truth. "I met her in Jackson Square because I needed answers, and I wanted her to know she couldn't talk to you like she did. Of course, she had an agenda and didn't like me calling her out on her bullshit. I should've known she was behind the fucking paps following us around and the gossip columns posting the story. I just didn't think she'd stoop so low, but once I started putting it all together…"

I pause, letting out a humorless laugh. "I was pissed…couldn't believe I'd been so stupid. Then she came at me with a sob story about wanting me back and wanting to try for a baby."

Casey goes still in my arms and I pull her closer, not wanting her to put up any walls or space between us. "What did you say?" she asks, swallowing down her fears. I hear them and recognize them and immediately squash them.

"I told her that was never happening because I belong to someone else."

"You do?" she asks, letting out a shaky breath.

Pulling her hand up, I kiss her fingers, then place it on my chest, hoping she feels it beating… just for her. "I do," I say, my voice sounding like it's being raked over gravel. "You own me, Casey Carradine, body and soul. And, if you'll have me, I want to be yours... I love you."

A tear rolls down her cheek and she lets out a tiny sniffle before smiling up at me. "I love you."

Three words.

The best three words in the world and when they spill from her mouth, my world rights itself—everything shifting into place and changing me forever.

I feel complete.

Not able to hold off any longer, I kiss her, claiming her just as she claims me. It's an all-consuming kiss full of emotion and promises and I never want to stop.

"Ross, I need you," Casey moans when I start kissing down the column of her neck.

I pull back and look at her, wanting to be sure. I want her so badly I can barely breathe but I want to be certain it's safe for her and the baby.

"Can we still do that?"

She giggles, the sound and the look on her face as she gazes up at me making my dick harden even more. "We can and we definitely should. Many times, in fact."

That's all I need to hear. Running my hand up her thigh, I slip my fingers under the hem of her panties and cup her ass.

"But first, I have some things I need to tell you too," she groans, tipping her head back as I kiss my way down her neck, heading straight for her glorious tits.

Those are growing too and I fucking love them.

And I've missed them.

"Can it wait?" I ask, already losing myself to the haze of lust I feel every time I'm with her.

She lets out another breathy moan, shaking her head. "No, I need to talk… talk first, then sex… lots of sex."

Reluctantly, I pull back. Looking down at her, I brush a strand of hair out of her face. "You have the floor."

With flushed cheeks, she smiles up at me looking more gorgeous than any woman should have the right to. Taking a deep, fortifying breath, she exhales. "This is my two-week notice."

Pulling my head back, I frown, wondering if I misread something. "What are you talking about?"

"I don't want to work for you anymore," she continues. "Well, at least not for pay… I want to take care of you, which means I'll still check your emails and make your coffee and schedule your interviews… and pay your bills." Pausing, her eyes lock onto mine. "I want to wake up every morning in your bed and sleep every night in your arms… well, at least when you're not on the road."

She places her hand on my chest, right over my heart.

"And I want a life with you, whatever that looks like. The good, the bad… the reporters and gossip columns," she says with a laugh and I hug her to me, kissing the top of her head.

If I could, I would protect her from all of the bullshit that comes with my job, but the fact she's willing to accept all of it and is going in with her eyes wide open, makes me the happiest man on earth.

She sighs into my neck and I feel her mood shift before she continues. "I don't want you to ever doubt my love for you… or wonder if I'm going to leave you, because I'll always love you and you won't ever get rid of me. It's me and you," she whispers.

"And Peanut," I add.

"And Peanut," she agrees, melting into me.

Needing her naked, I tug at the bottom of the shirt until she leans up and lets me take it off, tossing it to the floor behind me. "I want more babies with you," I confess, as I crawl down her body. "All the babies."

"All the babies," she whispers.

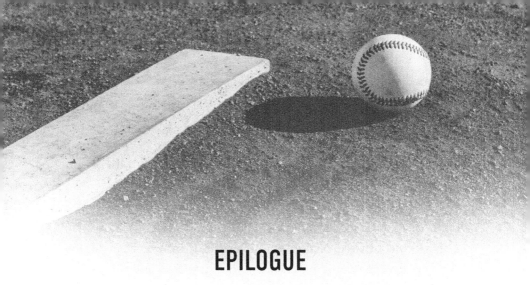

EPILOGUE

Casey

"CAN I GET YOU ANYTHING?" JACK ASKS, FOR THE UMPTEENTH TIME SINCE WE SAT down in the box where our seats are located.

Smiling, I shake my head as I rest my hand on my very large belly. "I'm good, Jack. Thank you, though."

"Just let me know if you need anything."

I nod, "I will, don't worry."

I swear, this kid is trying to evict me from my own body, instead of the other way around. I feel like I don't have room to breathe, and even though I'm always hungry, I don't feel like I can eat.

This morning, instead of kicks, I got my first Braxton Hicks contraction.

Of course, Ross freaked out, but I assured him it was normal. When he tried to talk me into a visit to the OB, I pulled one of my trusty books off the nightstand and proved they're nothing to worry about.

I'm pretty sure he put his parents on Casey Watch, because neither of them has left my side since we left the house.

He's not been much better over the last couple months.

Since our big talk, he's enforced new rules, which include me never being truly alone. When they go on a road trip, he insists on me going to Charlotte's or her coming and staying with me. When he's home, I'm basically an appendage of him.

He even moved all of my things from the guesthouse into his house and emptied out my boxes from Charlotte's attic. According to him, he didn't want any of my belongings anywhere other than next to his.

Not going to lie, it made me a little emotional.

But that doesn't take much these days.

When he surprised me on my birthday last month with an interior designer for the nursery, I bawled.

"Feeling okay?" Charlotte asks as she takes the seat beside me, the one Jack just vacated especially for her.

I sigh, kind of tired of the same question from every single person I know. "Yep, except for the part where I swallowed a basketball... and the indigestion... and I only slept three hours last night..."

"So, nothing's changed since yesterday," she says, unphased by my bellyaching. "Good."

Feeling a tightening in my belly, I wince and take a drink of my water.

"Are you okay?" Joann asks, turning in her seat as the players take the field.

"Fine," I tell her, with a smile. "Just excited about this game."

She pats my arm and turns back to the field. "Me too," she says, focusing on the team as they line up for the National Anthem. "Just think, next year, we'll have a little one up here with us."

Just the thought puts a smile on my face and brings my hand back to my stomach. I have a feeling Joann and Jack will be spending a lot more time in New Orleans next year. With the guest house empty, it gives them their own space in our backyard. Who knows? They may split their time and fly south for the summer.

When Ross takes the mound for the beginning of the first inning, the atmosphere in the box shifts and everyone's attention turns to the game. The excitement of playing in the Wild Card game is palpable. If the Revelers win tonight, they'll advance to play in the Division Series.

Ross strikes out the first batter and I exhale a small sigh of relief.

He looks focused, poised, and incredibly sexy.

By the second inning, I have to relieve my bladder, and Joann and Charlotte insist on accompanying me to the bathroom. On our way back, we hear the crowd roar. Waddling as fast as I can, I get back to the box to see a replay of Ross crushing a ball. The outfielder dives to catch it, but misses, allowing Ross to get to second base and sending Freeman home.

Go, baby, go.

I don't want to jinx anything by saying I had a premonition about this game, but I did. Ross woke me up this morning with some amazing, lazy morning sex. Due to the size of my belly, our positions are limited, but we make it work… boy do we make it work. And the orgasms are mind-blowing. I mean, they have been since our first night together, but lately, they've been intense.

Like, out of this world… hold my calls… see you next Tuesday.

But, I digress.

After the sex and orgasms, we cooked breakfast together for his parents.

Then, I had a nice Facetime chat with my own, who thankfully have warmed up to the baby and Ross. My mom wanted a virtual tour of the nursery and to see the crib they bought for us and had delivered. I talked to her and my dad while I sat in the middle of the floor and folded a small basket of onesies.

It's weird that laundry can make you happy, but those tiny pieces of fabric that smell like baby powder make me happier than any tub of Oreo ice cream topped with crushed-up Thin Mints.

When I walked outside, the sun was shining and it actually felt like fall.

To top all of that off, there were no reporters stalking me on our way into the game.

AND I found a penny heads-up on the ground just outside the entrance to the field.

Of course, I don't even let my mind go to the possibilities, because I'm now a firm believer in the stupid baseball superstitions.

The jersey I'm wearing is one of Ross's old ones from his first season in New Orleans. He said the night he wore it, he pitched seven innings and struck out eleven batters. I also have on the same socks I wore from the night Ross almost had a no-hitter.

"Come on!" I yell when there's a bad call. "Open your eyes. I thought only horses sleep standing up!"

Charlotte snickers. "That's a new one."

"I have to get creative," I huff, settling back into my seat. "They make me sound like a broken record with all of their horrible calls."

For four innings, the Revelers go three up, three down, and as Ross takes the mound in the seventh, I swear he looks straight at the box. There's even a long pause as he takes his stance and I wonder what he's thinking.

I can't imagine having that much pressure on me with thousands of people watching. The thought makes my stomach hurt a little. If I could take any of it away for him, I would, even though he doesn't need me to… I would.

Proving my point, he throws a fastball that zips by the batter, making him swing.

Jack fist pumps the air and I smile, loving the pride he has in his son, and thinking, not for the first time, that I hope Ross and our son have that kind of relationship.

I hope they're close and remain that way, regardless of the path our son chooses.

Even if they don't always see eye-to-eye, I hope that unconditional love parents have for their children is there and that it's reciprocated.

Resting my hand on my stomach, I watch as Ross finishes off the rest of the batters, still not allowing anyone to make it to first base.

During the seventh inning stretch, I do just that. Over the past half hour or so, my lower back has started to ache. When I stand to rub at the tension, I feel a wetness seep down my leg.

Horrified, I bend down as far as I can to try and see what's happening and my black leggings are a darker shade of black down the center from my thigh to my ankle.

"Uh…" I start and stop, not knowing what to say. My heart begins to pound as I think of the possibilities. I've either peed myself, which is mortifying, or my water just broke, which is terrifying. I'm not ready… I didn't bring my go-bag, Ross is currently pitching one of the best games of his life… the Revelers might be going to the playoffs… and I have four more weeks to go… "This can't happen," I mutter to myself, finally getting the attention of everyone around me.

It's Charlotte who notices first and she drops her nachos to the ground, hands flying to her mouth.

Joann gets on board next and seriously climbs over two chairs in one long stride. "It's fine," she says, taking my hands into hers as she talks to Jack over my shoulder.

"Call a car," she instructs. "Wait until the game is over and bring Ross to the hospital."

"What?" he asks, sounding confused until he sees where Charlotte's eyes are still glued—my wet leggings. "Oh… oh." As realization dawns, he pulls out his phone and gets to work.

"I can't," I breathe out, feeling panic seep in. "I'm only thirty-six weeks… this can't happen."

A twinge of pain hits me about that time and I wince. It's not strong, kind of like what I've experienced all morning, but it's enough to throw everyone into action, even my sister gets onboard, looping her arm through mine and ushering me out into the corridor.

Everything after that is a blur until we make it to the car Jack called for us.

Charlotte helps me into the back and Joann climbs in on the opposite side.

"I need Ross," I say, emotion thick in my throat. "I can't do this."

Charlotte grabs my hand and holds it firmly. "Yes, you can."

"I promise everything is going to be okay," Joann says calmly. "Thirty-six weeks isn't too early and I'm sure Ross will be there as soon as he can."

"He can't know," I say, feeling an immediate sense of urgency. "He has to finish the game. Tell Jack that. I don't want to mess this up… I have a good feeling about it."

That's when tears prick my eyes.

Ross is going to get his no-hitter and I'm not going to be there.

"He won't," she assures me. "And I'll tell him to get everything on video."

I nod, blowing out short, choppy breaths as I try to calm myself. The only thing I can control at this moment is how I react to the situation. Ross would want me to focus on that… focus on me and getting our baby here safely. I can do that. For him… for me… for us.

We're a team and I've got to play my part.

"Please hurry," Joann says to the driver as he pulls out onto the street. "We're having a baby."

As he zips through traffic, I practice the breathing techniques Ross and I learned while taking a private Lamaze class last month. Honestly, as we were taking the class, I wasn't sure if I'd even need the things we were learning, but of course, I wanted to be prepared. Now, I'm glad we did it…

practiced breathing seems essential right now as the pain in my back and pelvis increase.

"Just a few more minutes," Joann assures me, still holding my hand.

"This is definitely not how I saw things happening," I say as I see the hospital come into view.

Charlotte gives my hand a squeeze. "Sometimes, things don't go as planned. Fate steps in and takes over... I mean, it's pretty perfect if you think about it."

Huffing out a laugh, I shake my head. "You're right."

It is pretty perfect, or perfectly imperfect.

Mine and Ross's entire relationship has been a series of curveballs, nothing landing where expected, but somehow being exactly where we need it.

If someone would've asked me a year ago where I saw myself now, I never would've come up with this scenario on my own. It wasn't until I threw caution to the wind that my life took a sharp turn, leading me down a path to happiness and purpose and love... so, so much love, in all different capacities.

A love for my soulmate.

A love for my unborn child.

A love for my new family.

And a newfound love for myself and all the possibilities my life holds.

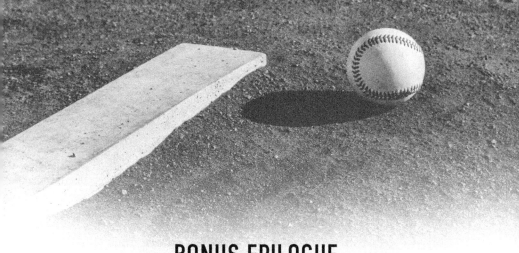

BONUS EPILOGUE

Ross

THE PAST COUPLE OF MONTHS HAVE BEEN AN ABSOLUTE BLUR.

Samuel Cy Davies was born two months ago. He's named after me, my dad, and my favorite pitcher of all time. Most people would tell you he looks just like me, but I see his mother in him too. He has her eyes and her spirit. There's never been a more laid-back baby. Even when he's hungry or wet, he's still pretty chill about it and he can sleep anywhere.

Between becoming a father and the Revelers winning the division and then losing in the championship series, I've barely had time to breathe, let alone sleep.

But the guys planned a post-season party at a bar down in the French Quarter tonight and Casey basically pushed me out the door, stating I needed to get out of the house before she kicked me out.

Things have been going great, but there's a chance I've been a little bit of a helicopter parent.

A year ago, I would've told you I'd never be one of those, but look at me now.

Casey told me I need to practice what I preach—balance. I've always been a big advocator about finding balance in life and in the game. She said I need to do the same with Samuel. But as much as she guarantees me he'll be okay, I still worry and I want to be there for, well, everything.

I had no clue the second he was born I'd feel like my heart is walking around outside my body. Well, he's not walking… yet. Thank God, because just the idea of him rolling over on his own is enough to worry about right now.

As the car pulls up at the corner closest to the bar, I tell the driver thanks and hop out.

Tucking my hands in the pockets of my jeans, I duck my head and make my way toward the bar. Mack and a few other guys organized the night and got the owner to shut the whole place down for us. It'll be nice to have a few beers and celebrate the season.

Sure, we didn't make it to the World Series, but we came damn close and left it all on the field.

And like they say, next year is our year.

When I open the door to the bar, the first thing I notice are all the familiar faces and then the banner.

Huggies and Chuggies

What the fuck?

"He's here!" Mack calls out, coming up to my side and slapping me on the shoulder as he forces a beer into my hand. "Casey said you were on your way and we thought about hiding and yelling surprise, but you've already had the ultimate surprise… am I right?"

His cocky grin makes me want to punch him, but instead, I shake my head and laugh, while accepting the beer and doing what the sign says. Chugging.

"Congratulations!" The greeting comes from everywhere and I realize I've been duped.

"This is supposed to be a celebration," I tell Mack.

He laughs. "It is… of your super sperm and our team kicking ass this season," he says, pointing to a large, blown-up picture of the team on the field the night I threw my no-hitter. Mack is lifting me off the ground while the rest of the team rushed the field.

Everyone was celebrating.

Gatorade was flying.

Jerseys came off.

My son was born.

It was a good night… the best night.

"We thought we'd double-up since it's the holidays and everyone is busy."

"It's great," I tell him, tipping my beer up to finish off the last of it. "Thanks, man."

During the season, when they all found out I was going to be a dad, they respected mine and Casey's privacy, offering quiet congratulations, but let us navigate that new road as privately as someone in my position can. I was grateful, both for their support and their discretion. But once we went public and Sam arrived, everyone came out of the woodworks.

Some of the wives and girlfriends of players brought food over.

Casey's hospital room was full of flowers and balloons, so much so she donated a lot of them to the hospital to give out to patients who were in long-term care.

Gifts, both large and small, were sent to the house.

The outpouring of love was an added bonus I never expected.

"Drinks are on us tonight," Mack says as he slaps my shoulder before walking off to cheer on some of our teammates who are playing what looks like a fierce game of beer pong.

Turning to the bar, I find a taller man with a thick dark beard and muscles bigger than Mack's drying some glasses. When I walk up and ask for a refill, he gives me a nod. "Sure thing, man."

"Is this your bar?" I ask, looking around the place. There are dark wood tables and floors with an old-fashioned jukebox in the corner. Dartboards, a pool table, and a long, well-stocked bar. It could be any dive bar in any city, but the large fleur-de-lis embossed into the wall screams New Orleans. Other than that, there's just something about the place that is quintessentially the French Quarter.

"It is," he says, his stern expression firmly in place. "Is this your party?"

I chuckle, accepting the beer he sets in front of me and taking a sip before answering. "I guess it is."

"First baby?" he asks.

"Yeah," I say, fighting a smile at just the mention of Sam. "Do you have kids?"

That's what gets him. His perpetual scowl finally softens as he says, "One."

"How old?"

"Almost two," he replies, crossing his burly arms over his chest. "You think you're tired now…"

That gets a full-fledged laugh, because fuck, am I tired. "I've never been more sleep-deprived in my entire life," I confess.

About that time, Thatch slides onto the barstool beside me. "It doesn't get better," he chimes in. "You go from the infant stage where they want to eat every few hours to getting days and nights mixed up. Then it's terrible twos, which is also false advertisement, because it can start early or run late, depending on the kid. And don't even get me started about the avoidance tactics of a five-year-old."

There's a chorus of laughs, but beneath the humorous façade is sheer and utter fear… fear of the unknown, fear of the sleepless nights ahead, fear of fucking it all up.

In the span of a few minutes, a comradery is formed and I get now why women join mommy groups. You need peers, people who go through the trenches with you and help you feel like you're not alone.

"I'm Ross," I say, reaching across the bar to shake the owner's hand. "And this is Owen Thatcher… Thatch."

"Shaw," he says with a firm shake and nod. "Shaw O'Sullivan."

He turns to Thatch and offers him the same. "You've got more than one, I take it?"

"Two," Thatch offers. "And I'm now the mom and the dad."

"Oh, shit," Shaw murmurs. Without another word, he pulls out three shot glasses and lines them up on the bar, filling them with Jack Daniels. Scooting one to me and one to Thatch, he lifts his glass and dips his head. "To fatherhood."

"To fatherhood," we echo, tossing them back.

We both stare at the empty glasses for a brief moment, lost in thought.

It's Owen who speaks first. "It's worth it though," he says thoughtfully. "All the sleepless nights and diapers… bottles and spit-up. My mom told me with my first one that everything is a phase and it's over before you know it. One day, you'll look back and realize it all happened in the blink of an eye. Honestly, even on the hard days, when I think about how big my two are getting, it makes me a little sad."

"How's the nanny working out?" I ask, remembering him telling me he finally found one right before the season was over.

He groans, pushing his shot glass back across the bar in a silent request

THE ACE and THE ASSISTANT 243

for a refill.

Shaw obliges, filling mine in the process.

"We're currently on nanny number two… and I'm afraid to say, things aren't looking so great."

"Shit, man, I'm sorry," I tell him, clinking my shot glass with his before we throw them back. "If there's anything we can do, let us know. I know we have a new baby, but Casey is great with kids and she'd be more than happy to watch them if you need her to."

Sighing, he runs a hand through his hair. "I appreciate the offer, but I've got the off-season to figure this shit out. I can't be worrying about my kids while I'm on a road trip or playing a game. You and I both know the season is long and when you've got personal stuff going on, it messes with your head… which means throwing for shit… and I need this…"

This more vulnerable side of Owen Thatcher isn't something most people see. To everyone else, he's a broody son of a bitch who walks around with a chip on his shoulder, but underneath it all, he's a little troubled, kind of where I was before this season started, except I didn't have two kids to worry about.

"You'll figure it out," I encourage. "And like I said, we're here if you need us, especially during the off-season."

"And drinks are always on me," Shaw says, tossing a towel over his shoulder. "Solidarity and all that."

Solidarity.

"Thanks," Owen says, lifting his glass to Shaw and then to me.

Before the night's over, I've had more beers and shots of Jack Daniels than I've had in a long time, a new friend in Shaw O'Sullivan, and some awesome shit. The guys give me a set of Revelers onesies with my number on the back, a tiny ball and glove, and a carrier I can strap onto my chest and carry Sam around in.

It's fucking awesome.

Just like my team.

And my life.

This past year might've been unplanned, throwing curveballs right and left, but it ended up being everything I needed and wanted—Casey, Samuel… a family of my own. A great season. I honestly couldn't ask for more.

Except making Casey my wife and having all the babies.

But we'll get to that.

Casey

CHRISTMAS IN NEW ORLEANS IS MY ABSOLUTE FAVORITE.

Lights are strung up over anything standing, giving the city a warm glow, and there's little to no humidity, which makes it perfect for all the outside activities available. There are bonfires along the levee, holiday light tours, and my personal favorite, caroling by candlelight in Jackson Square. I can't wait to stand in front of the Cathedral and soak in the holiday spirit with my family, especially Ross and Baby Sam.

Samuel was born on the eve of his father's first no-hitter.

Ross told me later that he felt a shift in the atmosphere and knew he had to finish the game and get to me. I'm not sure if I believe all of that, but he did get there fast. So did my parents, who flew into New Orleans just in time to see their first grandchild born.

It was a magical day, even though nothing went as planned.

My epidural was even a bust, but none of that mattered the second I held my baby. My entire world righted itself. Colors seemed more vibrant. Emotions felt more real. And the future looked clear. Because in that moment, I realized the only two things that mattered were right there with me—Sam and Ross—and as long as we were together, everything else would continue to work itself out.

This evening, we're all meeting at Neutral Grounds, a coffee shop in the French Quarter where Ross and I occasionally meet up with Phil, the contractor from the guest house, and his wife. They've become a third set of grandparents to Sam and will be joining us tonight.

My parents are back for Christmas. This is the most I've seen them in person since Charlotte and I moved back to New Orleans. I wasn't sure what to expect once Sam arrived, but like everything else, it's worked out better than I could've planned.

They're not the super hands-on grandparents that Jack and Joann are. My mom still hasn't changed a diaper or been spit-up on, but she's here and that's all I could ask for. Her nurturing skills have kicked in a little more with each visit and she actually put Sam to sleep last night while the rest of us sat around and snacked on a smorgasbord of our favorite holiday foods.

"Are you almost ready?" Ross asks, walking into the bathroom where I'm putting on a little mascara and lip gloss. I've never been a super heavy makeup person, but since Sam arrived, I've dropped my usual moderate makeup to minimal.

"Almost," I say, finally catching a glimpse of Ross in the mirror and nearly swallowing my tongue.

He's standing there in a pullover sweater that's the perfect shade of green to match his eyes. His scruff is neatly trimmed, allowing the definition of his jawline to show through. And as my eyes travel down, I see he's wearing my favorite pair of jeans that hug his muscular thighs and incredible backside.

But the piece de resistance is what's strapped to his chest.

Sam is already nestled down in his baby carrier and fast asleep with a beanie on his head that matches Ross's sweater.

Smirking, I bite my lip to keep from groaning.

Our parents are downstairs and our baby is asleep on his chest. This definitely isn't the time for the thoughts I'm having, but I'm finding it impossible to ignore them.

"I think we should take your mom up on her offer of Sam sleeping in the guest house tonight."

Ross cocks his head and steps closer, placing a hand on my waist. "I like the way you think," he murmurs, dipping his head low and pulling the collar of my sweater over so he can kiss the exposed skin. "Actually…" he continues, peppering kisses up my neck. "I already told her yes."

"Well aren't you a cocky little planner," I mutter.

His eyes find mine in the mirror and he quirks an eyebrow. "Why, Casey Carradine, did you just say cock?"

My cheeks immediately go red at his accusation and my eyes go wide as they dart to our sleeping son, his little head barely peeking out of the carrier. "Um… I," I begin stuttering and stop, huffing out a laugh. "No, I didn't. I said cocky… two completely different words."

"I just heard cock," he mutters, leaning closer. "And so did my dick."

"Oh, my God, Ross." Turning, I can't help the laugh that escapes. "You're so bad and when Sam gets a note sent home on his first day of preschool for saying a bad word, my conscience will be clear because I'll know I had no hand in that."

With a wicked grin, he leans down and captures my lips. "He'll be perfect, just like his mama."

"I'm not perfect," I tell him as I look down at Sam and kiss him on the head. "But he is."

"You're perfect for him," Ross says, wrapping his arms around me and encasing the three of us in a warm embrace. "And you're perfect for me."

Sighing in contentment, I kiss his jaw and then pull away. "We better get down there. Charlotte is always complaining about us running late and I want to prove to her that parents of newborns can still be on time to something."

He chuckles, following me out of the bathroom.

An hour later, we're walking into Neutral Grounds to find Phil and his wife already at a table, thankfully, because the place is packed. I also spotted Charlotte and Bo walking up the sidewalk as we were coming through the front door. Naturally, I hurried inside so I could say I beat her here.

"Casey," Phil says with a smile as we approach the table. "Merry Christmas!"

"Merry Christmas," I tell him, leaning in for a hug, then moving over to give his wife, Sandy, one as well. When Joann and my mom aren't around, Sandy has become my go-to for baby advice. They have four daughters, so she's had lots of experience.

"How's Baby Sam been sleeping this week?" she asks, walking around to take a peek at him.

"Much better," I tell her, admiring him from where he's still sleeping in the baby carrier. I'm not the only one who thinks a man like Ross walking around with a baby strapped to his chest is basically porn. I'm pretty sure at least two sets of ovaries exploded on our short walk here.

"Swaddling him like you suggested definitely helped. He's been averaging about six hours at a time and that feels like the best Christmas gift ever."

"That's wonderful," she coos, more to Sam than me. "Whenever you're ready to stay with Phil and Sandy, you give us a call."

Babysitters will never be an issue around here.

Speaking of, Charlotte and Bo walk in about that time and join our growing group. As I look around the table, I see all the people I care about the most gathered together and my heart overflows.

"I'm going to grab a coffee," Bo says. "Does anyone else want anything?"

"I've heard they have an amazing egg nog latte," Charlotte says, standing on her tiptoes to see the menu board. "I'll have that."

"Me too," I chime in. "But make mine a decaf." Even though I'm no longer pregnant, I still try to limit my caffeine since I'm breastfeeding.

"I'll have what they're having," Ross says absentmindedly, most of his attention on Sam.

Jack goes with Bo to help him carry everything and the rest of us find a spot around the long table.

"Have I introduced y'all to the owners of this fine establishment?" Phil asks as a woman with dark hair and gorgeous eyes walks up, followed by a taller man with blond hair. It's obvious they're together and in love. The way he touches her back and practically orbits around her makes it blatantly obvious.

Funny, now that I've found love myself, it's easier to identify it in other people.

"This is CeCe and Shep," he says, reaching an arm out to them. CeCe smiles, stepping into his embrace, and then Shep reaches over to shake his hand. Phil then introduces everyone at the table. If CeCe or Shep recognize my sister or Ross or Bo, they don't act like it.

We visit for a few minutes as they tell us about a new coffee roastery they're opening up next door and then ooh and ahh over Sam. By the time Bo and Jack show up with our drinks, we all feel like old friends.

"Please come back soon and take a tour," CeCe says.

"We'd love that," my mom says, taking her americano from Bo with a grateful smile. "I was just telling Dean that we find something else to love about New Orleans every time we visit."

"The city has a way of pulling you in," Shep says, looking down at CeCe. For a second, I wonder if they're married, but then I see the rock on her hand as it catches the dim light. "The next thing you know, you never want to leave."

My heart does a fluttery thing at his words.

I want that… marriage, forever… I know Ross does too and it'll happen when the time is right, or if it's anything like the rest of our relationship, when we least expect it.

Laughing to myself, I draw Ross's attention and he silently asks me what's so funny. Shaking my head, I fight back a smile, because, yeah, we do that now… speak without speaking, read each other's body language…

It's like when I found Ross, I found the other half of myself.

When the sun begins to set, we all venture across the street to Jackson Square. Jack and my dad head off in search of candles and song sheets, while the rest of us find a spot where we can all stand together.

Sam woke up for a bit while we were at Neutral Grounds, but after a fresh diaper and some milk, he's now back asleep. He tends to sleep well around loud noises, so he might sleep through all of the caroling. Ross says it's because of all the baseball games and me yelling at the umpires, which could be true. But I think it's because he's so chill, just like his dad.

As the candles are lit and the entire square begins to glow in a warm light, I can't help but smile.

I also can't imagine a more perfect Christmas.

When the singing begins, Ross's hand finds mine and he laces our fingers together.

Somewhere between *Silent Night* and *O' Holy Night*, he lets go of my hand and leans down until his lips are at my ear. "I have something for you," he whispers, discreetly blowing out his candle and placing it on the ground at his feet.

When he stands back up, I catch his green eyes in the light of the candle I'm still holding and they're patient and kind, and full of so much love. The same love I feel, reflected back to me.

"I've had this for a while and I was trying to think of the perfect time to give it to you, but with this guy," he says, kissing the top of Samuel's head as he squirms a little. "We haven't had a lot of time to ourselves. And well, Bo told me he's going to ask your sister to marry him tomorrow…"

I gasp, my eyes growing wide as my heart begins to pound in my chest, not only from the news that my sister will be getting engaged tomorrow, but also from what I have a feeling he's getting ready to give me.

As my hand comes up to cover my mouth, he pulls it back and places a ring on my finger… the fourth finger on my left hand.

"I realized, regardless of where we are or how this happens, the only thing that really matters is that you know how much I love you and that I don't want to spend another day where our two last names aren't the same," he says, slipping the ring further onto my finger.

The crowd around us continues to sing, ignorant to the fact I'm experiencing the second-best moment of my life. The first being the moment we met our son for the first time.

"Casey Marie Carradine," he continues. "I love you more than anything in the world. I love Samuel with a kind of love I didn't even know existed… I want this forever… I want us forever."

He pauses for a moment, his voice growing thick with emotion as he holds the ring in place. Leaning forward, I rest my forehead against his, soaking in this magical moment.

"Please make me the happiest man on earth and be my wife."

"Of course I'll marry you," I gush, a tear slipping down my cheek as I take in the gorgeous ring on my finger. It's simple, not too big or flashy, and exactly something I would've picked for myself. "If I could marry you right now, I would."

"Let's not wait," he says, taking both of my hands in his. "All of our family is here… we can do it the day after Christmas, before our parents fly back home."

A rush of excitement floods my body. "Are you serious?" I ask, unable to stop looking at my ring. I want to show it off and scream from the rooftops—ROSS DAVIES JUST ASKED ME TO MARRY HIM!

"I would've married you months ago," he chuckles. "Don't make me wait any longer… marry me."

"I can't freaking wait."

Ross slips Samuel off his chest and passes him off to his mom, then he takes me into his arms, lifts me off my feet, and kisses me like I'm his last breath… and his first… and every single one in between. There are so many promises packed into that kiss—to love, to cherish, for better, or worse… forever.

The End

Acknowledgements

First and foremost, we'd like to thank our families. They're the ones who have to put up with our lack of domesticity while writing words. Thank you for being so understanding and supporting our dreams.

We'd also like to thank our pre-reader and amazing friend, Pamela, we're so thankful for your continued support and encouragement. Thank you for being the best cheerleader!

As always, we'd like to thank our editor, Nichole. Thank you for all you do! We appreciate your insight and that you always push us to do our best.

A big "thank you" to Juliana Cabrera for doing an awesome job on this cover… and the recover of The Rookie and The Rockstar!

And YOU… we're so thankful for you. Writing is what we love to do, but having readers is what makes it worthwhile. Thank you for reading our words!

Much Love,
Jiff and Jenny Kate

About the Authors

Jiffy Kate is the joint pen name for Jiff Simpson and Jenny Kate Altman.

Jiff was born and raised in Louisiana, but she now lives in Texas with her two teenagers and her two English Bulldogs, Georgia Rose and Jake. She loves Project Runway, Queen, 80's music and movies, and the color purple. When she's not shaping the lives of our future generation, you can find her planning her next vacation to Disney.

Jenny Kate is a small-town girl from Oklahoma. She's a self-proclaimed coffee junkie/connoisseur. Her husband stays annoyed at her taste in music and her teenager thinks she's weird, so basically, she's winning at life. Between a full-time job as an accounting assistant and her three rambunctious fur babies, she's often dreaming about maid services and vacation days.

Together, they spend their evenings and weekends spinning tails and hoping one day they hit a best-sellers list.

You can connect with them and follow along with their shenanigans on social media.

Made in the USA
Monee, IL
26 August 2021